Para Handy Sails Again

THE CONTINUED VOYAGES OF
THE VITAL SPARK

*Chronicled with affection,
acknowledgement and apology
to Neil Munro
by*

STUART DONALD
Foreword by Lesley Lendrum

Neil Wilson Publishing Ltd • Glasgow • Scotland

© Stuart Donald, 1995

Published by Neil Wilson Publishing Ltd
303a The Pentagon Centre
36 Washington Street
GLASGOW
G3 8AZ
Tel: 0141-221-1117
Fax: 0141-221-5363

The moral right of the author has been asserted.
A catalogue record for this book is available from the British Library.
ISBN 1-897784-47-3

All photographs courtesy of Argyll and Bute District Libraries, Dunoon,
with the exception of page 93, courtesy of Dan Macdonald Collection
and page 213, courtesy of Hulton Deutsch Picture Library

Typeset in 11/12pt Caslon 224 Book by The Write Stuff, Glasgow.
Tel: 0141-339-8279
E-mail: *wilson_i@cqm.co.uk*

Printed by Scotprint Ltd, Musselburgh, Scotland

BY THE SAME AUTHOR

In the Wake of the Vital Spark, Johnston & Bacon Ltd (1994)
A topographical, historical and literary companion to
Para Handy and his world

PARA HANDY SAILS AGAIN

Dedication

To the memory of my parents

MY FATHER
who had the kindness and good sense
to introduce me to Para Handy at an early age

MY MOTHER
who worried about my childhood wanderings on the Firth
but still encouraged me to make them

THE AGE OF THE VITAL SPARK — *This fine picture of passengers disembarking from Williamson's turbine Queen Alexandra captures perfectly the atmosphere and the ambience of the turn-of-the-century Clyde as Para Handy knew it. Here are the well-dressed daytrippers he longed to carry, the gentry en route to their estates, the curious crowds thronging the pierhead for the social event of the day, and the confident elegance of the new breed of ships, with the grace and the silhouette of liners in miniature. Sadly we shall never see their like again!*

Contents

Acknowledgements

The greatest acknowledgement — and indeed apology — must be to the late Neil Munro, the 'only true begetter' of the marvellous world of Para Handy, his crew, his ship and his age.

Nobody could ever manage to recreate that world with the same matchless quality of craftsmanship, affection or accuracy. My hope is that my own efforts in that direction will entertain rather than irritate, and provide an acceptable extension to the Para Handy repertoire.

On practical matters, for the opportunity once again to 'raid' the MacGrory collection of turn-of-the-century photographs held by Argyll and Bute District Libraries I am indebted to District Librarian Andrew Ewan. Local Studies Librarian Bill Scott continued to proffer the advice on authenticity and guidance as to the most appropriate source material, which he generously gave when I was researching my previous Munro-based book, *In The Wake Of The Vital Spark*.

I am grateful to Fiona and Gregor Roy of Bookpoint, Dunoon, and to Bill Jardine of Rothesay, Clyde enthusiast (and pragmatist) *par excellence*, for encouraging me to persevere with the manuscript, and helping to restore my confidence in the dark hours of doubt.

For the highs of creative energy, when I never allowed mundane matters such as mealtimes, family or friends to interfere with the flow, and for the lows of mental blockages spent staring at the study wall into the small hours, I apologise to my wife Maureen. What follows owes everything to her tolerance!

Foreword

It is always good to meet an old friend in an unfamiliar place. A welcome, then, to these stories in which Stuart Donald has set Para Handy and the crew of the *Vital Spark* off on new ploys. In a way I would previously have held to be impossible, he has captured an amazing amount of the elusive flavour of the originals. His earlier book *In the Wake of the Vital Spark* shows the affectionate familiarity with my grandfather's tales — and with West of Scotland waterways — that enabled him to do so.

In 1927, answering a query from an English reader who knew only his historical romances, Neil Munro described the Para Handy tales as "humoursome Highland character sketches...written solely for the amusement of West of Scotland sea-board folk...they have sold, and still sell, extraordinarily in this part of the world". He would have laughed sceptically if a seer had told him that these sketches would still be in print 70 years later or that Para Handy would become a part of the latter-day Scottish mythology. Scottish newspapers still refer to the *Vital Spark* and her skipper without further explanation. For instance, the *Sunday Post* declared, two years after the Falklands conflict, that the *MV St Brandan* was "affectionately known as the '*Vital Spark* of the South Atlantic' ", while in 1983 the *Glasgow Herald* had a headline "Reluctant Para Handy puffer coaxed into last port of call."

Para Handy himself, though, having attained a curious brand of immortality, will never sail into a "last port of call". He has already had several reincarnations: I agree with Stuart Donald that the film *The Maggie* was the best attempt to "transfer Para Handy from the printed page", even though its debt to Neil Munro was never acknowledged.

The factnotes which Stuart Donald provides at the end of each tale help to recreate the atmosphere of the West of

Scotland as it was in Para Handy's day. He has also followed Neil Munro's topicality by introducing actual events such as the launch of the *Lusitania* and the discovery of Piltdown Man.

A contemporary of Neil Munro's, Rosslyn Mitchell, wrote: "So much has his writing the expression of his mind that he would forget things he had written himself. One evening in Arran he read aloud a Para Handy sketch, 'The Wet Man of Muscadale', and it was so fresh to him that he chuckled and enjoyed it as if he had never seen it before. Indeed, he had to stop because the fun of it was too much for him." If he could see these new tales by Stuart Donald he would likely be eager to find out what further high jinks the crew of the *Vital Spark* had got up to behind his back. He would be amused to find the second *Lord of the Isles* figuring in 'The Downfall of Hurricane Jack'. It was on the first steamer of that name that he came to Glasgow from Inveraray in 1881 to seek his fortune, and on the second that the Munro family used to travel from Gourock to spend the summer in Inveraray. Being a little of a feminist himself (as close study of 'The Daft Days' will reveal), 'The March of the Women', in which Para Handy encounters suffragettes, would appeal to him, being a sort of companion-piece to his own 'Land Girls'.

What next? Will it be great-grandson of Para Handy? A job at sea would have to be found for him, though it is hard to think of any to equal the magnificent independence enjoyed by the captain of the *Vital Spark*. And how would a late twentieth-century MacFarlane react to nuclear submarines, windsurfers, roll-on/roll-off ferries and wave powered generators? Over to you, Stuart Donald!

Lesley Lendrum

Introduction

Anyone who is planning to tamper with a national
institution approaches the task with some trepida-
tion and, in my efforts to extend the repertoire of the
much-loved tales about the Clyde puffer *Vital Spark*
and her kenspeckle Captain and crew, I am no exception.

Neil Munro's characters are a national institution to many
Scots, and the tales have a remarkable provenance. They
were first created to feature in Munro's anonymous columns
in the *Glasgow News*, on which paper he rose to become
editor. Although they were dismissed as 'slight' by their creator (who saw them as an interruption to the writing of his
serious, and nowadays sadly neglected, historical novels)
they have rarely, if ever, been out of print for three-quarters
of a century. Year on year new generations of readers are cap-
tivated by the gentle humour and kindly atmosphere of these
chronicles of a long-lost world and a gentler society, on
which we tend to look back with much affection, and nostal-
gic regret for what has gone for ever.

Trying to live up to the expectations of such enthusiasts
while having the impertinence to try to recreate Para Handy
and his people was always going to be a daunting task.

However, at the risk of offending the purists, I have to say
at once that writing these stories has been great fun —
which, in an ideal world, all writing should be: and that there
were occasions when they wrote themselves, in the sense
that I would embark on a particular tale with no clear idea of
where or how it would come to its conclusion.

In retrospect, however, I am surprised that a volume of
new Para Handy tales has not been attempted before this.
There have been no less than three television reincarnations
of the *Vital Spark* and only in the most recent of them was
there any serious attempt to dramatise some of Neil Munro's
original story-lines: the others were, basically, 'new' creations. The most faithful of all the attempts to transfer Para

Handy from the printed page was, in my view, the 1953 film *The Maggie* which, though never formally acknowledged as being based on Neil Munro's own characters, so obviously and so successfully in fact was.

Whether I have succeeded in creating an acceptable extension to the original tales will not be for me to judge, and I offer no attempt to defend my efforts in terms of their authenticity or readability. That is a matter for the personal judgement of those who may read them.

I would, however, defend the concept of writing new tales built round Neil Munro's creations, for I believe it has in fact been done before — and during his lifetime. In my documentary volume *In The Wake Of The Vital Spark* I put forward the proposition that the 18 'new' stories published for the first time in the recent Birlinn Edition of the original tales were, in fact, the work of hands other than Neil Munro's. I won't reiterate the arguments here, but my conviction about that point was one of the factors which encouraged me to proceed with the present work.

I close the case for the defence by stressing that I believe Neil Munro to be one of the finest writers of humorous fiction which this, or any other, country has ever produced. I grew up with the Para Handy tales, and know them — literally — almost off by heart. I therefore approached the whole task with both affection and respect for their creator. I like to believe that Neil Munro would not be taken too aback by imitation, for it is, we are told, the sincerest form of flattery.

And I am certain that he would not look too unkindly on whoever was rash enough to attempt it — for that surely is the kind of sympathetic and forgiving man he was.

I certainly don't ask the readers to be either sympathetic or forgiving, however — but simply to read on, and come to their own conclusions and form their own judgements!

My one intention and my only wish is that these new tales might entertain and amuse, for if they fail in that, then they fail in everything.

Sandhaven, Argyll
September 1995

1

The Encounter at Inveraray

As the *Vital Spark* chugged past the hamlet of Newtown, tacked almost as an afterthought onto the Lochgilphead road at the southern limits of the Burgh of Inveraray, the town's capacious pier came into view. Para Handy was astonished to see a huge crowd thronging both that structure and the stone quayside onto which it abutted, all of them staring across the water towards the approaching puffer.

"My Chove, Dougie," he said, "we've not always been such a centre of attention in the past! But I've always said, the time would come when the finer points of the shup would at last be recognised by the public at large. I'm glad we gave the lum a fresh coat of pent at Tarbert yesterday mornin', for she's neffer looked bonnier and plainly the news hass got around!"

"It's either that, or the Inveraray polis huv managed tae work oot jist whose punt wis up the mooth of the river Shira wi' a splash net efter the Duke's salmon the last nicht we wis by here," called a doom-laden voice from the engine-room at the Captain's feet. "Is there no sign of a Black Maria at the head of the quay?"

"I'll thank you to attend to your enchines, Mr Macphail," said Para Handy with some dignity. "And Jum! will you look lively and break out our best heaving-line ready for when we tak' our berth. There'll be no problem today findin' someone to catch it for us seein' ass we're the star attraction at the pier!"

The traditional place for the puffers at Inveraray is on the inner, west side of the pier and the *Vital Spark* was manoeuvred round the quay-head with just a little -

difficulty, for the tide was turning and the current threatened to push her back out. In the event, with some dexterous application of the helm and a touch of extra power to the propeller, Para Handy brought the boat safely into the slack water of the inshore berth.

"Right, Jum," he called, "stand by to heave the line!" And he turned triumphantly towards the pier preparing to wave a happy acknowledgement to the crowds who must have been watching his manoeuvres with interest and approbation, and who would now be surging forward to welcome the little vessel to her Inveraray berth — only to find that he was looking at some 200 disinterested backs, for the people on the quay had taken not the slightest notice of the approach and ultimate arrival of the puffer, but were still standing, as they had been when he had first caught sight of them, staring out towards the middle of Loch Fyne as if hypnotised.

"The Chook of Argyll himself must be expected aff a yat," said a somewhat chastened Para Handy to Dougie once they had finally secured the puffer to the quayside — Sunny Jim, as usual, having to leap for the jetty with the handline and haul the hawser in to the first bollard on his own. "And this iss his loyal lieges with their reception committee."

Squeezing their way through the crowd, the crew managed to gain a viewpoint, but found themselves staring across an empty loch with not so much as a fishing smack in sight.

Para Handy was just turning to seek some enlightenment from the nearest bystander, when there was a collective gasp from the assembled throng, followed immediately by a ragged cheer.

A squat, grey rectangular object was rising slowly out of the waters of the loch about 200 yards offshore.

∼

The Captain had heard all about submarines: but this was the first which he and the crew had ever encountered at such close hand. They watched in awed fascination as the conning-tower, then the gun, and finally the hull of the vessel emerged from the sea.

When the figures of the submarine captain and three seamen appeared on the bridge there was another spontaneous cheer from the Inveraray crowd, and the vessel turned in towards the pier where eager lookers-on fought for the privilege of catching and securing the heaving-lines which two seamen now threw ashore from bow and stern of the grey hull.

Half-an-hour later the onlookers had dispersed homewards to discuss the excitement of the day over their teas.

On the pier, the submarine crew had deployed a spick-and-span gangway from her foredeck to the quay, a small pillar placed at the head of it carrying a coat-of-arms and the ship's name, *HMS Bulldog*. The white ropes which looped from posts at either side of the gangway were finished with turk's head knots and two seamen, immaculate in white jerseys and navy-blue bell-bottoms, stood guard at either hand with grounded rifles. On the ship's deck sailors in fatigues were polishing glass and brass on the bridge of the conning-tower, and from somewhere deep within the vessel came the constant deep throb of one of the new-fangled diesel engines.

The crew of the puffer, crammed into the wheelhouse, stared with undisguised and undiminished curiosity at their unexpected neighbour on the far side of the pier.

Eventually Para Handy squeezed his way out on deck without a word and vanished down the hatchway to the fo'c'sle.

Ten minutes later he reappeared in his best — indeed his only — pea-jacket, and wearing the cap with the white top and the splash of gold braid which he had picked up cheap at the Barras in Glasgow some years previously, but (thanks largely to the considerable amusement with which his crew had greeted its acquisition) had rarely had the courage to wear.

"Boys," he said, scrambling up the iron ladder let into one of the pier uprights, "it iss only right that I should present my complements to a fellow captain when we find oorselves neebours in a strange port."

And he straightened his shoulders, puffed out his chest, and marched across the quay towards the submarine's gangway.

~

Later that evening, in the bar of the George Hotel, the Captain and Dougie sat in a corner by a narrow window nursing two halves of beer. Sunny Jim they had left on the pier fishing, more in hope than expectation, for the makings of the next day's breakfast. Dan Macphail was in animated conversation at the far end of the bar with one of the engineers from the submarine and had been promised a guided tour of her diesels the following morning.

Para Handy's reception at the submarine's gangway had exceeded even his wildest imaginings.

"Whit way are they all keepin' at the Admirulity?" had been his opening sally to the sailors on guard duty. Before either could think of an appropriate reply, the submarine's Captain had appeared on the conning tower to take a breath of air, seen the puffer's skipper on the quayside, and invited him on board.

"A proper chentleman," Para Handy now enthused to the mate. "A proper chentleman, Dougie. But a hard life. They have no space at aal on the shup. Chust like livin' in wan of the caurs on the Gleska Subway, but wi' watter aal round ye.

"I would not wish to change places with them, for aal their chenerosity" — the Captain had enjoyed the hospitality of the wardroom, including the very first Pink Gin he had ever encountered — "for why would ye want to run a smert shup and then hide her under the watter where naebody can admire her?"

The immediate effect of his kindly reception aboard *HMS Bulldog* had been a change in the attitude of the burghers of Inveraray towards the puffer. From the moment that Para Handy was spotted leaving the submarine and shaking hands with her Captain at the foot of the gangway, the status of the *Vital Spark* was revised upwards.

As if to underline that fact, the landlord of the George Hotel now appeared with a cloth in his hand, wiped the top of the table at which the Captain and Dougie were seated, and placed two drams on it.

"Compliments of the house, gentlemen," he said, and whisked their empty beer glasses away.

"My Chove," said Para Handy. "What's got into Sandy McCallum tonight?"

"You were goin' to tell me why the submarine iss in Inveraray at all, Peter," prompted the mate.

"It's because the loch iss so deep," said Para Handy. "They iss going to use it for the diving trials of aal the new submarines built on the Clyde. *Bulldog* iss the first, but there will be plenty more.

"They are putting something aboot it aal in the papers, which iss where the Captain hass gone tonight. There iss an Inveraray man who iss quite namely ass a writer, and who does some work for the Gleska Evening News. Captain Morris from the submarine hass gone to have an interview with him, which iss why he wass not able to choin us for a dram."

~

Just at that moment the street door opened and the submarine Captain walked in, flashing more gold braid than Inveraray had seen in many months.

With him was a man of middle-height, aged about 40, with a high-domed forehead, a receding hairline, and a mild and kindly countenance.

The submariner looked round the crowded, smokey room and caught sight of Para Handy.

"Ah," he said to his companion. "There he is, that's the chap I was telling you about. I'm sure you'll be able to get a lot of interesting material from talking to him. He certainly kept me well entertained. He's a real character, and a bit of a teller of tall tales too, I would think!"

And, taking the other man by the arm, he pushed his way through the crowd and, reaching the corner table, clapped Para Handy on the shoulder.

"Captain, here's somebody I've been telling all about you, and he's very keen to meet you. I'm sure the pair of you will have a lot to talk about!

"May I introduce: Captain Peter MacFarlane — Mr Neil Munro!"

FACTNOTE

Certain minor liberties with chronology must be admitted to in this story. Firstly it is unlikely that a submarine of the size hinted at would have been around the Clyde in the years before the First World War: secondly it was not till after that War that submarines were given names. Previously they were identified simply by their Class Letter followed by a numeral.

The Firth has, however, been closely associated with submarines for almost 100 years. Many were built in the Clyde yards such as Fairfield, Denny, Scott and Beardmore. The deep waters of the sheltered lochs — particularly the Gareloch, Loch Fyne and Loch Long — were ideal for diving trials and the testing of torpedos produced by the huge factory at Fort Matilda, Greenock, which Neil Munro referred to in the original Para Handy story 'Confidence'.

Much later, the Americans moved in to Holy Loch and for 30 years this was the European base for the US Nuclear Submarines which were such a crucial element of the NATO deterrent during the cold war. Now the Americans have gone, but Faslane on the Gairloch, and Coulport on Loch Long, serve the United Kingdom submarine fleet in a similar if lower-key capacity.

～

The real liberty taken in this tale, of course, is to place Neil Munro himself in it — but the temptation was absolutely irresistible! He must have revisited many times the community which meant so much to him and made such a lasting impression on him and influenced everything he did.

He was born and brought up in Inveraray and his first job was in the town, working in a lawyer's office. At the age of 18 he left for Glasgow, to lay the foundation of his future career as a working journalist and a talented novelist seen by many critics at the time as the natural inheritor of the mantle of Robert Louis Stevenson.

The chronicle of the gradual public indifference to his serious writing, and the rapid growth in their esteem and affection for works which he saw as slight and ephemeral, is well known. The tales of puffer skipper Para Handy: of waiter/beadle Erchie MacPherson: of commercial traveller Jimmy Swan, were all written for his regular columns in the Glasgow *Evening News*. And written anonymously for he did not wish to tarnish with trivia his reputation as a novelist of significance.

The real strength of his short stories, and the reason for their undiminished popularity, is that as well as being both highly amusing and beautifully crafted, they bring to life the people, places and pleasures of a long-lost world.

2

The Marriage at Canna

It was a Friday evening in July and the *Vital Spark*, on one of her rare sorties beyond the Firth, lay alongside the inner arm of a Skye pier which she was visiting for the first time.

An atmosphere of lethargy appropriate to the hottest day of the summer was evident not just in the village but particularly on board the puffer. Macphail thumbed the pages of a new romance with little enthusiasm, his eyelids heavy and his head nodding with the effort of staying awake. Sunny Jim sprawled across the tarpaulin covering the hatchway of the hold, sound asleep and spasmodically producing a staccato series of loud snorts to Para Handy's considerable annoyance.

The only cloud on the crew's horizon was that they had just returned from the local Inn and now faced a dry weekend, having spent their last coppers on a small canister of beer. With little prospect of more where that came from.

∾

It had been a bad week for the puffer. More accurately, it had been a very bad week for her owner — but a splendid one for the crew — and all because of a partly-deaf clerk in the main Post Office in Glasgow.

The previous Monday, after shedding a cargo of coals at Crarae, Para Handy had gone ashore to telegraph the owner's Broomielaw office for instructions. Two hours later the postmaster's son appeared on the quayside with the reply. "My Chove," said Para Handy as he perused the familiar yellow form,. "it's foreign perts for us, boys."

What the telegram should have said was "Proceed Immediately To Ormidale To Load Pit Props".

What it actually said (thanks to the aforementioned clerk's hearing difficulties) was "Proceed Immediately To *Armadale*…"

Thus the *Vital Spark* lay at a Skye pier two days steaming from Loch Riddon on the Kyles where her cargo awaited. Her owner's language on receipt of Para Handy's telegram complaining that nobody at Armadale had ever heard of the puffer or her pit props is best left to the imagination.

However, as a man of some resource (or more accurately a man unwilling to see the costs incurred in getting the puffer to Skye becoming a total loss) he had told the skipper to wait for further instructions: and was now hunting the Highlands and Islands for a cargo she could profitably bring back to the Clyde, while the crew enjoyed an unexpected holiday.

His most recent telegram had promised a decision about their next move on Monday morning, with money wired then too: but since that was a promise that neither the innkeeper nor the grocer at Armadale regarded as adequate collateral for 'tick', the crew faced a thirsty and hungry weekend.

"There's no food on board save yon barrel of salt herrin' from Campbeltown," Para Handy complained to the mate. "And nothin' to quench the thirst it gi'es ye except tea. Tea!" And he gave a shudder of distaste.

At that point came a discreet cough from the quayside and, turning, Para Handy was surprised to see a handful of men with the innkeeper at their head. "Captain," said this worthy, "we hae some business tae propose. May we come aboard?"

~

"Man, Dougie," said Para Handy early next morning, "this iss the life, eh?" The *Vital Spark* was an hour out from Armadale heading west into the Cuillin Sound: the sun shone on a bright blue sea: the puffer's deck was crowded with a throng of smartly dressed men, women and children — all in holiday mood.

"This iss what she wass built for," he enthused, beaming with pride. "The *Vital Spark* wass never meant to cairry

coals an' stane an' sichlike ass if she wass a common gabbart. People iss oor merket — passengers! MacBrayne himsel' would be prood to have her in his fleet if he could see
her noo!"

He leaned from the wheelhouse to gaze fondly at the
colourful pageant below. A gaggle of children played a bois-
terous game of tag despite the protests of anxious mothers,
and young couples promenaded arm-in-arm. A huddle of
men in shiny blue and brown suits passed a bottle surreptitiously from hand-to-hand, with a wary eye on the hatch
where their prim womenfolk sat silently knitting. Perched
at the very point of the bows, Sunny Jim was obliging with
a virtuoso performance on the melodeon.

The innkeeper's 'business proposition' had been simple.
There was a wedding on Canna, one of the small islands to
the south of Skye, on Saturday: his own son was marrying
one of the island girls. The Armadale men had never seen
eye-to-eye with the men from Canna till now: here was a
fine chance to heal old wounds.

But the Mallaig fishing smack which had been booked to
ferry the wedding party to and from Canna was late getting
back from the herring-grounds thanks to the calm and
windless weather. If the *Vital Spark* didn't come to their aid
there would be no wedding. Of course, there would be a
generous whip-round for the crew and in the meantime
drinks would be 'on the house' at the Armadale Inn.

～

"If she chust had another lum sure you would tak' her for
the *Grenadier*," enthused the captain. "I wish we'd room
for wan of they Cherman Bands: at least we've got Jum's
melodeon — but I'm vexed we cannae gi' e them a cup of
tea."

"It's no tea they're wantin'," cried a cheerless voice from
the engine-room below. "When did ye ever see a Skye man
wi' a *cup* in his haunds? Ah'm tellin' you Para Handy, ye'll
be gey sorry aboot this trup afore it's over, wait and see,
there's troubles tae come."

"Chust keep stokin', Macphail, and leave dealin' wi' passengers to them that ken what they're at," said the skipper
with some exasperation. "You're nothin' but a right misery!"

And indeed so it seemed. They tied up alongside Canna's

jetty just three hours out of Armadale after a crossing as calm as if they were sailing a millpond. The crew were invited to join the wedding party at the hall after the nuptials in the little church. There was an accordion band, and two pipers: pretty girls a-plenty: tables groaning with the weight of the food on them and a most astonishing quantity of whisky from the illicit stills for which the island was notorious.

"Man, Jum," said Para Handy as he reached out for another glass later that evening, "this Canna iss some place for high jinks!"

Even the morose Macphail had come out of his shell and was in animated argument with the bride's father — himself a retired engineer: Dougie had been coaxed onto the floor for a polka by the bolder of the two bridesmaids.

∼

The shattering of the idyll began a couple of hours before their planned departure for Armadale, when Para Handy stepped out for a breath of air. Behind him the jollification was ever more raucous and the first casualties of the bride's father's hospitality were to be seen, propped up in various stages of inebriation against the dyke which surrounded the hall.

The first warning of impending doom came when the skipper felt a fresh westerly wind on his face and saw, looming over the horizon, a growing mantle of ominously dark cloud. He returned to the wedding-party to give Dougie the bad news and see if the Armadale folk could be persuaded to leave sooner than planned.

It was too late.

Afterwards nobody could say what had happened, nobody was aware of hearing the first harsh word or seeing the first blow, but when Para Handy got back to the hall battle had been joined with a will and now the bride's and bridegroom's friends and relations were trading insults and punches. The women and children of Canna fled to the adjacent church, those from Armadale headed for the jetty.

Not even the puffer's crew could escape involvement in that general melee.

"You're to blame, bringin' godless Armadale men here at all!" cried the bride's father to Macphail, loosing a haymaker which that worthy luckily side-stepped. Two sidesmen frogmarched Para Handy to the doorway and threw him out with threats of horrible vengeance if he ever returned. Sunny Jim ran for the boat as if the hounds of hell were at his heels, but the slower mate was caught by the brothers of the girl he had been dancing with and given a very undeserved black eye.

From the comparative safety of the deck of the *Vital Spark* they eventually watched in disbelief as the Armadale men were forced to fight their way to the pier and back on board.

"My Cot," exclaimed the skipper, as the warps were loosed and the puffer moved out of the harbour. "Cross Canna off the charts, boys: we never daur put in there again! Thank the Lord that's over."

Something almost as bad was still to come, however. The calm water of their outward journey was now a sea of white horses and with a rising wind dead astern the puffer, riding light, was tossed hither and thither uncontrollably as a cork. In the late evening light the deck began to look like a battlefield, strewn with moaning, whey-faced bodies as the relentless pitching and tossing took its toll.

"You and your bluidy passengers," protested Macphail from the engine-room. "D'ye see the state of this boat! She'll hae tae be hosed doon when we get tae port!"

∾

Armadale was a ghost town on Sunday, a dead, deserted community on which the combined effects of over-indulgence and mal-de-mer wreaked dreadful havoc. The crew of the *Vital Spark* passed most of the day in the fo'c'sle, snapping at each other, reading old newspapers, or indulging in desultory games of cribbage or whist.

"I'm tellin' you it's me'll be glad to see the back of this place the morn," said the skipper. "Islands! I've had enough of them to last a lifetime. It's the Clyde for me from now on."

Following an early night — there was nothing else to do — the crew were up sharp on Monday and waited with anxiety to hear from the owner.

The telegram arrived just after nine and Para Handy eagerly tore open the flimsy envelope. His mouth dropped open in horror.

"Have we no' got a cargo, then?" asked Dougie anxiously.

"Oh, he's got us a cargo all right," said the captain. "A cargo of sand. From *Canna*!"

FACTNOTE

Armadale remains the terminal for the southernmost ferry crossing to Skye, from Mallaig at the terminus of the famed West Highland Railway Line. Run by Cal-Mac, the route offers a vehicle ferry in summer, with a smaller vessel providing a passenger-only service over the winter months.

Of the four inhabited islands which lie between Skye and the Ardnamurchan peninsula Canna is the most westerly: Rum, huge and mountainous and with its Victorian 'castle' of Kinloch now run as a very up-market hotel, is the best known. Smaller Eigg and tiny Muck lie south of Rum. Properly known collectively as 'The Small Isles' they are often (for obvious reasons!) irreverently referred to as 'The Cocktail Isles.'

Poetic licence has been taken in order to allow the wedding to be located on Canna. The island has the finest harbour of any of the Small Isles, and is a green and fertile spot, but even in Para Handy's day the population was too small to sustain the sort of spree which the story suggests. Things would have been different just 50 years previously, when the island peaked at a population of almost 400: however within two generations that figure had plummeted to less than 100.

Whether there were many illicit stills on Canna in years gone by, I do not know. But there were stills a-plenty throughout many parts of the Highlands well into the twentieth century and there may be a few in business yet! My first paid employment, in my student days in the late 1950s, was as a waiter in a (then) very well-reputed hotel in Wester Ross. The allocation of the weekly days-off for individual members of the dining-room staff hinged on the needs of the one permanent, year-round waiter — a local — to attend to the still which he 'ran' (if that's the word!) in the hills above the village. By custom and usage, he always had first choice for his day off, so that the still was properly cared for as and when the need arose.

Occasionally, too, puffers really did have the chance to carry large numbers of deck-passengers — though this was never in accordance with the rules or with the approval of the relevant authorities! At the time of the 'strike' against the resort of Millport on the island of Cumbrae by the Clyde steamer fleets in early July 1906, the puffers *Craigielea* and *Elizabeth* each carried about 100 residents and holiday-makers across to the island from Largs. The reasons for the boycott (reaction to demands for heftily-increased pier charges at Millport) are too complex to go into here, but the whole story is well chronicled in Alan Paterson's seminal *Golden Years of the Clyde Steamers* (David & Charles, 1979)

3

The Race for the Pier

I was strolling along Princes Pier at Greenock, waiting for the arrival of the Dunoon steamer, when I noticed a familiar figure seated on a bollard, attempting to light a clay pipe with an expression of great concentration.

"Home is the sailor, home from sea, eh, Captain? But where is the *Vital Spark* berthed today?" I asked, for there was indeed no sign of the puffer anywhere on the long frontage of the pier.

"Well, she's no chust exactly berthed," said Para Handy. "She's on Ross & Marshall's slupway gettin' her shaft replaced. We kind of blew the main bearin' off Bute last week and had to get a tow home."

"Not by any chance from the *King Edward*?" I asked.

The captain's face reddened. "Aye, chust that," he said, and resumed his efforts to get his pipe to light.

"I should have guessed when I heard about it that it was likely to be the *Vital Spark* that was involved," I said. "You'd better tell me exactly what happened, Captain. There's some very strange stories going about Glasgow, and this could be your chance to put the record straight."

Para Handy sighed. "Aye, I heard it wass aal the talk o' the steamie, as ye might say. But none o' it wass by any streetch of the imagination the fault of the shup. If Dougie wass here he would tell ye himself.

~

"This wass the way o' it," he said, returning the stubborn pipe to the pocket of his pea-jacket. "I'll no' devagate wan single iota from the facts and maybe ye'll can pit it in the

27

papers and clear the good name o' the *Vital Spark*. I'm vexed that such a namely boat should be reduced to nothin' but a laughin' stock for the longshoremen. It wass no laughin' matter for us at the time, I can tell ye.

"We had been to Skipness wi' a cargo of whunstone, and wass headed back to Bowling in ballast when chust off Garroch Head, at the sooth corner o' Bute, there wass this most monstrous crunchin' sound in the enchine-room and then chust silence, and we started to druft.

"Macphail came burstin' out o' his cubby like a thing possessed and it iss chust typical o' the man that he tried to blame me for the breakdoon.

" 'Ah've telt ye for years,' he shouted, 'Years! And ye've never paid a blind bit o' heed tae me, naw, nor spent a penny on the engines and noo ye see the result! Ah've worked ma fingers tae the bone tae keep yon antiquated tangle o' scrap-iron turnin' ower, wi' nae thanks for it: but this time yer chickens is come hame tae roost for she's feenished, feenished. Yon's the shaft gone and since it cam' oot o' Noey's Erk in the first place ye'll no' find a machine shop tae fix it. It's the breakers' yerd for the shup, and the scrap heap for us!'

" 'My Chove, Macphail,' says I, quite dignified, 'that's quite a speech for you: but maybe you'll stert thinkin' about what we can do to stop her goin' ashore, and leave the highsterix till we've more time for them.'

"And sure enough, what wi' the southerly wind and the floodin' tide we wass setting quite fast onto the Head, her bein' light, and things wass lookin' pretty bleak.

"Macphail retired below to nurse his feelin's — there wassn't a lot he could do to nurse the enchines — and Dougie and Jum got the lashin's off the punt so that we would be ready for the worst if it came to it. I wass near greetin' mysel', I'll admit it. This looked like a terrible end for the smertest boat on the Firth, and her wi' a brand new gold bead on her paid for out o' my own pocket chust last week.

"Suddenly there was a roarin' noise astern like aal the steam whustles on the Clyde goin' off at the wan time, and when we aal recovered oor composure and turned to look, what wass it but the *King Edward*, inward-bound from Campbeltown, and closin' doon on us like a bat out o' hell.

" 'Puffer ahoy!' came a megaphone from a young officer on the brudge, a real toff by the sound o' him, 'are you in some sort o' trouble?'

"The upshot o' it all wass that in chust a matter of three or fower meenits the *Edward* had thrown us a line and sterted to pull us safely awa' from the Head.

" 'We'll give you a tow into Kilchattan Bay,' called the toff on the brudge, 'We're putting in there to pick up an excursion party but we can't take you any further up the Firth because we'll have to slow right down to tow you safely, and we can't afford that sort of delay in arriving at Gourock.'

"And off we went at a very douce eight knots or so which to the folk on the steamer must have seemed ass if they wass standing still.

"Well, it's me wass the mighty relieved man I can tell you, for though the owner wouldna be right pleased at havin' to pay for a tug to come doon and fetch us up the river, at least it wass better than the shup broken to bits on Garroch Head: and he'd have to do somethin' aboot the enchines at last.

"So I wass even beginnin' to think the break-doon might be a blessing in disguise, when we heard another great blatterin' o' whustle blasts astern. Comin' up on us very fast indeed wass the *King Edward*'s great rival, the *Duchess of Fife*, on her way hame from Brodick, the beat o' her paddles like chungle drums and the crowds linin' her rails to cheer as she swept past the turbine steamer ass if she had been lyin' at anchor.

"The paddler's Captain wass out on the wing o' the brudge and he doffed his kep and bowed very courteous-like to Captain Wulliamson in the wheelhouse of the *Edward* as he went by, but when he put it back on he waved very mockin', and blasted oot a sarcastic toot-toot-toot on the steam whustle.

"Even from the deck o' the *Vital Spark* two cables astern, you could hear the murmur of anger goin' up from the truppers on the *King Edward*, and I saw Captain Wulliamson come runnin' oot to the enchine-room telegraph on the starboard wing: it wass plain he wassna in good trum at aal: next thing I could hear the shrill bell of it clanging furiously ass he rang loud and long down to the boys in the enchine-room.

"Ass you know the *Edward* hass three propellers aal druven by this new-fangled turbine enchine, and she hass aal the go of a greyhound. Wulliamson had called for emergency full speed ahead and she near enough lifted her bows out of the watter as she took off after the paddler.

"The trouble wass, of course, that she near pulled the bows of the puffer *under* the watter ass soon ass the tow rope tightened — which it did so fast I feared it wud snap: and I could wish it had, for I thocht every last wan o' the next fufteen minutes wud be my next. If Dougie wass here he would tell you himself."

I nodded: "The laws of physics, Captain," I said. "If I remember aright, any smaller vessel towed at speed by a significantly larger one is liable to be dragged under by the downward distortion of its normal centre of static gravity caused by the stress momentum associated with any uncompensated horizontal acceleration..."

I am glad to say that the Captain looked unimpressed by this explanation.

"Whateffer you say yourself," he said at length. "But we were near sinking and the bows wass gettin' lower and lower in the watter as the *King Edward* went even faster. Things wass lookin' black for the shup! Wulliamson had completely forgot we wass there at aal, and we had nothin' which we could cut the steel hawser he wass towin' us wi' and no' way o' sluppin' it."

"So Captain Williamson just couldn't resist the challenge to the turbine's reputation?" I asked.

"It wassn't chust that," said Para Handy. "He knew fine that the *Duchess of Fife* was making for Kilchattan Bay chust like himself, and if she got there first she'd lift Wulliamson's excursion perty, and leave the *Edward* sadly oot o' pocket. So they were both hell bent on gettin' the first berth at the pier, and each had a man on the brudge keepin' a close lookout on the pierhead semaphore boards to see which o' the two the piermaster wass givin' the right o' way to — the *Duchess of Fife* in the offshore poseetion, or *King Edward* inshore of her.

"Wan o' these days there'll be a colleeshun, the way they boats iss aye racing to the piers. But aal I wass worried about wass what wass likely to happen to the *Vital Spark*, and I had chust wan way o' remindin' Williamson that we wass there, so I hauled doon on the steam-whustle and held it wide open. But we wass chust like the banshee howlin' in the wilderness, as it says in the Scruptures, for Wulliamson neffer heard a thing but kept the steamer flat out for the pier, an' by now the sea wass running green over our bows.

"It wass the piermaster at Kilchattan Bay who saved us,

for ass the two steamers rounded the point and lined up for the pier he must have realised that there wass effery likelihood of a real smesh, and so he closed up both their semaphores and brought in the old *Texa* instead as she came limpin' in from Glasgow on her cargo run to Loch Fyne.

"Mercifully Wulliamson's eyes were better than hiss ears and he bided by the piermaster's instruction. It's us were the happy men when we saw the way come off her, and our own bow liftin' above the watter again ass the tow-line slacked off. But it wass a near thing.

"Ass it wass, both steamers were late on their run home for by the time the *Texa* had finished unloading they were sadly behind their schedules, and I'm told both Captains got a reprimand from the owners efter passengers had complained aboot the delay — and the piermaster had protested aboot the race.

"But — for all the pierhead gossip I hear aboot — it wass not the blame off the *Vital Spark*. How could it be?"

∿

I shook my head sadly.

"You've obviously not heard the full version of the story as it reached Glasgow, Captain," I said. "The Kilchattan piermaster's report didn't blame just the two steamers.

"He said he had been confronted with three vessels racing for the pier."

I took a crumpled copy of the previous day's Glasgow News from my pocket, found the report I was looking for, and read aloud: "The Kilchattan piermaster reported to the Clyde Port Authority that he had denied access to the pier to the packet steamers *Duchess of Fife* and *King Edward*. Though they were racing each other for the first berthing opportunity, this was standard practice and not in itself his reason for turning them away.

"His fear was that the presence of a third vessel could have had serious consequences and indeed threatened the safety of all involved. 'The two steamers were neck and neck at about 20 knots,' he told our reporter this afternoon. 'Though it is hard to believe, there was a Clyde steamlighter immediately astern of the *King Edward* which, with her whistle blowing a demand to be given right of way, was clearly attempting to overtake both passenger ships at once. In the circumstances the only course of action open to me was to close the pier to all three.' "

~

I am sorry to say that Para Handy has made no effort to deny this report but, rather, has enjoyed the kudos of the qualities which certain credulous individuals now ascribe to the puffer.

My duty, I feel, is to set the record straight.

FACTNOTE

There was intense competition on the Firth at the turn of the century, the heyday of the paddlers and the first of the new generation of screw steamers on the Clyde: and of course these years were the zenith of the puffers too. Keen races for first berthing opportunities at the piers between passenger vessels operated by rival owners were common-place — and notorious.

For the steamers, the prize was not simply the prestige of superiority in speed: it was commercial success. The faster ships attracted the greater attention and publicity and thus by reputation the greater — and more loyal — following. Of more immediate concern to the captains was that, if two steamers were closing down on a pier crowded with trip-pers awaiting the chance to return to Gourock or Glasgow after an excursion for the day 'doon the watter', fortune favoured the first arrival, which would scoop up the poten-tial passengers and leave her unsuccessful rival with an empty pierhead.

A trial of speed in open water was one thing: but a high-speed convergence in the narrow confines of some isolated pier was very different and there were regular (though thankfully almost always minor) collisions: there were also frequent near-misses or, to describe them with rather more accuracy, near-hits! One collision, documented in the pages of the Glasgow Herald, did actually take place off the Garroch Head, in 1877, between the *Guinevere* and the *Glen Rosa*, when they side-swiped one another with conse-quent damage to their paddle-boxes.

The advent of the turbines inevitably sharpened the rivalries as the hitherto unchallenged crack paddlers found themselves under threat from the new upstarts.

Probably the greatest duel of all, however, was played out

on an almost daily basis between the established paddle-powered speedsters *Lord of the Isles* and *Columba*. They both ran daily services from Glasgow to Bute and on through the Kyles: the *Columba* to Tarbert and Ardrishaig, her rival continuing north to Inveraray.

Their schedules usually found them leaving Rothesay on the outward passage at exactly the same time, and from there it was a race to reach the Kyles piers (the first of these being Colintraive) ahead of the opposition. The passengers invariably took up an extremely partisan stance but, as the contemporary newspaper accounts testify, they were as ready to heap abuse on a losing Captain as they were to cheer a winner's triumph.

TURBINE ELEGANCE — King Edward was launched from Denny Brothers' Dumbarton Yard in 1901 — the world's first turbine-powered merchant vessel — and ran the daily service from Greenock Princes Pier to Campbeltown and return. Capable of over 20 knots, she is seen here edging into the Kintyre capital's pier with a 'standing room only' crowd on board. Note the vessels on the stocks of the shipyard in the background.

4

Trouble for the Tar

From the deck of the *Vital Spark* the crew watched with interest as a large gaff-rigged ketch, having successfully and skilfully negotiated the deceptively narrow opening into the inner harbour at Rothesay, nosed in to the stone quayside, one of her hands standing in the bow pulpit making ready to throw a line ashore. In the capacious cockpit immediately astern of her substantial main cabin stood three elegantly turned-out men with a fourth, presumably the owner, at the wheel.

"A chentleman's life," said Para Handy., "There iss no better way to see the world than in a yat! They'll no' have problems wi' harbour-masters or ship's captains. Welcome whereffer they care to go, and steam aalways gives way to sail!"

Dan Macphail, with a watchful eye on the derrick as he swung another swaying bundle of fencing-stobs outboard to the waiting cart on the quayside, nodded agreement. "Aye, they huv it easy compared wi' the likes of us. The workers is aye the worst aff in this world, It's the gentry that comes oot best. Ah wudna say no to a poseetion on a yat!"

"Me too," cried Sunny Jim from the depths of the hold. "Just imagine no' havin' tae work wi' a cargo of coals ever again! A life of ease!"

"Mind you," said Para Handy, "even the lads on the yats have problems sometimes. Take your predecessor Jum, your kizzin Colin Turner 'The Tar', for instance. Crewin' on a yat nearly cost him his merriage…"

"Tell us the baur," said Jim, peering over the coaming of the hatchway. On the quayside the now fully-loaded horse-and-cart was heading for the town, and since there was as yet no sign of the second cart returning, a few minutes of rest and relaxation were in prospect.

Para Handy scratched his ear reflectively. "Well, it wass like this…"

~

"Ass you aal know, The Tar got merrit on wan Lucy McCallum, a Campbeltown gyurl, and left the shup soon efter the weddin'. He took a chob in a distillery in the toon ass a cooperage hand and he learnt his tred and for three years efferything went fine for the young couple. They rented a single end chust off Main Street and Lucy had two weans, a boy and a gyurl. Mercifully it seemed they wud tak' efter her rather than their faither in character ass well ass in looks, for he wass idle, The Tar, idle — and blate wi' it.

"But it wassna his fault he lost his chob at the distillery, for it wass at a time o' sleck orders in the spurits tred and the man that owned it chust shut it doon — not for good, but for a few months till there wass demand for spurits again, and he paid off all the hands and told them to come back in 10 weeks.

"Lucy wass fair dementit when the Tar gave her the news, but she couldna blame the boy, though it wass goin' to be very hard to get ony ither work, for there were fower other distilleries layin' men off at the time and there were chust no chobs to be had in the toon.

"Her mither wass a widow-woman but she helped the young couple ass much ass she could, and it wass she who heard that there wass to be a new boat-yerd opened up at Inveraray by a kizzin o' her late husband, and she wrote and asked if he could find a chob for the Tar, chust for a few months till the distillery opened up again.

"And he wrote back and said yes, if the Tar got himself there within the week he'd tak' him on in the framin'-shed.

" 'But hoo am Ah tae get up tae Inveraray,' asked the Tar when she gave him the news. 'Me wi' no wages comin' in?'

"She had even sorted that oot for him. 'Wan o' the English chentlemen that comes up for the shootin's in September bought a yat last year and it's been lyin' at Machrihanish effer since then,' she said, 'Noo he's wantin' it taken to Tarbert to wait for him comin' up there next month.'

"Wan o' the Campbeltown fishin' skippers wass pickin'

the yat up the next mornin' and sailin' it up to Tarbert while hiss own skiff wass on the Campbeltown slup for her annual overhaul, and he'd agreed wi' her that the Tar could crew for him. And of course wance he wass in Tarbert it would be easy to tak' the two hoor trup on to Inveraray on the *Lord of the Isles* any day of the week.

"There wassna mich the Tar could do to get oot of that, so next mornin' he wass up sharp and steppin' oot the six miles ower to Machrihanish wi' his tin box on his shoulders.

"Vickery, the skipper, wass there before him and within the hour they were off. The Tar wass a bit worried when he saw who the skipper wass, for Vickery was weel-kent for his fondness for the high jinks, but he wass a successful fisherman and a good seaman. The yat wass called *Midge* but in spite of that she wass a smert boat wi' a midships cabin wi' a couple of berths and a wee punt in tow.

"They made good time round the Mull of Kintyre and chust aboot two-o-clock they had Davaar Island dead ahead, and then the mooth o' Campbeltown loch openin' up to port.

"Vickery looked at his watch. 'We've made good time, Colin,' he says to the Tar. 'What d'ye say we chust look in to the toon for an hour and I'll see how they're gettin' on wi' the repairs on the skiff?'

"There wassna anything the Tar could say, he wassna skipper, so they tacked up the loch and moored the *Midge* in the harbour and rowed ashore in the punt. Ass fate would have it they met a brither o' Vickery's who'd chust got hame from Gleska that very mornin' on the *King Edward* efter a year at sea, and before the Tar kent what was what, they wass aal ensconced in the nearest Inn at a table by the window — 'So I can chust keep wan eye on the yat', said Vickery — and the drams kept comin' ass soon ass aal the brither's friends foond oot he was back in toon and came in for a yarn.

"Five in the afternoon came and Vickery gave the Tar the keys to his hoose and sent him to fetch a gallon jar so they could tak' some refreshments back on board wi' them. And the first person he met ass he wass comin' back along the street wi' the jar wass his mither-in-law! 'What are you doin' still here, Colin,' she cried briskly, 'when you should be well on your way up Kilbrannan Sound — and whaur are ye goin' wi' that jar?'

"The Tar tried to explain in a way that wouldna incriminate him but she gave him a sharp look and reminded him that the chob at Inveraray wouldna wait for effer. 'Get you to Tarbert, Colin Turner' she said. 'Or you'll answer to me for it!'

"Here and when they left to go back to the yat did Vickery's brither and anither couple o' his cronies no' come wi' them, and wi' their ain jars, and the perty sterted aal over again. At eight o'clock Vickery consulted his watch and annoonced that it wisna worth settin' off that night, they'd wait till next mornin' and get awa' sharp: and he went back ashore wi' his brither and left the Tar in charge.

"Next morning, the Tar woke at seven and there wass no sign of Vickery at aal. But within the hour he wass back, wi' a grey face, a short temper and a heid as spiky as a bagful o' old spanners. 'Iss this Campbeltown or Cairo,' he cried, 'and am I comin or goin'? Be a good lad, Colin, and nip ashore and get a can o' mulk at the dairy and a pooder frae the chemist, and if I can find where I pit ma heid we'll mak' a start."

"Who did the Tar meet on the quayside but his wife Lucy, wi' the elder wean on her shoulder and the baby in a pram full o' dirty washin', on her way to the laandry.

" 'Colin Turner!' she shouted on him, 'You should be in Tarbert by noo. Wait till I tell my mither on you!' And though the Tar tried to explain she chust stormed off in a real tizzy but not afore she'd gi'en him the bleckest look he'd effer seen on a wumman.

"When he got back on board the *Midge* he managed to persuade Vickery to loose her from her moorin' and off they set.

"But ass luck wud have it the winds wass against them, and then when they were off Carradale at aboot fower in the afternoon, the sea haar cam' doon like cotton wool and they couldna see the tap o' the mast.

" 'It's nae use, Colin,' said Vickery. 'Ah'm no riskin' the boat in fog like this.' And he picked his way into the harbour at Carradale.

"Pretty soon the Tar foond himsel' in the Inns at the head of the pier and again efferybody seemed to know Vickery and in no time at aal there wass a spree goin'. Wan o' the company wass a Campbeltown cairter caaled McCallum, wi' the by-name o' the Twister, who wass a kizzin o' the Tar's mither-in-law, and a man wi' a dreadful reputation for a dram, so soon they wass aal in full flight.

"The poor Tar had had enough of it and he tried to get his skipper back on board. 'I will no' be long at aal, Colin,' said Vickery. 'Why don't you chust awa' ootside and streetch oot on McCallum's cairt and have a snooze? I'll gi'e ye a shout when we're ready to go and we'll be in Tarbert in no time at aal.'

"Well, the Tar went and did chust that, for he wass aalways a man wi a great capacity for sleep. If Dougie was here he would tell you himself. The cairt wass half full o' sacks o' corn so he made himsel' a comfortable bunk and snugged doon.

"So he slept and better slept.

"When he finally woke up it wass seven o'clock next mornin' and broad daylight! He sat up at wance, feart that Vickery had sailed withoot him — and foond they wassna even in Carradale at aal! The cairt was stood at the foot of Main Street in Campbeltown! They wass outside the Ferry Inn and what had woke him wass the din ass Vickery and McCallum kept bangin' on the door to get the Landlord to open and gi'e them their mornin's!

"Chust then, who came roond the corner from the close leadin' to his ain single end but his wife and his mither-in-law!

"They both clapped eyes on him at the same time and let oot a shriek that even stopped Vickery and the Twister deid in their efforts to break into the Inn.

" 'Colin Turner!!! Whaur's your sense o' responsibeelity to your wife and weans! You've mooths to feed and aal you can do iss chust cairry on wi' drink like a Cardiff stoker!'

"It wass ass well for Colin that the cairter, at least, wass chust sober enough to tell his kizzin and her dochter that the poor Tar wass innocent of ony devagation, that he and Vickery had been thrown oot o' the Inn at Carradale at midnight and, having forgot aal aboot the *Midge*, and the Tar asleep in the back of the cairt, had let the horse do the navigation and meandered doon hame to Campbeltown in the wee sma' hours.

"So the Tar neffer made it to the chob at Inveraray, and the chentleman that owned the *Midge* wass in a right tirravee for he had to send a new crew doon frae Tarbert to pick her up from Carradale.

"The only thing that saved the Tar's skin wass that the spurit trade picked up (probably lergely due to Vickery's singlehanded support) and he got his old chob back the next week when the distillery re-opened.

"So, Jum, remember it's not aalways plain sailin' on a yat!"

FACTNOTE

Now that the network of steamer services on the Firth of Clyde is but a distant memory, the Mull of Kintyre is unquestionably the most isolated community not just in Scotland, but in all of mainland Britain, and Campbeltown the country's most remote town. In fact in some respects it is more remote from Central Scotland now than it was 100 years ago, when daily services by fast steamer from Glasgow, 80 miles by sea, were usually faster and certainly more comfortable than today's tortuous 140 mile bus journey — which takes 4½ hours each way.

The Tar's journey from Campbeltown on the eastern coast of the narrow peninsula to Machrihanish on the western side must have taken place before August 1906, for otherwise he would not have had to walk!

That month saw open to passenger traffic the splendidly-named Campbeltown and Machrihanish Light Railway Company's services on a narrow-gauge line, an extension of the track originally laid to transport coal for export across the peninsula from the Drumlemble pit to the docks of Campbeltown harbour.

Inevitably christened 'the wee train' the line remained open for passengers for 25 years, finally closing in 1931 after the shut-down of the coalmine during the 1929 depression.

Carradale lies roughly half-way between the southern-most tip of Kintyre and Tarbert, where the peninsula 'rejoins' the mainland at Knapdale, and was an established port of call for steamers on passage to Glasgow. Today it remains a popular destination for visitors in the summer months and maintains its traditional fishing industry year-round.

Discussing this story-line with a resident of Campbeltown prior to publication I suggested it was rather far-fetched that I had the horse bring the cart all the way home from Carradale by itself. "Not at all," he said: "they used to do that from the Tarbert Fair in the old days — and that was twice the distance!"

The seas around the Mull are exposed and subject to violent storms. Hence the construction almost 200 years ago of the Crinan canal, which allows small vessels to move between the Clyde and the Western Highlands in sheltered conditions. The hazards of the Mull are perhaps best exemplified by the fact that in the years before the development of powerful, fast rescue vessels there were not as today, just one, but *three* lifeboat stations within a few miles of each other at its southernmost limits — Campbeltown, Southend and Machrihanish.

DREAMLAND FOR DRINKERS — *This panoramic view of Campbeltown and its bay shows, behind the mother and her two infants, an unbroken phalanx-in-depth of distillery after distillery: there were more than 20 in the town in the years around the turn of the century and grain to supply them was a frequent cargo for the puffers, and larger vessels too.*

5

Up for the Cup

It can be — depending on the particular circumstances at any particular time — either an advantage, or a disadvantage, to be the skipper of a West Coast puffer. In the remotest communities the arrival of the little vessel is a major event, the social (and business) highlight of the month or, in some instances, the year. She may be delivering the bits and pieces of the material world, from mangles to mattresses, which the community has anxiously been waiting for: or she may have come to load a cargo, be it timber or whinstone, barley or roofing slate, the eventual sale of which will provide the cash income necessary to keep the village economy going for another season.

As almost the only link with the outside world, the puffer provides often the sole opportunity such communities have to maintain even the most basic social communication with distant family and friends. Thus the *Vital Spark* has been known to carry a few jars of rhubarb jam (and, most important of all, the recipe for it) from an old lady in Colonsay to her newly-married niece in Greenock, or a border collie pup from a farmer in Ayrshire to his cousin in Appin.

Sometimes Para Handy is flattered by such requests, sometimes irritated by them: it depends on his mood. But, being of a kindly disposition, most of the time he is happy to help.

What can test his generosity to the limit, however, is when the little extra something he is asked to carry is neither animal nor inanimate — but human.

"I've had mair trouble wi' the occasional supercargo than ye'd hae wi' a barrowload o' monkeys," he told me when I encountered the crew recently in a Gourock hostelry, "but

the wan we had last week wass the giddy limit. Neffer, neffer trust a man frae Colintraive. Chust ask Macphail!"

Hearing mention of his name the engineer, who had been
sitting hunched over the niggardly fire in the far corner of
the bar, turned round and in so doing displayed a monstrous 'shiner' on his right eye.

"How on earth did Dan come by that?" I asked in astonishment.

"Och, he didn't exactly come by it," replied Para Handy.
"He didn't have to go and look for it at aal, at aal. Somebody
gave it to him. Neffer, neffer trust a man from Colintraive."

And, with only a little further coaxing, he told me the
tale.

～

"It wass partly Dan's own fault, of course," said the skipper with a nod in the direction of the figure at the fire. "It
usually is. You ken yoursel' what he's like. Not exactly full
of the milk of human kindness, no, nor exactly the soul of
tact or discretion.

"It all started last Friday when we wass picking up a
cargo of oak bark at Colintraive.

"You wud see in the papers that the Kyles Athletic fitba'
team had managed to get to the third round of the Scottish
Cup by beatin' Dunoon Rovers, and then Renfrew Thistle.
And who were they drawn to play next but Gleska Rangers
themselves! And at Ibrox Park!

"You can imagine the excitement all along the Kyles. The
team had gone up to Gleska the day before on the *Minard
Castle* and they were stayin' in wan o' they Temperance
Hotels — a very wise precaution given their reputation for
a spree — ass guests of the Gleska Highlanders Association.
Friday afternoon, when the *Columba* called in on her way
back from Ardrishaig, maist o' the men of the Kyles villages
wass waitin' on Colintraive pier wi' their tin boxes in one
hand, and the addresses of their Gleska cousins wrote doon
on a bit o' paper in the ither.

"By the time we finished loading on Friday afternoon, the
Kyles wass a deserted place indeed. We wass all doon in the
fo'c'sle at wir tea when there came a shout frae the pier and
Jum went up to see what wass up.

"Here wass Ferguson the innkeeper — and a quiet weekend he wass facin', what wi' all the menfolk awa' tae Ibrox

and it too early in the year for ony towerists to be aboot — wi' a young fellow maybe in his early twenties scuffin' his feet beside him.

" 'I dinna think ye've met Hamish, my youngest', says he by way o' introduction.

"The upshot of it wass that Hamish had been up in Glendaruel on a chob wi' the Forestry and had got back to Colintraive too late to catch the boat to Gleska wi' the rest o' them, and him a desperate keen supporter o' the Kyles Athletics team.

"I could see which way the wind was going to blow but I owed an obleegance to Ferguson for the time he'd subbed us till the wages cam' through from the owner so before I could say eechie or ochie aboot it, young Hamish was aboard the boat and we were to gi'e him passage up river when we left at dawn the Saturday mornin'. In truth it wass no great inconvenience, for we wass to unload oor cairgo at Govan on Monday mornin' and so we'd planned to berth the shup there for the weekend ass it wass.

"Noo ye'll mind that afore Macphail moved to Plantation he'd spent all his years in Govan so, though he'd never been to a fitba' game in his life, he coonted hissel' a supporter o' the Rangers. 'Brutain's finest', he wud say when the papers showed them winnin' some new trophy or ither: 'Rangers iss the boys!'

"So he didna' take too kindly to a Kyles supporter installed in the fo'c'sle, specially wan festooned in the favours o' the Kyles team, in a kind o' roarie yellow colour like the skin of a custard and wi' a stripe or two o' purple through it.

"Dougie wass ashore visitin' a cousin so Jum and me did oor best to keep the peace but Macphail was aye needlin', needlin' at the young fellow. It wass 'At least you lot'll see fur wance whit way a real team plays fitba' tomorrow' — and — 'See in yon strup o' yours, the Kyles boys'll look like naethin' so mich as a set o' kahouchy skuttles or a cageful o' canaries!' — and — 'Whit nicht wull ye be haudin' the wake in Colintraive?'

"I tell you I wass that worried they wud come to blows then and there I took Hamish to wan side and made him promise to keep hiss hands in his pockets and off the enchineer. 'Ye'll have to mind he's an older man and you wud lose face if you laid wan on him,' says I. 'Michty,' says Hamish. 'It's him that wud lose face — and a' the component pairts o' it — if I did.' But he promised me he'd swallow the insults ass if they wass water off a wally close and sit on his hands if needs be. 'You have my word on it, Captain MacFarlane,' he says: 'I swear I'll no' lay a finger on the auld fool.'

"To be on the safe side and to keep them apart I took Macphail up to the Inns and treated him oot of my ain pocket. When we got back aboard the young man wass sound asleep in the spare bunk and I thought that was that, for we had a very early start the next mornin', and Macphail wud be snug doon in his enchines wi' the latest novelle and oot o' herm's way.

"Everythin' went sweemingly on the Saturday, we made a quick passage up the river and put in to the basin at Govan at aboot two o'clock and set the young fellow ashore within an easy walk o' Ibrox Stadium.

"His faither had promised to send a telegraph to wan o' his Gleska cousins and get him to meet him at the quayside and sure enough there wass another yellow-and-purple bedecked figure waiting for him at the dock gates.

" 'Whateffer you do, dinna' staun' behind the Kyles goal' was Macphail's parting shot. 'For there'll be that mony holes in the net in nae time that ye'll be sittin' targets like ducks in a shootin' gallery! Or canaries raither!'

"But chust two minutes later the young fellow wass back! Here and wass it no' an aal-ticket game! His cousin had chust the wan ticket so there wass nothin' for Hamish to do but drum hiss heels. 'I've arranged for cousin Gordon to come back doon here to collect me wance the game's over,' he said, and him near to greetin' wi' the disappointment of it all. 'I hope it's all right for me to wait on the boat till then?'

~

"Mercifully Macphail went aff to sulk among his enchines and the rest of us sat doon in the fo'c'sle and had a baur.

"Come five o'clock the young fellow went up on deck to look oot for his cousin comin' back. Dougie and me went up too, and began gettin' the shup ready for the unlading on Monday. Dougie started to loose the tarpaulins on the cargo hatch, and I freed the jib o' the derrick from its bracket at the fore end of the wheelhouse.

"Chust then Macphail came out on deck. 'I thocht you'd have been ashore tae get your black armband and your weepers,' he cried to Hamish. 'But at least I can gi'e ye plenty o' coaldust tae mak' yer ain!'

"I'll say this for the boy, he never stirred, chust drummed his fingers even-on on the jib-arm of the derrick.

"And then hiss cousin appeared at the gates, and walked up to the side of the quay. You chust needed to see the way that he walked to ken he certainly wassnae the bringer o' glad tidings frae Ibrox."

"Hamish looked up anxiously. 'Whit wis the score, Gordon?'

" 'Seventeen-nil.'

"Hamish said nothin', chust kept drummin' his fingers even-on on the jib-arm, but there was a great guffaw from behind him where Macphail stood on the other side of the deck by the bulwarks at the after end of the hold. 'Seventeen-nil! *Seventeen-nil!* Go on, Hamish — are you no' even goin' tae ask him — *who fur?*'

"It took just seconds. The young fellow spun round, seized hold of the jib-arm, and with a mighty shove swung it outwards and towards Macphail. It caught him chust at head-height, as you can see from the state of his eye: and knocked him overboard into the basin.

" 'I'm right sorry, Captain," said the young fellow: "but a man can take only so mich: and I kept my promise. I didn't lay a finger on him."

"Since Sunny Jum wass ashore gettin' the groceries, and I'm the only wan o' the rest of the crew that can swum, it was me that had to dive in and fish him oot. And ruined my best pea-jacket in the doin' o' it.

"Like I said at the beginning: you can neffer trust a man frae Colintraive."

FACTNOTE

The quiet Kyles village of Colintraive has a number of particularly fine houses, many of which were originally built as summer homes by wealthy Glasgow merchants and professional men. The shortest ferry-crossing on the Clyde operates from here to Rhubodach on the island of Bute, less than five minutes away across the narrows.

The most unexpected teams can occasionally reach the later rounds of the Scottish Cup, and they can find themselves drawn to play established, senior clubs. This helps to give the Cup (at least from the point-of-view of the neutral bystander) a sometimes surreal serendipity.

In 1995, for example, a non-league Fife team called Burntisland Shipyard (named from the years long gone, when it was a 'works' team in the days when Burntisland *had* a shipyard) reached the third round of the tournament. Sadly for those whose sympathies lie with the underdogs, that was the limit of their progress.

Inevitably some of these fairy-tale teams have gone down to crashing defeats. The most notorious score-line of all dates from 1885, when Arbroath (playing at home) beat Aberdeen Bon Accord by 36 goals to nil — which was equivalent to a goal being scored every two-and-a-half minutes of playing time. The *Guinness Book of Records* account of the event comments: 'But for the lack of nets and the consequent waste of retrieval time the score must have been even higher.' Arbroath still play senior football today, though in one of the lower divisions.

Two years later the equivalent record for the English Cup was set by Preston North End with a 26 to nil victory over Hyde.

I hope that any supporters of Rangers who may read this story will excuse the placing of a totally fictional game at the very real Ibrox Stadium: I am sure they will, particularly when it involves such a convincing victory! And I doubt very much if there would have been any 'all-ticket' games in Para Handy's day, but sometimes a little anachronism becomes a must in the telling of a tale!

It has also to be admitted that the Kyles area is better known for its Shinty traditions than for any pretensions to football. Shinty is perhaps best loosely categorised, for those unaware of its finer points or even of its existence, as a version of hockey which seems to have few rules and scant consideration for the safety of the protagonists. A game with a Physical Contact Quotient which makes almost any other team-game seem a pansy pursuit, and enjoying a strong loyal and local following in the Highlands (to which area it is largely confined), it has been described by uninitiated critics as legalised mayhem. To those brought up with, and devoted to, the traditions and the finer points of the game, such a comment is as a red rag to a bull. So I unreservedly withdraw it!

6

An Inland Voyage

On occasion, the *Vital Spark* left her familiar Clyde haunts for the sheltered waters of the Forth & Clyde Canal. Sometimes she was bound for the farther shores of the Firth of Forth to load barley for the distilleries back at Campbeltown. Sometimes she would pick up a cargo of timber from the seasoning basins at the port of Grangemouth. Sometimes her business was within the canal network itself, taking coals to the Carron foundries or uplifting pig-iron from Bonnybridge.

Whatever the reasons for her presence on the Canal, Para Handy viewed such journeys with an unremitting and quite remorseless loathing.

The other members of the puffer's crew looked on these inland voyages as a welcome relief from the more demanding environment of the open waters of the Firth, and the associated problems of wind and tide. To chug effortlessly through the countryside along a smooth ribbon of never-ruffled water was sheer paradise compared with the purgatory of battering round Ardnamurchan in the teeth of a howling headwind and a steely, rolling swell.

For the skipper, though, the Canal was hell: for here, in every town and village through which the little vessel passed, he was at the mercy of the unfeeling urchins who watched the approach and greeted the passage of the puffer with undisguised derision.

At least on the river and in the firth the sarcastic cries of "*Aquitania* ahoy!" from boys fishing from piers or hanging over the stern of the crack paddlers shooting past the lumbering puffer could be ignored. The puffer would eventually be out of earshot of the piers, and the paddlers would much sooner be just a dot on the distant horizon as they sped away, carrying his tormentors with them.

On the Canal the taunts were ever-present. The *Vital Spark* was easily outpaced by the ragamuffins of Avondale or Twechar, who assembled on the banks in droves as she approached and then ran alongside her with their merciless, mocking cries as she wheezed her way towards the next set of locks. Her looks and her speed were compared unfavourably with the elegance and pace of renowned passenger-vessels like the *Faery Queen* or the *May Queen* and Para Handy could only escape the verbal onslaught by retiring to the wheelhouse, tightly shutting door and windows however hot the weather, and feigning a lofty disdain that he certainly did not feel.

"Man, Dougie," he would protest, as he watched the gang race ahead and line up at the parapet of the next bridge the puffer must pass under, "ye wud think their faithers and mithers wud bring them up wi' some sense of the dignity o' the sea! They've no more respect for the *Vital Spark* than if she wass a common coal scow or a cattle barge!"

∾

Thus a fine May morning found the captain in a foul mood as the puffer approached Camelon on the Forth and Clyde Canal, their destination the Rosebank Distillery on the outskirts of Falkirk with a cargo of the best Fife barley. Her progress through the locks at Grangemouth had involved running the usual gauntlet of taunt and insult and the skipper's patience was exhausted.

The *Vital Spark* nosed in to the quayside at the Rosebank basin where two horse-drawn drays stood waiting to start carting the sacks of grain to the adjacent distillery warehouse.

Para Handy, once the unloading had started to the accompaniment of the noisily hissing clatter of the puffer's temperamental steam-winch, made tracks for the distillery office to report his arrival.

"You're looking a bit out of sorts today, Peter", commented the manager, who was well acquainted with the skipper and his crew over many years.

Para Handy explained the reasons for his ill-temper and, to his surprise, found he had a sympathetic ear.

"I know exactly what you mean," said the manager. "We

have just exactly the same problems with the little terrors. Thirty years I've been here, and 30 years of splendid service we've had from generations of our Clydesdales. But now these new-fangled motor wagons are all the rage, honest horses aren't good enough for the kids of Camelon.

" 'Peep, peep! Oot o' the way!' or 'Can ye no' get them oot o' first gear then, mister?' are the least of the insults my men have to put up with when they're out on the roads with the drays."

"No respect, chust no respect at aal," agreed Para Handy. "It's a peety we couldna gi'e them a lesson they'd remember, a lesson to shut them up next time they felt like givin' lip to their elders and betters."

"Dreams, dreams, Peter," said the manager and, reaching into a drawer of his desk, produced a square bottle of the colourless straight-from-the-still whisky and poured them both a generous dram.

∼

Unloading the barley sacks took till late afternoon, and so the *Vital Spark* lay overnight at the Rosebank basin. As the crew were preparing for an early start the following morning Para Handy was surprised to see the distillery manager come running up. Behind him, two workmen were pushing along the towpath a strange-looking machine mounted on four small wheels.

"Could you do me a wee kindness, Peter? Could you put this fire engine off at our Maryhill bottling plant for me?"

Half-an-hour later the puffer cast off and headed towards Lock 16, junction with the Union Canal to Edinburgh, on her journey westwards to Glasgow and the Clyde.

Macphail the engineer was of course the only man aboard able to even begin to comprehend the workings of the machine which now perched on the hatch of the puffer's empty hold. Leaving his engines to their own devices he prowled round the little contraption, cap in hand, scratching his balding pate.

"Two horse power," he read aloud the inscription on the brass plate riveted to the platform on which the device was mounted. "Two horse power fire pump."

"Whit does it dae, Dan?" queried Sunny Jim.

"Ah've read aboot them," said the engineer. "It's wan o' they new-fangled petrol injins the same as they hae on caurs, but this wan's for pumpin' watter." He gesticulated to the hoses coiled round drums on opposite sides of the frame. "It's tae pit oot fires. Ye stick the end o' wan o' they hoses intae the watter, caw that haundle on the end tae get the injin sterted, and point the ither hose at the flames. The watter gets pumped up and the fire gaes oot."

"Man, man," said Para Handy in some surprise. "An infernal machine, my Chove! Whateffer will they think of next?" And he resumed his contemplation of the spring countryside as it slipped by at the rate of 4 knots.

They had a peaceful passage across the central heartland of the Forth and Clyde valley but the canal urchins appeared again as they approached Kirkintilloch.

"Would you look at that," cried the exasperated skipper as a gang of young boys raced along the towpath beside them, pulling faces and catcalling, "a skelp behind the lug's what they're sair in need o'." And he pulled up the sliding windows to shut himself into the cramped wheelhouse.

The door opened and Sunny Jim squeezed in.

"Captain," he said, "I've got an idea..."

⁓

Five minutes later the puffer glided into the Townhead locks in Kirkintilloch. Sunny Jim jumped for the iron ladder let into the stone walls of the lock and climbed to the towpath. Pushing his way through the assembled crowd of young boys he helped the lock-keeper to swing the wooden gates shut at the stern of the boat. The lock-keeper opened the sluice in the gates above the puffer's bow, and water started to pour into the lock to lift the little vessel up to the level of the next stretch of the canal.

Jim peered down onto the deck of the puffer 10 feet below him. There was surprising activity taking place on the hatchway.

The mate was uncoiling one of the water hoses on Para Handy's "infernal machine" and Macphail was preparing to swing the iron starting-handle. The skipper himself, with a suspicious glint in his eye, was cradling the brass nozzle at the end of the second hose in his hands.

The puffer continued to rise up the surrounding lock walls as the water flooded in from the higher level. Rows of grinning faces to either side awaited her coming as the Kirkintilloch urchins prepared to subject the hapless Para

Handy to another torrent of abuse.

Sunny Jim had a quick, whispered consultation with the keeper as the level of the water in the lock rose higher. That worthy quickly took shelter in his nearby hut, and Sunny Jim, with a last check of the levels, jumped six feet down onto the puffer's deck and shouted: "*Now!*"

Macphail swung the starting-handle, the little petrol engine fired, the water pump got down to business, and in a matter of seconds a powerful jet of water shot from the brass nozzle in Para Handy's grip.

With a whoop of triumph, he directed the jet to left and right, sweeping it across the ranks of his tormentors who, caught totally by surprise, were quickly drenched through before they hesitated, broke, and fled in disarray.

"Let that be a lesson to you," called Para Handy with a grin of triumph. "Two horse-power and an auld man, that's aal it takes to send you packing! Maybe next time ye'll think twice before you give any lip to the men who run the horses and puffers on this canal, eh?"

And, turning the pump off as the lock gates ahead of him swung open and Macphail headed for the engine-room to put some way on the little vessel, he returned to the wheelhouse and began to rehearse the very satisfying story he'd have for the manager of the Rosebank distillery next time they met.

FACTNOTE

Only two of Scotland's Canals — the Crinan and the Caledonian — remain fully navigable today, though some stretches of the Forth and Clyde, and Union, Canals have been restored and there are some pleasure sailing opportunities.

The Crinan and the Caledonian remain in use because they still fulfil the purpose for which they were built — to offer an alternative, for smaller vessels, to what would otherwise be a long and exposed sea-passage. Scotland's other major Canals had provided for the convenient transportation of raw materials in bulk, such as timber, steel or coal: and the speedy and more comfortable movement of passengers.

Since both these functions were, in the course of time, better catered for by the railways and the road networks, the canals became outmoded and eventually abandoned.

THE NEW HORSE-POWER — Here is the precursor of the juggernauts of today, an early brewer's lorry with, perched on the fence, some of the urchins whose taunts on and off the Firth could make life such a misery for the beleaguered Para Handy. But it would be 50 years before the last horse-and-cart disappeared from the streets of Glasgow.

Thus were lost the Forth and Clyde Canal from Grangemouth to Bowling: the Union Canal which (across beautiful countryside and over some quite spectacular aqueducts) linked the centre of Edinburgh to the Forth and Clyde Canal near Falkirk: the Monkland Canal from Glasgow to the coalfields of Lanarkshire: the Paisley Canal from Glasgow to Johnstone, all that was ever completed of an ambitious project to link Glasgow by canal to Ardrossan on the Ayrshire coast: and the less-well-known Aberdeenshire Canal which ran from the Granite City northwards to Inverurie.

At the height of the canal 'boom' there were proposals for many other, smaller scale, projects throughout Scotland from the Solway in the south and as far north as the Moray Firth. Some of these, such as a 2 mile cut to carry coal from the Ayrshire mines to Saltcoats harbour: a 3 mile waterway, again to carry coals, across the Mull of Kintyre from the Machrihanish mines to Campbeltown: and a 2 mile canal at Cupar in Fife, to convey limestone, were actually completed.

Two hugely ambitious projects came to nothing: but it is

quite intriguing to speculate how the economic history of the country might have been altered if they had. One, first mooted at the beginning of the nineteenth century, proposed a cross-Scotland canal linking Dumbarton on the Clyde with Stonehaven, south of Aberdeen, by way of Stirling and Perth. The second, which was actively promoted for over 60 years and only finally buried for good in 1947, was for a Canal linking the Firths of the Forth and the Clyde, a through route for ocean-going vessels, a huge waterway which would have been on the same scale as the Manchester Ship Canal in England. Several alternatives were considered: by far the most dramatic, not to say controversial proposal, would have taken the waterway from the head of Loch Long and through Loch Lomond to debouch into the Forth near the village of Fallin a mile or two east of Stirling.

7

Those in Peril on the Sea

Conditions had deteriorated throughout the October night and when the crew awoke in the morning it was obvious that there could be no question of the *Vital Spark* beginning her return journey to Glasgow. Far from her usual haunts, she lay against the wooden pier at Scarinish on the Inner Hebridean island of Tiree, where she had unloaded a cargo of winter coals.

The prospect was chill and cheerless. A south-westerly wind of storm force howled mercilessly across the treeless, blasted machair of this flattest of islands, and savaged the scattered clusters of croft houses which huddled together as if searching (in vain) for some element of shelter from the worst excesses of the weather. Occasional flurries of rain were swept across the bleak landscape in stinging horizontal sheets.

Most frightening of all, though, was the state of the sea itself. Between Tiree and Mull, 15 miles away, the ocean seemed to boil in fury as the wind whipped the tops off the steep waves: and the rocky sentinels of the tiny Treshnish islands which lay off the Mull coast at times disappeared under the cataracts of flying spray exploding from the mountainous breakers which disintegrated against their low black cliffs.

"My Cot," said Para Handy, as he slammed the fo'c'sle hatch behind him after a quick peek out to assess the situation, "I doot we're goin' nowhere today, laads: indeed I doot if even Mr MacBrayne'll be goin' anywhere. Heaven help any shup that's been caught oot in this."

Macphail — whose stock of novelettes lay out-of-reach

for the moment in the engine-room — looked up from his perusal of the only reading matter to hand, a copy of the Oban Times which the Mate had purchased the previous day in the Scarinish shop. "If the *Mountaineer* so mich as pits her nose oot o' Tobermory in this, they're askin' for trouble," he agreed. "This is aboot as bad a storm as I can mind of for mony years."

Sunny Jim, whose previous sea-going experience — as a hand on the Cluthas — stopped at Yoker, was mightily relieved to have confirmation that the puffer was not intending to venture into a storm the very sound, never mind the sight, of which had given him an apprehensive, sleepless night.

"Whit's the worst experience at sea that ye've ever had wi' the *Vital Spark*, Captain?" he asked.

Para Handy scratched his right ear reflectively.

"That would have to be a time a few years back, when we wass bringin' a cargo o' brand new herrin' boxes from a Campbeltown factory up to wan o' the fush-merchants in Oban. But it wass a bad experience not because it wass dangerous at aal, Jum, but chust because it wass so doonright vexatious.

"We had to sail to Oban roond the Mull o' Kintyre, because they wass repairin' wan o' the locks in the Crinan canal and it wass closed to aal shups for three weeks. For several days afore we set oot from Campbeltown, there wass a steady wund from the west: not a gale, you understand, but chust this constant, constant wund.

"Caairyin' a bulky, light cargo like herrin' boxes meant that even wi' the hold cham-packed wi' them we still had a lot of freeboard, so we wass able to pile up a great mass o' them as deck cargo as weel. Even then, though her stern wass doon, her bows wass still up, and there wass a wall o' the boxes aboot eight foot high streetched right across the hatchway.

"Ye couldna see a dam' thing ahead of the shup from the brudge, and the Tar had to sit on the tap o' the deck cargo to gi'e us directions.

"Effery time we roonded the Mull and the wund hit us, we chust got pushed back! Even wi' Dan's predecessor, McCulloch, pilin' on the coals and near burstin' the biler wi' the steam pressure we couldna get enough power to mak' ony headway into thon wund! The pile o' boxes wass chust like a sail and we wass doin' mair speed under wund-power

— but goin' astern — than we effer did under steam-power goin' ahead!

"I wass bleck-affronted. Effery mornin' for fower days we left the harbour at Campbeltown, and effery evenin' for fower days we had to turn back there to anchor overnight and try again the next day. I have neffer been so embarrassed aboot the shup even though it wass not her fault — it wass the wund. And when the fishermen in Campbeltown foond oot what wass goin' on they took a real rise oot o' us. My Chove, wan night someone cam' oot in an oarin'-boat while we wass aal asleep and pented oot the name o' the shup on the stern and pented on *Cutty Sark* instead! And the local paper printed a piece sayin' the vessel should be caalled the *Bad Penny* because she kept comin' back, and that if we stayed ony longer we'd chust as well get a Cooncil licence to give roond-the-bay trups to towerists!"

Sunny Jim turned to the engineer. "Whit about you, Dan?" he asked: "wi' you goin' foreign for so mony years you must have seen some sights!"

"The worst experience I can mind wis nothin' to dae wi' a storm either," offered Macphail. "I wis an apprentice at the time, on a Union Castle liner tae Capetoon, and we lost the propeller aff the shaft aff the Skeleton Coast. There wisnae a dam' thing we could dae aboot it. There wis no wireless in them days, of course, so we jist had tae wait till anither shup appeared, and then hope she could gi'e us a tow.

"There wisnae a breath o' wund, and the sea jist like glass, but there wis a swell ye wudnae believe unless ye saw it! The sea had a run o' thoosands o' miles frae Sooth America tae build up a swell, and it wis like a roller-coaster at Hengler's but mich, mich bigger. The taps o' the swells wis aboot a mile apart, and aboot a hundred feet high! When ye were doon in the troughs you couldnae see a thing but the slope o' the swell either side. We went up and doon and up and doon jist like a twenty thoosand ton yo-yo, and at the same time she wis daein' that, she wis rollin' like a pendulum, and the maist o' the passengers wis that ill they thocht they wis deein'.

"In fact some o' them *hoped* they wis deein'. I wis on the poop deck wan evenin' and there wis a poor cratur hingin' ower the rail, jist as green as grass, and I said to him, no' tae worry, naebody ever died o' the sea-sickness.

"He gave me a look I'll never forget, and groaned 'Dinna

say that, boy, for peety's sake: it's only the hope o' deein'
that helps me tae keep goin' !'

"When we finally got a tow in, the swells wis that deep
that there wis times the shup that wis pullin' us jist disappeared frae sight completely: ye couldna even see the taps
o' her masts!"

Dougie, a notoriously timid sailor and a man who had
spent his entire career on the puffer routes in the west,
shuffled his feet and looked uncomfortable when Jim swung
round and looked enquiringly in his direction.

"You needna be askin' Dougie," said Para Handy, "for he
hass nothin' at aal to tell you aboot the perils o' the deep.
Whiles some of us hass been stravaigin' across the oceans
o' the world — I've been to Ullapool masel', and twice to
Belfast — here iss a man who could be feart for hiss life
crossin' on the Govan Ferry on a summer's afternoon! Iss
that no' right, Dougie?

"Onyway, while you're tryin' to think up some heroic tale
for the laad, I will chust tak' a dash up to Harbour House
and see what my old friend the Piermaster is thinkin' the
weather might be doin', for if we are to be marooned mich
longer we wull have to speak nicely to his good-wife aboot
the len' o' some proveesions."

And the Captain pulled on his heavy oilskin coat and
clambered up the companionway and out into the wild of
the storm.

"He thinks he iss very funny," said the embarrassed
mate, "but I have a story for you Jum, for aal that: and by
the time I've finished tellin' it Para Handy wull be sorry he
needled me in the first place!

"The worst conditions that ever I experienced had nothin' at aal to do wi' the weather — but a very great deal to do
wi' a certain steam-lighter Captain!

"Before oor time on the *Vital Spark*, Jum, Para Handy
and I wass workin' for a man in Girvan that had a sailin'
gabbart caaled the *Elizabeth Jane*. Wan time we wass in
Campbeltown wi' a load o' lime from the quarry at Glenarm
in Antrum, and wass due to sail back ower to Ireland for
anither wan.

"The herrin' fushin' in Kilbrannan Soond and Loch Fyne
wass absolutely in its prime at the time. The skiffs wass
comin' in each mornin' nearly sinkin' under the weight o'
the fush they had on board. There wass such a glut o' herrin', you couldna give the fresh fush away in Gleska, and

the kipperin' sheds and the picklin' factories couldna keep up wi' the supply.

"Para Handy wass chust a young man, and he wass aye lookin' for ways to turn a coin. He had an uncle that wass a fush merchant in the toon and when he saw the glut o' fush there wass, Para Handy went to him wi' a proposition. The *Elizabeth Jane* would cairry a load of fresh herrin' in barrels ower to Glenarm, where there wissna mich o' a fushin', and sell them there, and the pair o' them wud split the profit on the trup.

"I didna like the soond o' it, and said so. But Para Handy wass convinced he wass aboot to mak' his fortune and he wouldna listen to reason. So off we went on Tuesday afternoon wi' aboot a hunder barrels o' fresh fush in the hold, which wass to be sold in Glenarm ass soon ass we docked the next mornin'.

"It was a bonnie day, wi' chust the right north-easterly breeze to gi'e us a good passage.

"But by mudnight, the breeze had dropped tae nothin' and we wass chust druftin' aboot wi' aal sails flappin' and us gettin' nowhere. For three whole days there wassna a breath o' wund and we lay like a piece o' druftwood, goin' a mile here and a mile there wi' the tide and the current, and the sun wass chust bakin' doon!

"We could see the hills of the Irish Coast to the sooth, and Kintyre to the north, but they could have been the mountains o' the moon for aal the chance we had to reach them. We got the sweeps oot and tried to row her, but wi' the weight of the fush we had in the hold we didna mak' a hundred yerds an hoor and we dam' near drapped wi' the effort o' it.

"By the third day the fush wass in an interestin' condeetion and there wassna mich fresh air on board, I can tell you! They wassna fresh fush at aal by noo, those herrin': they was in gey poor trum, cooped up in barrels in yon hothoose o' a hold under a bleezin' sun. By the fourth mornin' you chust tried no' to breathe, if at aal possible.

"On the fifth day, thank the Lord, the wind got up again, from the sooth-west: there wass no point in tryin' to sail against it to Glenarm, for naebody wud buy the fush noo, so Para Handy headed back for Campbeltown to dump the cairgo — before it got up and waalked ashore on its own. Ass we came in the harbour you could see the folk on the quayside stert sniffin' and then run for cover, and the piermaster wouldna let us berth the gabbart, never mind unload it!

"We had to pit oot to sea again, and spend the night wi' a scairf tied over our noses and mooths, winchin' the barrels oot o' the hold and drappin' them quick ower the side o' the boat. The smell wass chust unbelievable!

"It aal cost Para Handy a pretty penny, he had to pay for the barrels, but worse we both lost oor chobs, for the owner foond oot why we wass so late gettin' back to Glenarm and when we reached Campbeltown wi' the second load of lime there wass a new skipper and a new mate waitin' to tak' oor berths.

"And though, for all Para Handy says, I have neffer in my life been *sea-sick* I can tell you Jum, that for the maist of that particular trup I wass sick at sea. Very sick. And so wass the Captain!"

FACTNOTE

The Minches, those stretches of water which separate the long arm of the Outer Hebrides from the Inner Hebrides and Mainland Scotland, can be unpredictable and stormy at almost any time of the year. Littered with islets and rock skerries they were a maritime graveyard for centuries, and despite the proliferation of light-houses and automatic lights as an aid to their safe navigation they still claim the occasional victim.

The Treshnish are a group of tiny, uninhabited islands a few miles west of Mull. They cannot rival world-famous Staffa and the dramatic basalt columns of Fingal's Cave closer inshore but their dramatic silhouettes do make an unforgettable sight. One, also known as the 'Dutchman's Cap', has every appearance of the traditional 'pirate' hat made familiar to cinema-goers in all Hollywood manifestations from Treasure Island to Captain Blood. Only the skull-and-crossbones is lacking!

Tiree has a wild beauty but is also notorious as the windiest place in Scotland: and the flattest island in the Hebrides. It is less remote today than in Para Handy's time, with a regular vehicle ferry service from Oban and plane from Glasgow.

Largely due to their lack of power, and a lack of 'grip' in the water caused by their hull shape, the puffers were notoriously unmanageable when riding 'light' in even a moderate wind and the problems faced by Para Handy as he attempts to round the Mull of Kintyre are based on the actual experience of a Ross & Marshall puffer in the 1950s.

Off the west coast of South Africa the Atlantic swells running in from the Roaring Forties have been known to reach gigantic proportions in which a 10,000-ton ship can apparently, and frighteningly, 'disappear' with ease as she drops into the trough of the waves.

At the height of the herring fishing on the Clyde there could be such a glut of landings that the shore stations were unable to cope with them. I never had experience of that but when we lived in Shetland I saw at first hand just how enormous herring landings could be, given the right circumstances. In the early days of purse-netting, Icelandic and Scandinavian boats brought in quite unbelievable catches. None more so than a Reykjavik purser which came in to Lerwick harbour with only the whaleback and the poop above water: her main deck was actually submerged with the weight of fish on board. When her skipper discovered that he could only sell the catch for fish meal and not on the more lucrative processing market (I cannot remember the legal details but such was the position at the time) he then actually tried to put to sea to sail his catch home — and had to be forcibly prevented from doing so by the harbour authorities!

8

Macphail to the Rescue

The *Vital Spark* had never visited Loch Etive before, but Para Handy knew enough of the reputation of the fierce tide-rip in the shadow of the railway bridge at Connell to time his arrival at the narrows to coincide with the slack of the tide, when the otherwise steeply rushing waters lay relatively at peace.

In this he succeeded: but nevertheless took the precaution of whistling down the speaking-tube to Dan Macphail in his noisy domain to ask for full power.

"Power!" a contemptuous voice echoed back: "the day there's ony power on this hooker Ah promise you'll be the very first to know aboot it! It's a miracle we've got this far but hoo the owner has the nerve tae send this tub ony-where ootside Garroch Heid is beyond me. Wan o' these days we'll jist no' get back, she'll peg oot on us and dee o' auld age."

"Chust so, Dan," said the Captain in a placatory tone, "but I am certain you will see us safe home again —" and turning to the Mate who was standing at his side he whispered "— Dan's in duvvelish bad trum this week! What iss wrong wi' the man?"

"He's no been himsel' since he visited yon spae-wife at Minard Fair last week," said Dougie, "and had his hand read."

"He should have more sense," said Para Handy, "than to pay ony attention to the ravin' of a wumman wi' nae mair knowledge o' his future than he has o' the workin's of a turbine enchine."

The Mate tactfully resisted the temptation to remind Para Handy of the occasions on which he himself had slipped into a Fortune Teller's candy-striped tent at country fairs, with his shilling grasped firmly in the grubby hand which he was about to present for a mystical interpretation. Such a service was usually offered by the wife of the round-about proprietor, disguised in spotted red head-kerchief and borrowed floral robe, prodigally (and deliberately) burning so much incense for atmosphere that it was almost as difficult to breathe as it was to see.

By now they had entered the wider, sheltered upper loch and the vessel was headed towards the pier at Bonawe. She was scheduled the following morning to load a cargo of granite setts from the nearby quarry for Glasgow Corporation roads department. By five o'clock the puffer was snug at the pier and the crew, with the exception of the Engineer (who refused to be persuaded to join them under any circumstances), set out to walk the mile or so inland to the inn at Taynuilt.

They had scarcely settled themselves at a corner table with glasses of beer and the landlord's best set of dominos when the outer door burst open and an worried-looking man in a yachting cap came in almost at a run. He banged the bell on the bar loudly and urgently and when the land-lord appeared had a brisk and anxious exchange with him, the two of them hunched across the counter so that their heads were almost touching.

Finally the landlord straightened up, shaking his head.

"I'm sorry, Captain Forbes, but there's no' an ingineer this side o' Oban. Go you there on the next train," and here he consulted his watch, "You'll be in the toon by eight o'clock and if you're lucky in finding a man you'll be back before 10."

"Ten!" cried Forbes. "I can't leave a touring party strand-ed on the ship till then! They're due back at the Hotel for their dinners at eight!"

Para Handy cleared his throat. "Where's the shup, chentlemen," he asked, "and what seems to be the trouble? We have a sort of an enchineer wi' us — he's no' here but he's no' far away — and I am sure he would not see you stuck."

~

Half-an-hour later Captain Forbes, Para Handy and Macphail (the last still in the same ill-humoured temper)

were clattering through the Pass of Brander in a pony and
trap.

Forbes was indeed in a predicament.

The small Loch Awe pleasure steamer, of which he was
captain and part owner, was aground at the mouth of the
pass, where it opened out into the broad waters of the loch
itself. "We should never have come so close in shore," he
admitted ruefully "but I've done so often enough before
without any trouble."

The trouble stemmed from the fact that the engine had
died just as he was about to turn the little vessel back to
deeper water and, drifting with the momentum of her passage, she ran gently aground 200 yards offshore. The problem was seriously compounded when all efforts to get her
engine re-started failed

"We took a new engineer on for this season," said Forbes,
"and I don't think he has the experience he said he had."

The three rowed out to the little ship — imaginatively
named the *Lochawe* — in the dinghy in which Forbes himself had come ashore in search of another engineer. As they
clambered aboard the Captain was surrounded by a crowd
of passengers, some of them curious, some anxious and
some just plain angry.

"Why don't you chust tak' them below to the salong,"
suggested Para Handy, "and trate them to the wan wee
refreshment. A man aalways feels mich better when he hass
a gless o' somethin' in hiss hands! Macphail and me will
have a look at your problem.

"He may not look much," he confided as his Engineer
disappeared in the direction of the engine-room at the
stern, "but though I would neffer tell him to hiss face, in
case it would make him swoll-headed, he iss wan o' the very
finest enchineers in the coastal tred!"

So it seemed.

Twenty minutes later came the gratifying sound of the
shaft turning and, by dint of moving the passengers to the
stern of the little boat (which was in deeper water) and calling for maximum power astern, Forbes was able to pull the
grounded bows off the shoal onto which they had strayed,
and the vessel was soon under way and headed for the pier
at Loch Awe village, just beside the Hotel at which her passengers were staying.

"You and Mr Macphail can get the train from the village
station back to Taynuilt, Captain Macfarlane," said Forbes

with some warmth. "And I am sure I do not know how to thank you enough. You have saved my reputation! And probably my ship as well!"

"It wis nae problem," said Macphail, grudgingly. "Jist a broken linkage, and that on an injin gey like mah ain. Ah've telt your man whit went wrang so if it happens again, he should be able tae fix it. Else ye'd best look oot fur a new ingineer."

~

"Well, does that not make you feel better, Dan?" asked Para Handy as they sat in the Glasgow to Oban train for their short trip back to Taynuilt. "I am not referring to this —" he waved the crisp, white Bank of England £5 note pressed on them by the grateful Forbes "— but to the cheneral proof of your agility and your value. You have been in a foul mood for the last few days and we are aal most anxious to see you snep out of it!"

"If onything it mak's me feel worse," said Macphail miserably.

"Dan, Dan, what ails you?" asked the perplexed Captain. "We've been long enough at sea, Captain and Enchineer, that we should have no secrets."

Macphail sighed, long and deep.

"It wis yon spae-wife," he said at last. "she wisnae wan o' the usual rubbish ye get. She wis wan o' the real Gipsy Rose Lees! She telt me the names o' my wife and weans, she telt me the name o' the shup, she telt me we wis comin' tae Loch Etive for the setts.

"Worst, she telt me she saw me on a puffer wi' a broke-doon injin and an injineer no' able tae fix it, and the shup herself goin' on the rocks! Jist like whit happened tae that man this efternoon — but no' on a passenger boat like yon, on a puffer she said. That has tae be the *Vital Spark*.

"Peter, get anither injineer, at least till ye're all safe back tae Gleska, for sure as daith if ye keep me on we'll be agroond at the Connell tide-rip, or even a worse boneyerd, an' the shup'll be lost!"

"You're a haver, Dan," said the Captain, but taken aback by the Engineer's unfeigned, vehement despair. "Spae-wifes! They're aal rubbish!"

"No' all," said Macphail, "No' all of them." And he turned with a heavy sigh to stare miserably across the passing countryside into the dying evening light.

~

Para Handy came back to the corner table from the bar counter at the Taynuilt Inn, with four drams perched tantalisingly and precariously on a battered tin tray featuring the advertising slogan of a long-forgotten brand of chewing tobacco: a silver mountain of change from Captain Forbes' five pound note: and a broad and quite triumphant grin.

"Dan," he said, "I have the best news you've had for days and if you don't believe me you can ask himself over there himself and he'll tell you it iss aal true": and he gestured towards the landlord, who nodded and smiled back.

"Even if your spae-wife wass the chenuine Gipsy Rose, Dan, and even if effery single thing she told you wass true, you have nothing at aal to worry aboot! It hass aal happened already!

"The *Lochawe* wass wance a puffer herself, that's what she wass built ass! They turned her into a passenger shup years ago but orichinally she wass a puffer chust like the *Vital Spark*, which is why the enchines wass so like what you were used wi'. What happened today iss what your spae-wife told you aal about — but she neffer said it wud happen to you on *your* shup, chust that it wud happen to a puffer and that you'd be there when it did. And it has happened — but tae the *Lochawe* and her enchineer!

"That means it's not going to happen to you — nor to the *Vital Spark*!

"So cheer up, Dan, and let's have no more of your nonsense. And don't you effer, effer again let me cetch you goin' onywhere near a spae-wife while you're the enchineer on my shup!"

FACTNOTE

The railway bridge at Connell was completed in 1903. For more than half-a-century it doubled as a toll-paying crossing for motor traffic for which exorbitant tariffs could be (and were) charged in view of the near-monopoly situation which its owners enjoyed. The only alternative route for vehicles from Oban to Benderloch or Appin or Lochaber (or vice versa) was a tortuous road journey of nearly 100 miles. Eventually, in 1966 — after the closure of the railway line to Ballachulish — it became a normal, toll-free part of the road network.

The tide-race at this point, known as the 'Falls of Lora', is most noticeable at the spring tides, when it presents a quite daunting spectacle for any small boats contemplating the passage into Loch Etive.

The first major industrial venture attempted at the Etive village of Taynuilt, in the 18th century, was an iron foundry but this had a relatively short lease of life.

For decades thereafter, however, a large granite quarry on the shores of Loch Etive opposite Bonawe was the source for many of the cobblestones or 'setts' which paved the streets of Glasgow for many generations. A few now by-passed city backstreets and cul-de-sacs survive with these original surfaces: hardwearing, impervious to almost any abuse but quite notorious hazards for two-wheeled traffic (pedalled or powered) in the wet, when they turn swiftly into treacherous, ridged skid-pans.

The Pass of Brander runs westwards from the northern shores of Loch Awe just beyond the remarkable Cruachan Hydro-Electric Power Station, built inside the mountain and completed in 1965.

The small passenger steamer *Lochawe* served on the loch for half a century, finally going to the breaker's yard in 1925. Mystery surrounds her origins. She is registered as having been *built* in 1876, but there is evidence that she was in fact *converted* in that year for passenger duties, having been originally designed and constructed some years earlier as a steam lighter of 100ft overall.

Her lines and general appearance were certainly suggestive of a cargo rather than a passenger carrying ancestry. She had a very substantial freeboard, and a cavernous saloon and dining room which gave every indication of having been created in the original hold. Like every puffer ever built — and unlike almost every purpose-designed passenger vessel of the time — she had her engines aft. The Pointhouse yard of A & J Inglis was responsible for her conversion (or construction) in 1876, and she was then dismantled and transported in sections to Loch Awe for assembly on a lochside slip.

9

The Kist o' Whustles

It was several weeks since the paths of my own peregrinations had crossed with the passages of the *Vital Spark*, and I was out of touch with the latest news of the doings of her Captain and crew when I came across them loading a cargo at the factory pier of the fireclay works on the river Cart.

"It's drainage pipes for Cowal," acknowledged Para Handy with a deprecatory shrug, meeting me as I strolled up the quayside just outside Paisley, "and given the amount of rain they've been havin' on the peninsula this last week or two, it iss mebbe not before time."

Using a contraption consisting of a complex rectangle of netting made from webbing-straps the puffer was loading a cargo of ochre-coloured pipes of quite startlingly large diameter.

"They are going to Kilmun," continued the Captain, "for that Mr Younger, the chentleman that mak's his money from the beer: he iss puttin' mair gairdens into hiss Benmore Estate and with the amount of rain watter that comes pourin' off the hill, he needs aal the drains he can get, poor man.

"Macphail wass suggestin' that mebbe he iss goin' to divert the watter to the brewery but then Dan iss of the opeenion that aal beer hass been wattered, exceptin' perhaps when it's his favourite stout."

"They look an awkward cargo to handle," I suggested, watching as another dangling, precariously-secured bundle came swinging inboard, and ducking instinctively as it passed just a few feet above my head.

"There iss worse," said the Captain agreeably: "though at

67

the moment I wud find it very dufficult to say chust what. But at least they are clean.

"And in any case, it's aal chust in the day's work for the shup. Drain-pipes for Kilmun: or whusky from wan or ither o' the distilleries," he added emphatically and hopefully, — but I did not even offer to take the hint: "we can cope wi' it aal. If Dougie wass here..."

~

The Holy Loch cuts into the Cowal Hills just two miles north of Dunoon, the salt-water arm of a geological fault-line linking the estuary to Strachur on the upper reaches of Loch Fyne to the west. Between the Holy Loch and Strachur lies narrow Loch Eck, mirroring the steep and wooded hills which rise around it.

That freshwater loch, renowned as among the most beautifully situated of any in the country, also mirrors (in miniature) the attributes of its larger saltwater neighbours, for it boasts a modest passenger steamer service, provided for excursionists and round-trippers, by the *Fairy Queen*, a screw steamer little larger — though with much finer lines — than an ordinary Clyde puffer.

I was reminded of this on the occasion, some months after my encounter with Para Handy at the Paisley docks, when I came across the *Vital Spark* and the captain and his crew at Kilmun pier, where I had arrived aboard the steamer *Redgauntlet* on a Saturday morning, invited to spend the weekend on the coast with old friends who had taken a house for the summer.

Laid against the north side of the pier, the puffer was busily unloading a series of plywood boxes, little more than two feet square but as much as 12 or 15 feet in length. Dougie the Mate was operating the steam-winch with very considerable care, not to say delicacy, of movement. Sunny Jim, standing on a flat-bodied dray on the pier, guided the boxes as the jib swung them towards him, lowering and stacking them on the cart with as much concentration as if they had contained the very finest of bone china.

More surprisingly still, there was a goodly crowd on the pier to watch this process including, huddled together in a group, a number of distinguished-looking gentlemen — one even sporting gaiters — dressed in clerical clothing.

"My goodness, what sort of cargo is it you have today,

then, Captain?" I enquired as Para Handy came over to pass the time of day, "for I'm sure the ship is as much at the centre of attention as if it was the Crown Jewels themselves, and the crew are taking as much care of it as if it was eggs!"

"Well," he said, "conseederin' what the last cargo you saw us wi' wass, and that it wass consigned for Kilmun too, you could surely guess that it would be pipes. Chust pipes," he said, and then added mysteriously, "but mebbe a raither special sort of a pipes."

"Well, it's the first time I've ever seen pipes boxed up like that," I said. "so it's not drain-pipes for sure. Lead pipes for a plumbing contractor, is it? They must be very particular about where they buy their raw materials."

"Goodness me," said Para Handy, "it iss not plain water pipes we have in the boxes, Mister Munro. For wance the owner hass managed to get the contract for a dacent cairgo worthy o' the shup. Wan that iss mair in keepin' wi' her style and her cheneral abilities.

"These here iss organ pipes — sent doon from Gleska, for the new unstriment they're puttin' in at the Kilmun Kirk along the road there.

"We brought down the wud and the metal and aal the rest o' the materials for the insides of it last week, alang wi' two men that are buildin' it, and then last night we came back wi' aal these fancy bits!"

It was a pleasure to see how the Captain glowed with pride at the distinctive cargo which had been in his care: and to reflect that, given the enthusiasm of all on board the puffer for what the engineer would have called a "good tune", and the modest but nonetheless accomplished musical talents of Dougie and Sunny Jim, they were perhaps the most appropriate crew on the river to be entrusted with it.

"Ass weel ass these pipes for the front, and fancy carved wud screen-frame to hold them," continued the Captain, "there iss two keyboards, I'm tellin' you no lee, two o' them nae less. It seems chust a waste o' time to me for I have neffer yet seen an organist wi' fower airms. But that iss not aal! For then there iss what the men that's buildin' it tell me are pedals for the man that plays it to use his feet on to get a choon!

"If they were to pit it in a side-show in wan o' the fairs you would surely get the public-at-lerge to pay their saxpences chust to watch it in operation: for the man that plays it must have aal the agility and cheneral sagiocity o' the India Rubber Man at Hengler's Circus and Carnival!

"Obviously none o' yer common-or-gairden harmoniums iss good enough for the folk at Kilmun. This is a proper fantoosh organ, the like o' them that you wud find mebbe in St Mungo's where the Gleska chentry go, or in Paisley Abbey where the Coatses come from, or in a Kirk that's beholden to Mister Carnegie for the occasional contribution."

"Well, Captain," I said. "You must remember that Kilmun Church has been under some patronage from the Dukes of Argyll for many years, and so maybe it is His Grace that is paying for it as a present for the congregation!"

And, reflecting that it was perhaps just as well that the crew of the *Vital Spark* were not of the persuasion of the Free Church of the Western Highlands, (for then the care bestowed on the instrument in their charge might have been somewhat less painstaking) I shook the Captain's hand and headed off towards my friends' lochside retreat.

~

I had the pleasure of attending the recital given a couple of months later in Kilmun Church on the occasion of the official inauguration of the new organ.

The historic little kirk was packed and the instrument, safely installed in the choir gallery above the main door of the building, was resplendent with its banks of gleaming pipes, its rich wood carvings and fretwork.

What I think nobody was prepared for — or could have even begun to be prepared for — was the splendid sound quality and sheer magnificence of the organ itself.

The audience sat in rapt silence as the church filled with the most sublime harmonies and melodies, the sheer power and depth of the bass pipes almost outshone by the daring virtuosity of the contrasting melodic stops, brilliant in their cascading ripples, their soaring scales and shimmering arpeggios.

After two hours in which the listeners were transported, as it were, to another world, the concert concluded — fittingly and properly — with the singing of that most inspiring of all the master-works of the Scottish Psalter, 'Ye gates, lift up your heads on high' to the tune *St George's, Edinburgh*.

~

As the hushed crowd left the church and passed into the cool darkness, a sense of the infinite hung about the churchyard and the last soaring, triumphant notes of the great organ crescendo which had closed the evening seemed to hang on, still, in the silent night.

As I picked my way along the shore side of the church-yard wall, a dark silhouette — a familiar dark silhouette — detached itself from the trunk of a venerable tree which overhung the path, three other figures just discernible beyond it.

"I am gled they feenished with *St Chorge's*," said Para Handy quietly. "Anything else would chust have been a let-doon."

"I had not expected to see you here, Captain," I said. "Why did you not come into the kirk?"

"I do not think that wud have been right, Mister Munro, for we are chust Brutain's hardy sons, straight from a day's work perambulatin' aboot the river, and in no' fit state to be seen in among the Kilmun congregation alang wi' aal the chentry.

"But we were prood to have brought the new kist o' whustles doon here, and happy to have had the chance to hear it played. There iss some chobs we value more than ithers..."

"...and there are some men to whom we owe a debt of gratitude for the care and devotion with which they carry out those jobs," said a voice from behind us, and the Kilmun minister clapped Para Handy on the shoulder.

"We would all be very pleased, Captain, if you and your crew would come up to the Hall right now, and join us all for supper so that we can thank you properly."

FACTNOTE

The Loch Eck steamer was for decades an integral and essential link in one the most popular of all the 'round trips' on the Firth. Passengers sailed from Bridge Wharf down river and through the Kyles, then on to Strachur on Loch Fyne whence they transferred by coach or (later) chara-banc to the head of Loch Eck, and thence back to the Holy Loch or Ardentinny piers for their return passage to Glasgow.

PADDLE POWER — *This splendid picture captures the drama of a crowded paddler at full stretch. The steamer is one of the North British Steam Packet Company's Craigendoran fleet — Redgauntlet — referred to in the story about the Kilmun organ. She was built at Barclay Curle's Scotstoun yard and launched in 1895. She is listing to port as the crowds line that rail to watch the steamer from which this photo was taken vanish astern. Note too the huge diameter of the steering-wheel on her open bridge, requiring two helmsmen to handle it.*

The *Fairy Queen*, an 80ft vessel with generous saloon facilities for her patrons, was built in the upper reaches of the Clyde at Seath's Rutherglen Yard in 1878 and gave almost half-a-century of service before she went to the breakers in 1926.

Such excursions are a distant memory but the gardens at Benmore between the Holy Loch and Loch Eck remain one of Argyllshire's greatest treasures. The millionaire Edinburgh brewing family, the Youngers, gifted the estate to the nation in 1925. As well as being a spectacular attraction and an asset for visitors and locals alike, Benmore — managed nowadays as an adjunct to the Royal Botanic Gardens in Edinburgh — has an outstanding flora and is also a major research station, especially renowned for a rhododendron collection of 250 different species.

The church at Kilmun stands on the site of the oldest Christian foundation in this part of the country, established in the early seventh century by St Munn, an Irish monk who had previously served in the Columban community on Iona.

The present building, completed in 1841, is the third to have been erected on the site looking out across the Holy Loch. It is unusual in many respects, particularly for the way it has been constructed to encompass and shelter, on its north-eastern corner, the mausoleum built in 1795 as the resting-place of the Campbell Dukes of Argyll, whose ancestors used Kilmun as their burial-ground, and most of whose descendants are interred here.

The church is of great beauty and considerable interest: many thousands of visitors come to see it each summer. The stained glass and the woodwork are particularly fine. So is its organ, installed in 1909 and unique in being powered by a hydraulic pump — operated by the local mains water supply — the last such in the country. It is, quite simply, a splendid instrument, the unexpected jewel of a tiny kirk, and one which would not be out of place in any of the larger churches in the land.

How the organ and all its works was first brought to Kilmun I do not know: but it is perfectly possible that transportation was indeed provided by a puffer, for it could certainly not have arrived in any way other than by sea.

10

Hurricane at the Helm

I had arrived in Oban by train late one September afternoon on my way to Lochboisdale in South Uist. The MacBrayne steamer *Mountaineer* sets out on the 10 hour crossing three days a week — at 6.00 in the morning. I had reserved a sleeping-berth so that I could pass a comfortable night on board and avoid an unconscionably early rise in the morning, waking instead in time for breakfast as we approached Tobermory.

As I climbed up the gangway from the South Pier I happened to glance across the bay and, to my considerable surprise, saw a familiar but totally unexpected maritime silhouette. So it was that, a short while later, with my baggage safely stowed aboard the paddler, I made my way along an esplanade thronged with a great crowd of visitors enjoying an early evening stroll before dinner, and out onto the town's North Pier.

Para Handy was seated on the hatchcover of the *Vital Spark* with his pipe in one hand and a mug of tea in the other, studying the toes of his boots with apparent interest.

"Good evening, Captain," I said. "You are about the last person I expected to find in Oban."

"Well, well," he said, looking up with a start. "It's yourself then. This writing business must be doing well, eh, if you can afford a nice wee holiday at this time of year? Not that it's any of my business…

"Ah well then," he continued after a few moments, once he realised that I had no intention of unburdening myself of any confidences about my present financial condition, "Yes, we are chust here perambulating aboot the Sound of Mull for a week or thereby. The owner has got a contract to tak' in the winter coals to some lighthooses and so here we are.

"I wish I could offer you something but would you credit there iss nothing on the shup..."

It was not too difficult to persuade the Captain to join me in making the short journey to the bar of the Argyll Hotel.

~

"This iss not familiar watters for the *Vital Spark*," he said a few minutes later as we settled to a table near the fire, "but I have Hurricane Jeck with us on this trup and it iss certainly familiar to him."

I remarked that I had not been aware that that intrepid mariner had had much experience in the islands trade.

"Cot bless you, yes" said Para Handy. "For aboot eight months he wass aal over the Hebrides for Mr MacBrayne, chust after his spell as master of the clupper *Port Jackson*.

"Jeck had a hankerin' to settle doon, for that wass the time he wass walkin' oot wi' the widow MacLachlan from Oban, before the problem he had at the Gleska Mull and Iona Soiree, Concert and Ball wi' her and Lucy Cameron.

"Nothin' worked oot for him, he had the very duvvle's own luck ass usual, he lost the gyurl and then he lost the shup and in chust a matter of months he wass back goin' foreign again, this time on the *Dora Young*."

I indicated that I would be more than interested in the story by calling for the Captain's glass to be refilled.

"It wass this way," he continued, sniffing the amber liquid with some satisfaction. "Mr MacBrayne took him on ass skipper on the *Handa* when she wass on the Oban to Tiree service.

"You'll mind she wass aal hold, very broad in the beam and she carried only a couple o' dozen passengers, but Jeck ran her ass if she wass the *Columba* and his manners wass that sublime that folk thocht it a rare preevilege chust to be allowed on board the shup.

"Wheneffer Jeck took the pier at Tobermory he'd be oot on the wing o' the brudge, wi' his kep on three hairs and wi' a cheery wave for aal the world. When he had docked her he wud sweep off the kep wi' a most dapper bow to the gyurls on the quayside and it soon wass that the maist o' the weemenfolk o' Tobermory wud come doon each mornin' chust to waatch the *Handa* berthin'.

"It wassna chust his manners that wass sublime, it wass his cheneral agility ass well. Ass he came into Tobermory Bay he'd be leanin' maist elegant ower the enchine-room telegraph on the wing o' the brudge, and he'd run her in at full speed, headin' straight for the pier, and leave it till the very last moment afore he'd ring doon for full speed astern, and caal to the helmsman to birl the wheel, and lay her alangside ass delicate ass if she wass an egg.

"It wass a performance that became namely wi' visitors ass weel and efter a month or two of Jeck bein' on the run the pier wass bleck wi' folk each mornin' aal come to see the show. And he wass that dapper, and such a perfect chentleman, that it wass a preevilege to watch it aal, though Jeck's critics (maist of them ither captains who was chust jealous for his success) said he wud get his come-uppance wan o' these days.

"You probably ken that the *Handa* is no chicken. She wass built in 1878 at Port Gleska, and ass the years went on she has needed mair and mair upkeep.

"That wass Jeck's undoin'. Wan mornin' he wass oot on the wing of the brudge ass usual, waitin' till the last meenit to ring for full power astern, and when he chudged the last meenit had come and pulled on the telegraph lever, did the dam' thing no come awa' in his hands, the base of it aal rusted to nothin', and wi' the force o' the pull Jeck went tumblin' backwards doon the brudge ladder and landed sprauchled oot on the main deck.

"It wass aal of a half-meenit afore the folk on the pier realised that the *Handa* wassna goin' to pull up in time that mornin' and there wass wan richt clamjamfrey ass they aal struggled to get out o' the path of the shup!

"She rammed the pierhead bow first, and embedded hersel' eight feet into it! It wass two days afore they could get her pulled oot and two weeks till the pier wass fully repaired!"

"Mr MacBrayne would be none too pleased," I ventured.

"He wass really quite reasonable," said the Captain. "It had to be admutted that if the telegraph-handle had stayed in the wan piece the accident would never have happened, so part of the blame had to be wi' the shup.

"Forbye, the reputation o' the man had reached Gleska and the clerks in the Heid Office wass able to see that the *Handa* wass earnin' more money than ever for Mr MacBrayne, what wi' aal the folk thinkin' it wass a privilege to sail wi' sich a chentleman for Captain.

"So while the *Handa* wass awa' bein' repaired, Mr MacBrayne made Jeck First Officer on the *Flowerdale* on the Outer Isles service. Though she wassna his own command, she wass a much bigger shup wi' a lot o' prestige, and Jeck took to her to the manner born.

"Pretty soon he wass enchoyin' the same sort of reputation wi' the *Flowerdale* in Castlebay ass wi' the *Handa* in Tobermory. She used to lie over at Barra from six in the evening till early the followin' mornin' and Jeck wass aye welcome in the hooses in Castlebay, for he wass a fine cheerie chap and carried a perty aboot wi' him whereffer he went. There wass many a gyurl in Castlebay had her kep set on Jeck but he wass havin' too mich of a spree to be thinkin' o' settlin' doon, and mony's the hert he broke in the months that followed.

"The trouble came at the year's end. The *Flowerdale* tied up at Castlebay on Hogmanay evenin' and since she wassna sailin' till fower o'clock next mornin' Jeck went ashore to tak' a ne'erday dram or two with a wheen o' his Barra friends. He took the enchineers wi' him, for Jeck wass aye verra considerate of the boys who made possible aal the speed he could get oot o' the shup, and aal the manoeuvrability she had, for Jeck could turn her on a postage stamp, her havin' two propellers.

"He could caal for full astern port, full ahead starboard, and spin her roon' in her ain length like a peerie in a close. Jeck took great pleasure in showin' his agility wi' the shup and it's a good thing that Captain McKissock was fast asleep in his cabin when Jeck wass in cherge, for he wass a true chentleman of the old school and would not have looked kindly on Jeck's high-jinks and cheneral frivolity.

"Onyway, that Hogmanay nicht, Jeck and the enchineers got back on board chust before sailing time. Jeck wass in fine trum, but he could carry his dram like a chentleman and nobody wud have known it. The enchineers wass feelin' no pain either, but since they were oot o' sight o' the cheneral public it didna really matter what they looked like.

"Jeck headed for the brudge, the enchineers for their control room, and at fower o'clock off they set off like hey-ma-nanny for Coll and Tiree.

"For more than three hoors *Flowerdale* tore through the watter like a greyhound, Jeck hummin' a whole repertaree

of Gaelic song to himsel' in the wheelhouse and the helmsman on watch tap-tappin' the time wi' his feet.

"Chust gone half past seven in the mornin', wi the dawn
comin' up fast over the hills of Ardnamurchan, Jeck wass
connin' her into the bay at Arinagour on Coll at near on 18
knots, a beautiful sight for the folk launchin' the passenger
flit-boat aff the beach, as the shup came hurtlin' roon' the
headland wi' a rake on her like Jeck's kep on a Setturday
night.

"The lads in the flit-boat had seen the sheer poetry and
drama o' Jeck's arrivals at Arinagour often enough in the
past weeks but it wass aalways an impressive performance.
He wud head her straight for the beach and wait till the
very last possible moment on the brudge wing afore he rang
doon for full astern port, full ahead starboard, and spun her
roond in her length and dropped the anchor.

"He wass determined to get the New Year aff wi' a bang
and he hung on and on, draped casual across the brudge
wing and never movin', till even the boys in the flit-boat
began to get anxious: but then he snapped to like a sodger,
rang his instructions to the enchine room, and gave the flit-
boat a smert naval salute.

"And nothin' happened. She kept racin' for the beach at
a good 18 knots. Jeck rang and better rang on the telegraph
till he wass near demented, but there wass neffer a cheep
frae doon below.

"He ran into the brudge-hoose and grabbed the wheel,
and spun it desperate-like to starboard to try and steer the
Flowerdale oot the bay. It wass too late. She had too much
pace and he had too little space to mak' it work, and he ran
her straight onto the sandbar at the eastern headland at full
speed. Mercifully it wass a chentle slope, and she slowed
doon ass sweetly ass if she wass under control. Nobody
wass hurt and there wass no real damage to the hull, either.
But they had to wait three days before the tides wass right
for the *Fusilier* and the *Chevalier* to be able to tow her
back into deep water.

"By that time, Jeck wass lookin' for another chob.

"Tuppical of the man's ill-fortune. You wud have thocht it
wass his fault, the way MacBrayne treated him.

"It wass the enchineers should have got the seck. There
wassna a man jack o' them sober doon below. There wassna wan o' them awake either, come to that. They'd all had
mair nor they could tak' at Castlebay, and they wass aal fast

asleep on the control platform. Jeck could huv rung the telegraph till he wass black in the face!

"He's neffer had a good word to say for enchineers till this day: I think that's why he's often so nippy wi' Macphail. But he still has the hert of a child, and the chenerosity of Mr Carnegie!"

At which hint, I felt it incumbent on me to arrange for the Captain's glass to be replenished.

FACTNOTE

Fact can sometimes be stranger than fiction — or maybe simply mirror it. Whatever the truth of the matter, the two incidents which provided me with the idea for this story were reputed to have happened to real-life MacBrayne ships and were told to me some years ago by a former MacBrayne seaman as historical fact.

The collision with Tobermory pier was said to have taken place in the early 1930s, exactly as described. The vessel involved was the regular Sound of Mull steamer *Lochinvar*, which had been built in 1908: and was fully refurbished in 1934.

She was a strange-looking ship, and a strangely-powered one as well. Only 145ft overall, she was originally constructed with three six-cylinder paraffin engines driving three screws: in 1926 these were replaced by 4-cylinder diesel engines. The engine-room was placed at the stern, with her cargo hold immediately forward of it: and the passenger accommodation and bridge forward of that again. Cargo was loaded and unloaded by a jib-crane and her only mast was a simple pole mast on the foredeck. As built, she had one very thin, very tall smokestack later replaced by the complete opposite — one very short, very squat funnel. In either guise she looked something of an ugly duckling, though her actual hull was finely proportioned.

The incident at Arinagour is reputed to have occurred in the 1960s and there must be witnesses who could confirm if it did really take place. The vessel was the *Claymore*, mainstay of the thrice-weekly link from Oban to Lochboisdale, the second ship to carry that name. Her predecessor gave nearly 50 years service to MacBrayne, mostly on the Glasgow to Stornoway run.

The second *Claymore* was commissioned in 1955, a handsome ship with comfortable accommodation in two classes — the last of her kind in that respect. However, she was notoriously tender in heavy weather. She had the fatal combination of substantial top-hamper (thanks to the generous public space offered in her lounges, dining-saloons and bars): linked to a shallow draft (necessary for access to island piers at all states of the tide, and to places like Coll which in those days had no pier but relied on flit-boats to attend ships — which came as close in shore as they could).

I can vouch for her lack of sea-going qualities! Blessed with the happy fortune to have been born a good sailor, I sympathise strongly with those who are not so lucky. I remember with wry amusement the throwaway line from the skipper of the *Claymore* to a passenger enquiring as we left Oban what the weather ahead was likely to be. "Well I hope you like rock-and-roll," he said, "for you're certainly going to get it today!" And indeed we did — not just on that occasion but on many others too.

MacBrayne's Gladstone Bag — Such, thanks to her carrying capacity, was the nickname bestowed on the little Handa, seen here at an unidentified pier somewhere on the West Coast. Though they lacked the glamour of the big paddlers such vessels were the workhorses of the Highlands and provided the crucial link to the outside world. The engine-room telegraph on the port wing of the bridge, and the ladder behind it, can be clearly seen!

11

The Vital Spark at the Games

It was a fine August morning and the *Vital Spark*, having made an early start from Colintraive where she had spent the last two days unloading a cargo of roadstone, was punching round Toward Point into a light northerly breeze.

There was something of a holiday atmosphere aboard, what with the sun glinting on the spray of her (modest) bow wave: but more particularly because the crew had succeeded in selling a few sacks of the owner's coal to the Colintraive merchant, and were planning a clandestine spree once they were docked at the Broomielaw and before heading for their weekends at home.

"Rothesay's gey quiet the day, Peter," said the mate, gesturing towards the curving esplanade and phalanx of boarding houses of Rothesay Bay in the middle distance. "No' mony steamers there at aal this mornin'."

Indeed, the usually bustling pier of the capital of Bute was all but deserted. Only the diminutive *Texa* lay alongside, her derrick swinging the crates of a mixed cargo to the quay, while MacBrayne's majestic *Columba* was edging out on her daily mail run to Ardrishaig.

"Well, Dougie," replied the Captain, " whit else wud ye expect on the last Setturday of August? Aal the boats'll be runnin' in and out o' Dunoon right noo, and since you've reminded me o' that, I've a good mind that we should maybe chust go to join them. What d'ye think yourself?"

"Mercy, I'd clean forgot what day it wass," said Dougie. "But aye — why not, why not indeed!

"Then that's what we'll do," said Para Handy: and after making a great show of whistling through the speaking tube to an engine room and an engineer he could have bent down and touched, he called down it: "Richt, Macphail, if for wance you can get that neb o' yours oot o' they novelles for a meenit, ye could maybe get up some steam and see if we can get to Dunoon sometime this month!"

~

"What's the great attraction aboot Dunoon?" asked Sunny Jim curiously, looking up from the forehatch, where he sat peeling an enormous potful of potatos which, with salt herring to encourage the thirst, had been planned for dinner prior to berthing in Glasgow.

"We're goin' to see Cowal Gaithering," replied the skipper.

"Cowal?" queried Jim with a puzzled expression. "Wha's Cowal? And whit's he gaitherin'?"

"Man, Jum," said the skipper. "There iss times when I think you are nothin' but an ignorant lowland neep to be sure: but of course I blame your time on the Cluthas. Your world ends at the Yoker Ferry. You havna the advantage nor the concept o' the great traditions of the west. Cowal's no' a person — it's yon whole lump o' land" — he pointed towards the hills on the port side — "and a Gaitherin's a Games. D'ye tell me ye never heard of the Cowal Hieland Gaitherin? It's namely aal over the world ass the snappiest Games of them aal, bar nane. Iss that not so, Dougie?"

"Whateffer you say, Peter," observed the mate agreeably. "For they're certainly the snappiest for a dram. Every time you find your gless iss empty there's aye somewhere fine and handy to get it refilled. If you've the coin."

"And that we have," rejoined the skipper, "for ye'll mind o' the wee deal we struck wi' Mackintosh in Colintraive, eh? But not a cheep tae the owner!" And he laid an index finger along the side of his nose with a conspiratorial grin.

"But whit happens at a Games," queried Sunny Jim, ignoring the snort of disgust which came echoing up from the engine-room. "Is it like the fitba'?"

"Jum, Jum, I despair o' ye. A Games iss what has made us Brutain's hardy sons. It's the very bedrock o' the nation, the true tradition o' the Hielan's. Bonnie lasses in tartan skirts louping aboot like things possessed: laddies skirling the pipes: big fellas that well built they wud mak' Hurricane Jeck look like a skelf tossin' tree-trunks aboot, chust the same ass if they were matchsticks: pipe baun's merchin' up and doon the streets: an' grown men that should ken better sneakin' off from their wives and weans to hae a few drams mair nor's guid for them."

"What he means," cried Macphail from the sooty depths of the boiler-room, "is that it's jist a lot of weel-oiled tumshies a' dressed up like kahouchy balls cavortin' through the toon, and frichtening the lieges: an' a bunch of wee nyaffs jumpin through girrs an' that."

"Ye're a leear, Macphail," cried the affronted skipper, "chust the nearest thing tae a Sassenach, ye should be right ashamed tae call yerself a Scot!"

"But I thocht a' these Games things wiz jist somethin' invented for the towerists," said Jim, "naethin' but chaps in hired kilts wi' the wrang legs for them and their behinds stickin' oot, and accents ye could saw wud wi'?"

"Naw Jum," said the Captain. "In Braemar maybe, or even Inverness forbye, for they're a' saft in the heid up there and the countryside's fair stuffed wi' toffs and sich. But no' at Cowal. Cowal's aal chust for the people. Brutain's hardy sons! Chust wait till ye see!"

And — the puffer by then being off Bullwood with the Gantocks rocks dead ahead — Para Handy concentrated on navigating safely through the twin hazards of the reef and the constant stream of paddle-steamers depositing their quota of revellers on the main Dunoon pier, till he coaxed the *Vital Spark* into the very last remaining space at the puffers' traditional berth, the little Coal Pier in the East Bay.

∽

The misanthropic engineer was more than pleased to nominate himself as the unanimous choice for shore watchman. Wild horses would not have dragged him to the festivities as he settled back into his bunk — for all that it was but mid-day — with the latest penny dreadful, an unread novelette, and a quarter of candy-striped balls.

The remainder of the crew, with Sunny Jim under the skipper's patient tutelage, fought their way through the colourful crowds on Argyll Street and on up to the Dunoon stadium: paid their admission moneys (with some reluctance) and spent the next few hours enthralled by a harlequinade of sight and sound as the very finest of Scottish music, dance and athletic prowess was put through its paces.

Frequent forays to the beer tent while funds lasted, and then a desperate but unsuccessful search for the 'Committee' when they ran out, kept them in the best of spirits in more ways than one.

When the Gathering climaxed with the traditional assembly and march past of more than 2000 pipes and drums even the normally taciturn Mate was observed to wipe a surreptitious sleeve across his eyes, Sunny Jim stood gawping at a spectacle so splendid, so sonorous and so stirring, and Para Handy himself was with some difficulty dissuaded from climbing onto a nearby cart and delivering 'Hielan' Laddie' in an enthusiastic but tuneless baritone.

It was dark by the time the throngs from the stadium made their way back to the esplanade. Across the water the lights of Gourock beckoned and at the pier the paddlers were banked three deep for the evacuation to come.

But one final ritual remained.

As the clock on the Parish Kirk on Castle Hill struck 10, the night exploded into a blinding light that would have challenged the mid-day sun, and a noise that would have shamed the opening barrage at Ypres.

The last tradition of the Cowal Highland Gathering, the Grand Fireworks display, ran its tumultuous course for 20 minutes. Then the crew of the *Vital Spark* picked their way through the crowds, and across the smouldering detritus of the display, back to the ship.

Spreadeagled on his back on the hatchway of the hold, with his hands pressed hard against his ears, his feet drumming on the planking, and his mouth open in a soundless scream, they found the engineer — bellowing, once he was able to speak again, that a world war had begun.

～

"Man, Macphail, ye' re an ignorant gowk so ye are," said Para Handy unsympathetically half-an-hour later, when they finally calmed him down enough to allow the administration of a stiff medicinal dram from the jealously-guarded bottle kept (with some exercise of will-power) solely for such emergencies.

"Surely ye knew what wass up when ye saw the ither puffer crews leave their boats and get awa' from the pier ass soon ass the darkness fell? Surely ye knew that the fire-works display iss aalways set up on the very Coal Pier itself?

"No wonder ye got the fright o' yer life an' thought ye were in an explodin' munitions factory. But let this be a lesson to you Dan! If you'd come ashore wi' the rest o' us ye might have had to pit your hand in your pocket — but at least ye wouldn't have pit your hert in your mooth!"

FACTNOTE

Traditional Highland Games are held in communities large and small throughout both the Highlands and Lowlands of Scotland and the Cowal Highland Gathering, which celebrated its Centenary in 1994, is the largest and most spectacular of them all. To Scots the name of Cowal is probably the best known but English visitors are perhaps more likely to be aware of the Braemar Games thanks largely to the 'Royal' connection. Senior members of the Royal family attend every year, as the event coincides with their holiday in nearby Balmoral Castle.

Similar Games are held throughout the world, wherever there is a strong Scottish community or connection, and many overseas competitors take part in the Games in Scotland — particularly at Cowal, which hosts the official World Championship Events in Highland Dancing as well as prestigious Solo Piping and Pipe Band Competitions. Other attractions at any self-respecting Games will include the traditional Heavy Athletic events (the tossing of the caber in particular) without which no Highland event would be deemed complete — and most certainly not by any visitors from south of the border!

Dunoon's wooden steamer pier still stands, though it is today a somewhat depressing mockery of its past glories, reminiscent of a Hollywood film-set: all facade and no substance. Much of its splendidly colourful and overstated Victorian superstructure of tea-rooms, towers and turrets lies sadly unused and some — most regrettably part of its long viewing-gallery — has been demolished. It is the terminal for Cal-Mac's work-horse vehicle ferry service from Gourock and, in summer months, an occasional port of call for the *Waverley,* the only operational sea-going paddle steamer left in the world.

Old photographs from the turn of the century show a

THE GENERATION GAP — *The great tradition of Highland Games continues unabated — the wardrobe of the participants might be unrecognisably different, but the programme of Highland Dancing, Pipes and Drums and Heavy Athletics celebrated every August in Dunoon Stadium today is the same as it was in the days when the Vital Spark sailed the Firth. Para Handy would be as much at home at the Cowal Games in 1995 as he was in 1905, though the outfits worn by today's dancers and pipers would seem as strange to his eyes as those in this photograph are to ours.*

different world — paddlers queuing up to come alongside, passengers streaming on and off in their hundreds (they still do, though now from the far-from-glamorous ro-ro ferries) and files of charabancs and horse-buggies awaiting them on the shore side of the pier gates. Even into the fifties Dunoon remained a steamer 'cross-roads', with day-long activity to watch, and many holiday-makers passed hours on the pier (with interludes in its tea-room or its bar according to taste!) enjoying the varied pageant of shipping on the Firth.

A few hundred yards north east of the steamer pier is the still older stone jetty which was used by generations of puffers, and their predecessors. Though it is decades now since there was last a cargo boat of any description calling at Dunoon this is still known locally as the "Coal Pier" — and the displays of pyrotechnics which climax the last night of Cowal Gathering are indeed constructed on this convenient platform.

12

A Spirited Performance

At once one of the most popular and the most frustrating tasks the puffer crews can be asked to perform is to carry cargos to or from the highly-reputed Malt Whisky Distilleries dotted around Argyll and the Inner Hebrides.

Popular, because a puffer with its hold full of barley for the malting loft, or of oak staves for the cooperage, is a welcome visitor with a badly-needed cargo: and skipper and crew are traditionally treated to a generous dram or two of clear spirit straight from the stills, and with a proof content which make the commercial blends seem like spring water by comparison.

Frustrating, because sometimes puffers are contracted to carry a load of whisky in cask from the remote distilleries to the bottling and blending plants in the upper reaches of the Clyde or in Glasgow itself. The agony of sailing atop a cargo ample enough to guarantee a lifetime of high-jinks, but guarded by customs seals and (sometimes) by customs officers in person and thus as unattainable as if it had been on the far side of the moon, is a frustration adequate to torture Tantalus himself.

The *Vital Spark* and her crew were in just that situation one fine summer's evening as the vessel lay moored alongside the private jetty of one of Islay's most respected distilleries.

On her arrival that afternoon in ballast the resident Customs Officers had boarded the puffer and all but stripped her from stem to stern.

"What on earth are they daein'?" spluttered an aggrieved Sunny Jim as he was summarily aroused from his comfortable cat-nap in the fo'c'sle and unceremoniously bundled on deck.

"Chust checkin' on us, Jum," said the skipper, "to see if we've a place somewhere handy for hidin' a barrel or two. I'm bleck affronted they should even think it of us. The *Vital Spark* hass something of a reputation in the coastal trade..."

"You can say that again!" boomed a sonorous voice from the echoing depths of the engine-room. "And some reputation it is, tae."

"Pay no heed to Macphail, Jum," said the skipper, raising his voice to ensure that that worthy would miss nothing of what he was about to say. "He's chust embarrassed because wan o' the officers found his secret store of novelles under that loose deckboard in the fo'c'sle and called all his colleagues down to have a good laugh at them."

The engine room did not respond to that sally.

"And have any puffer crews ever managed to steal something from a cargo of whisky?" asked Sunny Jim.

"I don't care for your language, Jum," said the captain. "Not steal, for sure and it wass neffer for selling that any spurits wass taken, but chust for drinking. Liberate would be a better word for it.

"Myself, I don't think there iss the same imagination in the puffer crews nooadays ass there wass when I wass a young man your age. Not the same spurit of adventure, you micht say. The modern sailors iss timid, chust timid. They're feared o' bein' caught, for a stert: and they're feared o' the Customs — not that I exactly blame them for that. Put a man intae a uniform nooadays and he behaves like an enemy sodger, all aggravation and aggression. Time wass when the Customs offeecials would use their mental agility tae ootfox the crews: today they chust come on board like this efternoon and kick the boat to pieces whether they've ony reason to or no'. There iss no subtlety left in what aye used to be a chenuine battle of wuts, when whicheffer side won, the ither respected them for it and swore to get even next time roond.

"I mind servin' ass an apprentice wi' a skipper caaled Forbes who had his ain boat: a sailin' gabbert it wass, and him and the mate and me wass the only crew on board her. Wan time we loaded wi' whusky in casks at Campbeltown and the Customs men came on board and pit their seals all round the hatch covers.

"You'll understand that these were inspected when we docked at the blenders in Gleska, and if the seals wass tampered wi' in any way, then it wass the high jump for aal the crew.

"We were hardly oot the harbour when Forbes grabbed me by the lug and pulled me to the fore end of the cargo hatch. Wan o' the planks in the hatch side-coaming wass a false plank — it had no tongue and groove to it, so it could chust slide oot leavin' a wee square hole into the cargo hold.

" 'In ye go, Peter,' says Forbes. 'This iss whit we employed ye for: ye're the only wan o' us small enough to get in through there. Tak' this wi' ye' — and he handed me a piece of rubber tubing — 'and when ye've prised the bung frae the top o' wan o' the whusky casks, siphon the spurits and pass us oot the end o this tube so we can start filling oor ain barrel up here.'

"I telt him I couldn't do that, it would be the jyle for me if I did, for sure.

" 'It'll be the jyle for you if ye don't,' says he. 'For ye're an apprentice disobeyin' the command of a superior officer on a shup at sea an' I'll hae ye up tae the docks polis in Gleska so fast your feet'll nae touch the ground.'

"And would you believe, Jim, I wass that feared of him I went and did it, though for weeks efter I didna sleep properly for fear the polis were comin' to get me.

"There was another gabbart, the *Amelia Ann*, that wass namely among the longshoremen for the quantity of whusky her skipper could liberate on a trup from Islay to Gleska: the Customs men was fair demented for, no matter hoo mony ropes and wax seals they put on the hatchway, there were aye two or three barrels less in Gleska than the manifest showed: but the wax seals wass neffer broken and the ropes wass always whole. The skipper of the *Amelia Ann* swore blind that there wass a Customs Officer at the loading berth in Islay who simply couldn't coont, and they'd no way of disproving it for the seals wass aye intact and they could neffer find ony trace of spurits on the boat.

"What none o' the authorities knew wass that the skipper had a brither that worked at the forge where the brass master seals for the Customs wass made, and the man chust cast wan extra set for his brither. And ass for the disappearing barrels, well, he simply hung them ower the side from what looked chust like an ordinary fender rope, and hauled them back in again when the inspectors had given up and gone home in disgust.

~

"Of them aal, though, there wass nobody could touch my old friend Hurricane Jeck for sheer agility when it came to liberating a drop of good British spurits.

"I mind fine wance when him and me wass crewin' on a puffer caaled the *Mingulay* that belonged tae a Brodick man. Thanks to Jeck she had the duvvle's own reputation at the distilleries and wi' the Customs men, and they always swore they'd catch us sooner or later and really put us through the girrs when we came into a distillery pier.

"Wan time we came into a jetty in Islay late one evening ready to load up a cargo of the very best malt spurits in cask the following mornin'.

"Well, they thocht they had the better of Jeck this time. The distillery had already waggoned the casks down to the pier, and they'd put an eight foot high wire and metal-framed fence not chust at the landward end of, but right roond the other three sides of it: and they'd two security guards inside it, sittin' on top of the stacks of casks.

" 'Let's see ye get somethin' oot o' that, MacLachlan,' said the heid Customs man wi' a smug grin. Jeck said nothin', but chust shook his head sadly.

"At two o'clock in the mornin', when the tide was fully out and the *Mingulay* was dwarfed by the jetty now rising high above her hull, Jeck shook me awake.

" 'Come on Peter, let's get oor share o' the spurits!'

" 'You're no' canny, Jeck,' says I. 'We'll get nothin' here. The spurits iss all fenced in and the guards iss still awake for I can hear them talking.'

" 'So much the better,' says he: 'the more noise they make, the easier for us.'

"And would you believe it, he produced an empty barrel and a big brace-and-bit. We climbed over the puffer's bulwarks onto the horizontal trusses on the framework of the jetty and worked the barrel till it wass under wan o' the gaps between the planks that made up the surface of the pier, right at the very middle of it. Then Jeck used the gap to drill a hole into the base o' wan o' the whusky casks from below, and ass the spurits poured oot he caught them in the barrel we'd brought with us.

"It wass much harder to get the full barrel back on board the boat — but we managed it efter a bit o' a struggle.

"Next morning we loaded the cargo on board in netting slings, the Customs men roped and sealed the hatches tight, and it wass long efter we'd unloaded in Gleska before the empty cask wass discovered. By that time it wass too late to blame anyone, and the Customs people finally decided it must have been liberated by someone at the blenders. They never jaloused that it would have been possible for Jeck and me to do what we did."

"What I don't understand," said Sunny Jim, "is where you got the empty barrel from — and where you hid it on board?"

Para Handy grinned. "Well, Jum, let's say that we didn't drink any tea on the way hame from Islay, long trup though it was. We had chust used the *Mingulay's* own water-barrel for the chob!"

"Happy days and high-jinks," said Jim a little despondently. "I wish we could enjoy some o' that sort of spree these days, but with these foxy Customs men that's jist a daydream."

Para Handy stood up from where he'd been sitting, hunched on the corner of the cargo hatch.

He looked round to ensure no unwanted ears were within eavesdropping range.

"What were you planning for supper the night, Jum?" he asked.

"Salt herring, I thocht," said Sunny Jim.

The captain grimaced.

"No, Jum, for peety's sake no. Naethin' salty, whatever you do. Naethin' to provoke a thirst. And, a word of advice — don't be tempted to drink ony of oor ain watter." He nodded towards the wooden waterbreaker lashed to the mast.

Sunny Jim stared in disbelief. "You don't mean...?"

Para Handy laid a forefinger against the side of his nose.

"But how on earth...?" Sunny Jim began.

"Wheesht, Jum," said the skipper anxiously. "Wheesht. That's for me to know: and for them neffer to find oot!" And he turned and waved to the three Customs men standing in animated conversation on the quayside.

FACTNOTE

Many puffers called upon to transport whisky really did

regard the operation as something of a challenge to their ingenuity and all of the subterfuges described in this tale were actually employed at one time or another by different crews!

There are about 100 whisky distilleries in Scotland today, a far cry from earlier days before rationalisation, take-over and the economies of scale saw mergers and buy-outs which decimated the numbers of individual enterprises. In Para Handy's time there were more than 20 distilleries in Campbeltown alone!

The majority of whisky is used for blending, with whiskies from a variety of other distilleries, to create the best-known proprietary brands. The blender's art is the most highly prized of skills, and the secret of the blending processes jealously guarded.

Only a minority of distilleries produce a whisky which will be bottled and marketed as a 'single': that is, unblended with the product of other manufacturers. Almost without exception those whiskies which are branded and sold as sin-

THE AGONY AND THE ECSTASY — *Two puffers waiting at the Caol Ila Distillery pier, Islay, for the most frustrating cargo in the world — casks of malt whisky straight from the bond. Though this photograph dates from the 1940s, the agony of proximity to such temptation (and the ecstasy of the generous dram which was the crew's expected bonus from the manager) were the same then as they had been 40 years previously.*

gles are malt whiskies, made from malted barley in copper pot stills, rather than grain whiskies, chief ingredient of the blends, which are made from maize and unmalted barley in continuous stills.

The character and quality of the familiar commercial blends is generally dictated partly by the quantity, but above all by the quality, of the malt whiskies which they contain.

As a rule of thumb, grain whisky is bland but malt whiskies are full-flavoured: most important of all, each malt has its own unique character which the experiment of centuries has proved impossible to duplicate. On Speyside, the major centre of malt whisky production, adjacent distilleries drawing their water from the same river and buying their barley from the same grower will produce totally different whiskies. And nobody knows why.

Some of the finest singles would have been as familiar to Para Handy as they are to the whisky connoisseurs of today — the world-renowned Islay malts, product of that fertile island lying west of the Kintyre peninsula. They are among the very greatest, the most distinctive (and, for many English or overseas visitors anxious to sample them in public house or off-licence, among the most unpronounceable) names in whisky lore and legend.

Lagavulin. Laphroaig. Bruichladdich. Bunnahabhain. Names to conjure with!

13

Things to Come

The whole of Arran seemed to be asleep this Saturday afternoon in August. An air of somnolence as heavy as the unexpected heatwave, now entering its second week, hung across the island and Brodick pier was deserted, but for a solitary black-hulled puffer lying, empty of any cargo, against its inner face.

A line of washing stretched from a hook on the forward face of the wheelhouse to the mast of the *Vital Spark* and water dripped spasmodically onto the tarpaulin covering her hold. As befitted a vessel on which all men were 'chust Jock Tamson's bairns, wan effery bit as good as the next' as her Captain put it, it was a very democratic line on which Para Handy's best jersey jostled for space with Macphail's socks, these latter having more holes in them than a gruyere cheese.

From the fo'c'sle chimney a thin column of smoke drifted upward and in the bows of the puffer Sunny Jim was rinsing the crew's dinner-plates in a bucket of sea-water. Replete with herring and potatos, the three other members of the ship's company sat on upturned fishing-boxes on the pier with mugs of thick sweet tea, and contemplated the view in companionable silence.

"There is nothin' in the world beats the Clyde," said Para Handy conclusively, "when the weather is in the right trum! You could not ask for a finer sight than Brodick Bay and the Goat Fell on an efternoon like this! You could be sellin' tickets to towerists chust for a look at the view!"

Macphail snorted. "Towerists is wantin' mair than jist a view nooadays," he said. "Wi' them it's all go! Jist look at whit's happened in Bute! Tram-caurs, an' sweemin' baths, an' concert halls, an' baun'staun's, an' gowf, an' boats an' yats tae hire, an' an aqua room."

"Aquarium," corrected Sunny Jim, as he clambered up the ladder and onto the pier.

"Or whatever," conceded the engineer, "but Ah'm sure it gi'es a richt fleg tae veesitors: there's plenty Glesga fowk think a fush is somethin' only tae be foond in cans, they dinna realise it's a wild animal that swums aboot in the watter jist as free as a burd!

"And besides, if it's scenery ye're wantin', Scotland's got a long way to go to be upsides on some o' the places Ah've seen when I went foreign." Macphail's much-aired experience of the world was at once an irritation and a challenge to the crew and in particular the Captain, who never knew whether to give total credence to the engineer's pronouncements in that area. Indeed Hurricane Jack had, on occasion, been known to hint darkly that he for one didn't believe the engineer had ever been furth of the Irish Sea.

"I wouldna be sure on that, Dan," offered the Mate who, though normally of a peaceful not to say diffident disposition, took umbrage at any criticism — whether direct or implied — of his West Highland homeland. "You would go far to find a finer sight than the view from Oban of a sunset over Mull."

"Or Brodick and Goatfell," repeated Para Handy.

"Mull! Goatfell! Ye've nae idea o' the world, neither the pair o' ye. If ye'd seen Capetoon an' Table Moontain, or New York an' the Statue o' Luberty, or Rio de Janwario and the Sugar Lump, ye'd no' be blawin' aboot yer ain kail-yerd."

"Rio," mused the Captain. "Jeck wass there wance: he said it wass awful over-crooded wi' foreigners o' every description and neffer a wan o' them spoke a word o' English and there wassna a dacent gless of whusky to be had! He thocht New York wass chust much aboot the same, for none o' the Americans he met could speak much English either!

"Go to ony o' those places indeed! I'd ass soon go to — iss it Spain? — onyway, where aal the Onion Chonnies come from, chust aal garlic and chokers and berets and bicycles! No: we are Brutain's hardy sons, livin' in the land o' the free, here we are and here we stay!"

"Man, Captain, you're jist a richt stick-in-the-mud," protested Sunny Jim. "Whit way d'ye think Brutain got the

Empire in the first place? It wisnae thanks to auld fogeys
that widnae stir frae their ain firesides. If it had been left up
tae the likes o' you, we widnae ha'e colonised the Cumbraes
yet!"

∼

The topic came up again the following week as the puffer
lay at Inveraray waiting for its cargo of oak-bark to be cart-
ed down from Glenshira.

Captain and crew were seated on deck enjoying the last
of the evening sunshine, and studying the latest crop of
Inveraray tourists with covert interest, in continuing good
weather. The fine spell, indeed, had now lasted so long that
local worthies seated on benches outside the Inns with a
schooner of beer were talking of record temperatures, and
local farmers nursing a whisky at the bar were complaining
endlessly to anyone who was prepared to listen about the
lack of rain.

It did seem, however, as if the weather might be on the
change for the clouds were gathering over the hills at the
head of Glenaray, and the drivers of tourist charabancs
waiting on the seafront were rigging their canvas awnings
— just in case.

Among the full house of summer visitors staying at the
Argyll Arms Hotel, which stood within sight of the pier, and
just across the road from the driveway leading to the
impressive castle seat of the Dukes of Argyll, was an
American family comprising father, mother — and two very
slender, very tall and very blonde daughters in their early
twenties.

The parents were a conspicuous addition to the attractions of Inveraray with their — by the standards of that
douce Highland town — garish and unfamiliar clothes,
nasal conversation never delivered at any level under a
shout, and a predilection for hiring boats or carriages at the
drop of a hat and tipping with a reckless generosity that had
the townspeople lost for words.

The girls in particular had made an immediate and overwhelming impact on the community — or at least on its
young men, many of whom took to hanging around the fore
shore opposite the hotel at all hours of the day in the hope
of catching just a glimpse of the objects of their admiration
as the family went about its peregrinations.

Jim, who had lost no time in calling at the public bar of the hotel in search of further information about the visitors, was able to report that the paterfamilias was originally of Scots extraction — a Campbell, no less — and that he had made his fortune in the United States steel industry.

"He'll have come back to Inveraray in search of hiss family's roots," suggested the Mate, digesting this snippet.

"Naw," said Jim who, seemingly seeking any escape from the pervading heat, had been soaking his head under the ship's pump and was now vigorously towelling it, "for he didnae stert oot as a toff, his roots is in Glesga, in the Gorbals accordin' tae the barman. He's come tae Inveraray tae try an' buy a piece of land frae the Jook, tae build a hoose tae use on his holidays, for the barman says the man's fair determint tae come back tae Scotland year on year frae noo on." And with that he stood up, stretching, and clambered down into the fo'c'sle.

"Neffer!" said Para Handy as Jim disappeared. "Think o' the expense, think o' aal the discomfort o' the journey."

"Havers!" chipped in the engineer. "For a stert, money's nae object wi' a millionaire: and the journey's a dawdle nooadays, since they built the *Lusitania*. You could jist as weel be in a hotel! We're no' talkin' aboot tryin' tae cross the Atlantic in a tarry auld tub the like o' the *Vital Spark*. We're talkin' aboot real shups!"

"She's aalways real enough for you when you iss collectin' your wages at the end of the week, anyway," said Para Handy with some anger. "That's no way to talk aboot a shup that's kept you and your femily in the way they iss accustomed to for mony a year!"

"She'll never be an ocean greyhound, that's for sure," replied Macphail heatedly. "Ocean tortoise, mair like!"

"Weel," said the Captain, "since you're the man that's supposed to be in cherge o' the enchines, dinna look to fault me on that score! Look to your own laurels iss my advice to you!"

"All Ah'm sayin'," retorted Macphail, "is that we'll be seein' mair and mair American veesitors in the future, wi' the fancy new ways o' travel that's aboot the noo. Wait you and see! The maist o' the towerists on the Clyde'll be frae overseas, and the Glesga fowk wull stert traivellin' abroad!"

"Away with you," said Dougie incredulously. "Where would they go? Spain, I suppose, to save the Onion Johnnies a journey?"

"And why not?" asked the engineer. "Ah've been tae Spain when I wis deep sea: there's mullions o' fowk livin' there so it canna be a' that bad a place. Lord knows, it's usually hot enough."

"It's hot enough here for anyone," replied the Captain. "I doot the average Gleska faimily wud have more sense than to trevel to a country that's chust choc-a-bloc wi' foreigners who canna even speak English — even if they had the money for it."

"You'll see," said Macphail darkly. "The Americans is comin' and the boardin'-hooses on the river'll hae tae set oot mair than jist a fush tea fur them, and the resorts mair nor a penny peep-show and a hurdy-gurdy man, if they want tae stay on in business."

"So what are they to do, then?" asked the Captain with heavy sarcasm. "I suppose you think restrongs'll stert dishin' out curries and rice and aal the other fancy gew-gaws you're aye blawin' that you ate when you wass on yon tramp-shup in the Indian jute trade? And that the Chook'll open up the castle doors at sixpence a time for folk to troop through and gawp at him and herself takin' their teas?"

As Macphail was flexing his thoughts in search of a suitably vitriolic response there came the most horrendous crash of thunder, which echoed off the watch-tower hill of Duniquaich and round the bay.

Within seconds the skies had opened and raindrops the size of pan-drops were bouncing off the parched ground: within minutes there was not a soul to be seen anywhere out of doors, puddles gathered on roads and paths, and the grassy area in front of the Argyll Arms Hotel was like a quagmire.

"My Chove," gasped Para Handy from the safety of the fo'c'sle, "that's some thunderbust! Check the diary, Dougie, and see if this iss no' the day o' the Argyllshire Gaitherin', for if it iss we should have known fine what wass comin'. It aalways rains for them in Oban, puir souls!"

"Which," said Macphail, resuming the thread of his earlier argument, "is exactly why the Glesga fowk wull soon be awa' abroad for the Ferr: sunshine guaranteed, no' like Loch Fyne. The only things guaranteed here is rain and mudges!"

"At least the Americans'll no' come back, wance they see rain like this," observed Dougie. "And when the word gets roond, aal the foreigners'll bide at hame."

"That's jist where ye' re a' wrang," said Sunny Jim, pulling on his jacket and picking up his melodeon from the shelf at the head of his berth. "Mandy and Carrie tell me that they come tae Scotland tae get awa' frae the constant heat o' their own place in Texas. And they dinna caal it rain, lads: they jist caal it Scotch Mist: and they love it!"

"Stop you a meenit," said Para Handy in surprise as Jim made his way towards the companionway. "Where are you goin'? And who are Mandy and Carrie?"

"Jist the American lasses at the Argyll Arms," said Jim: "I had a word wi' the family when I was up there earlier the day and I've been invited to gi'e them and their faither and mither a recital o' reels and strathspeys on the melodeon.

"Their faither says they fair tak' him back tae his youth and he particularly asked me tae jine them tonight, for their havin' a ceilidh before they leave tomorrow."

"But...but what about the rest of us?" spluttered the Captain. "Are we chust to be left here like lost sheeps?"

"Naw," said Jim. "A'body's welcome: but jist leave me a clear road wi' the lasses.

"You could fill in yer time mair better in fact, for the Jook wudnae sell Mr Campbell ony land: maybe ye could persuade him that the *Vital Spark* is a yat — and get him to buy her tae use her each time he comes back hame!"

FACTNOTE

It goes without saying that tourism as we know it today had not been invented in Para Handy's time — and that the weather on the Firth remains as unpredictable today as ever!

Patrons of the Clyde resorts at the turn of the century fell into two categories. Most day-trippers were from the 'working class' areas around Glasgow. Longer-stay visitors ranged from factory workers to professional men and came for anything from a weekend to a month, some in hotels or boarding-houses: some, the first self-catering holidaymakers, in rented property.

Many Glasgow business-barons, however, either rented a house for the entire summer, or built their own: and, while their families enjoyed the sea and summer air, they commuted daily to their office using the efficient, speedy steamer network.

Few tourists came from farther afield: Scotland was not

TECHNOLOGY, EDWARDIAN-STYLE — A Kintyre Motor Company charabanc arrives at the Campbeltown quayside, about 1910. This one has a solid roof, but many had canvas hoods which were folded down in fine weather. One lad runs alongside, the feet of another chasing the vehicle can be seen to the rear, behind the back wheel. Hanging onto the back of buses or lorries for a free ride was a popular, if highly risky, pursuit!

yet established as a holiday 'destination' for the English, never mind the overseas market. Long-distance travel was confined to the wealthy. Most English visitors and most of the very few from foreign countries, were 'gentry' coming either to their own estates, or those of their friends. Society moved north in season for the highly-specialised pursuits of the Fishings and the Shootings: and to a lesser degree, Yachting as well.

Macphail was right in seeing that increasing speed and comfort on the Atlantic passage would bring Americans over in growing numbers. There was fierce rivalry between the shipping lines of Britain, France and Germany to capture their share of the profits to be had in catering for the travel whims of wealthy Americans. Para Handy, however, could never have imagined that air-travel would open up Europe, and then the world, to all his countrymen, whatever their social or economic background.

'Onion Johnnies' usually came from the Basque country in the foothills of the Pyrennees and were a common sight throughout rural Scotland well into the second half of this century. They would travel as a group but then work as individuals, sharing a central base where they could store their stock-in-trade: and criss-cross the country on bicycles so festooned with strings of Spanish Onions that they could hardly push them, never mind ride them, at the beginning of each circuit.

The Dukes of Argyll, so far as I am aware, have never hosted expensive ticket-only dinner-parties for socially-hungry American or Japanese tourists, though some of their opposite numbers in the English aristocracy certainly have. However, in common with almost every stately home everywhere, only by opening its doors each summer to the curious tourist has Inveraray Castle been able to finance the repairs, upkeep and general investment essential to the maintenance and enhancement of its structure.

14

Look Back in Agony

The *Vital Spark*, all way off her, almost at a stand-still, was drifting the last few feet onto the fendered face of Rothesay pier when there came the most spine-chilling, ear-piercing howl from the engine-room under the wheelhouse.

Startled by-standers jumped in alarm, and heads swiv-elled towards the source of the banshee tocsin which sounded for all the world like the puffer's own steam whistle but set an octave higher and with a far greater capacity to discomfit the hearer.

"My Cot, Dan," shouted the Captain, bending down to peer into the stokehold at his feet, "if you've been and stubbed your big toe or whacked your foot wi' the shuvvle again, wull you for peety's sake keep the noise doon to a dull roar, for the Ro'say folk'll be thinkin' we've come to deliver aal the de'ils o' hell to the island instead o' chust a cargo o' coals!"

"It's no' ma toe, ye clown," howled the Engineer, "it's mah back: talk aboot white-hot pokers gaun' through it — Ah cannae move a muscle."

Some five minutes later, with the vessel safely secured at her berth, the crew assembled in the cramped engine-room to examine the stricken engineer, diagnose his problem, and offer their consensus advice.

Macphail was on his feet, but bent forward from the waist at a right angle so that the upper part of his body was vir-tually parallel to the deck, and his arms dangled loosely in a posture reminiscent of the ape in Hengler's Menagerie.

"Man, Dan," said Para Handy at length: "this is a fine to-do to be sure. How did you effer contrive to get in such a fix?"

"Ah'm sure an' Ah didnae contrive it," said Macphail with some exasperation, "d'ye think Ah'm enjoyin' masel'? Every meenit's jist agony an' Ah cannae budge! Ah'm stuck!"

"Well you cannot chust bide there for ever," said the unfeeling Mate, "it's your shout for the refreshments up at the Harbour Bar for a start and, besides, we need a fourth for dominos."

∾

However it soon became clear that the Engineer really seemed quite unable to straighten up and Para Handy's attempts to free him from his predicament by forced manipulation — "Chust the wan wee tug, Dan, and you'll be ass straight ass a ramrod again!" — had the effect of producing blood-curdling shrieks of protest compared with which the Engineer's earlier howling was as birdsong at evening.

Thus by-standers and passers-by on Rothesay pier, and on the esplanade itself, were treated to the remarkable spectacle of one adult male, body locked into a kind of inverted L-shape, being pushed along the pavement standing in a small wheelbarrow propelled by one, young, man while two older men, one at either flank of the barrow, held the stooped man by the arms to stop him from falling out of the conveyance to one side or another.

In due course, and not a moment too soon for any of those involved in it, the little tableau reached the chemist's in Montague Street.

Para Handy held the shop door open, and Sunny Jim heaved the barrow over the shallow lip of the step into the narrow gas-lit interior of the pharmacy. A low counter displayed a range of toiletries of every description and a stock of specifics for virtually every known ailment, real or imagined, which might afflict the citizenry of Bute. The wall behind the counter was lined with rows of small mahogany-fronted drawers to shoulder height, each with a lettered and gilded glass plate proclaiming its contents. The wall on the other side of the pharmacy was shelved from floor to ceiling and the light glinted on porcelain canisters and ribbed specie jars and bottles lettered in Latin and in gilt.

"Well, well, it's yourself then Mr Maxwell," said the Captain as the white-jacketed figure of the pharmacist

appeared from behind the frosted-glass screen which con-
cealed the dispensary at the far end of the shop. "You're
keepin' weel, I hope?"

"Can't complain, Captain," said Maxwell genially, pushing his horn-rimmed spectacles up onto his high forehead:
"and yourself too, I hope. What can I do for you all?"

Sunny Jim pushed forward past the barrow and its teetering occupant. "Ah'll hae twa pennyworth o' cinnamon,"
he asked, fishing in his trouser pocket for the coppers. The
chemist opened one of the drawers behind him, took out
half-a-dozen of the brittle brown sticks and wrapped them
in a screw of paper.

"And I'll have chust a smaal bottle of Bay Rum," said the
mate, "seein' ass we're aal here onyway," and handed his
sixpence to the proprietor.

A croak of protest from behind them suddenly reminded
the crew of the real reason for their presence in the pharmacy.

"Well," said Para Handy, "we have got ourselves chust a
wee bit of a problem wi' the enchineer here."

"It's no' you that's got the problem, you eejit," protested
Macphail through clenched teeth. "It's me that's got it, for
peety's sake, and if it wis you staundin' where Ah'm staundin' ye'd no' be callin' it a wee problem either."

"Whateffer," said Para Handy, "but we wass efter won-
derin', Mr Maxwell, if you have onythin' for a sore beck. The
poor man can scarcely move."

"An' there's a lot of coals needin' shuvvled afore this day's
oot," interrupted Sunny Jim pointedly, "an' Ah'm no' gaun
tae shuvvle them, that's for sure."

"There's not really a lot I can give him for a bad back,"
said the chemist, "except maybe some laudanum if he's in
pain. Are you in pain?" he asked, turning to Macphail.

"Naw, naw," said the Engineer with heavy sarcasm. "Ah
dae this for the fun o' the whole thing: ye can surely see jist
hoo mich Ah'm enjoyin' masel'?

"Pain? Of course Ah'm in pain! Or in purgatory, mair
like!"

"Have you tried ironing it?" Maxwell enquired of the
Captain. "Often a hot iron will simply lift the cramps out of
the pulled muscles, or ease any twisted tendons back into
place...

"There's nane o' this lot comin' near me wi' an iron, hot
or cauld!" spluttered Macphail. "Ah wudna trust ony wan o'

them for it. They'd be sure to scar me for life, or maybe drap it on my fit forbye, or whatever.

"See's yer laudanum, an' let's get oot o' here!"

$\sim$

"If you would just try to straighten up, Mr Macphail," said the Doctor, "I think you would find that once you'd done so, your problems would be over."

The Engineer, his shirt pushed up to his neck and his back laid bare as he clung to the top of the examination couch in the High Street surgery, said nothing.

"You've pulled a tendon," the Doctor continued, "just below the right shoulder-blade here..." he scarcely touched the spot with the tip of his finger but Macphail let out a yell which made the hairs on the back of the necks of his audience stand up to be counted. The crew jumped but the Doctor carried on just as if there had been no interruption "...but if you could force yourself to jerk upright, I am certain it would slip back and you would be right as ninepence."

Macphail turned his head slowly, cautiously, as if fearful of putting any sort of strain on neck or back, and favoured the Doctor with the sort of look that an early martyr might have reserved for his persecutors.

"We can only thank you for your time, Doctor," said the Captain apologetically, as they manhandled Macphail back onto the barrow with the sort of level of difficulty that might have been expected had rigor mortis already set in, "but I'm afraid Dan is thrawn, thrawn when it comes to his health."

$\sim$

"I am getting chust sick and tired of aal this," complained the Captain an hour later as he, Dougie and Sunny Jim leaned reflectively on the bar counter of the Harbour Inn. Macphail they had left outside, despite his protests, the wheelbarrow leant up against the Inn wall alongside a couple of push-bikes, a knifegrinder's hand-cart and a (sold out) stop-me-and-buy-one trike, the owners of all of which were now playing four-handed cribbage at a corner table.

Since leaving the Surgery they had been along to the Glenburn Hydropathic in a vain attempt to have Macphail admitted to its salt-water hot spa baths (they had been unceremoniously ejected from the hotel foyer by an out-raged duty manager) and then spent 20 fruitless minutes trying to persuade the Engineer that a donkey-ride along the sands of the west bay might just shoogle the twisted tendon back into place.

Ignoring the occasional calls of protest from their ship-mate in the street outside, and the now less-frequent and, it must be said, rather less-convincing howls of anguish as well, Para Handy called for beer and scratched his head in some perplexity.

"What in bleezes are we goin' to do wi' the man?" he enquired of nobody in particular. "I am thinkin' the Doctor iss probably right, if we could chust persuade him to move his beck, then it wud aal fall into place. But he'll no' do it, the duvvle."

His voice tailed off in mid-sentence and a sudden gleam came into his eye.

"Lads!" he cried: "I think I see the light! Drink up, and we shall see what we can do..."

~

"We will chust have to take you back to the shup, Dan," said the Captain two minutes later as they wheeled their ungainly cargo down towards the quayside.

At the Square beside the Esplanade the barrow dunted across the cobblestones and the gleaming metal rails of the double-track of the Rothesay tramway, each such tremor producing a croak of protest from the Engineer.

Then, at a signal from the Captain, Sunny Jim lowered the handles at the rear of the barrow and let it stand, sup-ported by its front wheel and rear legs, right between the rails of one of the tramway tracks at the very corner where the trams came hurtling round from the Esplanade and into the terminus.

The three men backed away, leaving Macphail teetering on the barrow, gazing after them beseechingly. From the near-distance and getting nearer all the time could be heard the distinctive and imperious clang of the bell of a fast-approaching tram.

"The Doctor said somethin' had to mak' you move, Dan, for your ain good!" shouted Para Handy. "And if you don't look lively and chump oot o' that barrow like a good laad, I think that wan o' the skoosh-caurs is goin' to fetch you a right dunt — ony meenit noo!"

There was the teeth-gritting screech of metal on metal as the still-unseen tram flung itself into the turn and the wheels bit at the rails in protest as it took the 90 degree curve. Just as the blunt nose of the speeding vehicle appeared round the corner, Macphail gave an agonised yell, an agonised leap — and threw himself out of the barrow in a desperate flurry of limbs and sprinted for the safety of the pavement, as swift and as supple as an athlete.

Within 30 seconds he was at the side of his fellows, all his back problems forgotten, heaving with rage.

"Ye left me to dee!" he roared, wagging an accusing finger.

"Not really, Dan," said the skipper. "For a start I knew fine that hearin' the skoosh-caur comin' wud mak' you leap for your life, if you were fit. And if you weren't fit then I knew what you obviously don't — that the wee bitty track we left you on hasn't been used for years, ever since they brought in the electric caurs to replace the auld horse yins! It's as deid as the dodo! They only use a single-track nooadays, no' the two, and the caur wud have passed ye on the ither side!"

FACTNOTE

It was only after I had finished writing this story that I recalled an episode in the TV series with Roddy MacMillan as Para Handy in which Macphail had a back problem (in Arran) and rolled off the pier on a luggage trolley. I remember no other details. I apologise for any unconscious plagiarism but I have kept this story in as I think it is sufficiently different, and above all since there is too much personal nostalgia in it for me to abandon it.

If there are any old-fashioned pharmacies left, I would be glad to hear of them. My father was a chemist with his own business in the village of Kilmacolm, Renfrewshire. He died very suddenly in 1962 and at that time the premises had been little altered since the turn of the century: certainly after he acquired the business as a young man in the 1930s he changed nothing. The interior was much as I have described the Rothesay pharmacy. Though not gas-lit, it had a small gas jet, used to melt the scarlet wax by which every prescription he dispensed, each wrapped meticulously in

AN EDWARDIAN LEGACY — I was unable to trace any 'untouched' pharmacies which might resemble my late father's shop in Kilmacolm or the pharmacy in Rothesay described in 'Look back in Agony', but the MacGrory collection includes this photograph — taken, presumably, on the occasion of the formal opening of the business — of Campbeltown grocer Eaglesome. It is still there in Reform Square, virtually unaltered in 90 years. The photographer and camera can be seen, reflected in the glass of the doorway.

shining white paper, was sealed using a metal monogram stamp. He was pleasingly old-fashioned in other ways too, sported a watch-and-chain daily and was most probably one of the last men in Scotland to wear spats — which he did, in winter at least, till the day he died.

He also devised and sold many specifics of his own, as did many pharmacists of that generation. I am told this would be illegal nowadays. More's the pity. My father's hand lotion, headache powder, midge repellent, cough mixture and many more were much in demand in the village, and were mailed to customers not just in this country but overseas as well. Sadly, the secrets of all of them died with him.

Kilmacolm was once well-known for its Hydropathic or spa hotel sited on a prominent hill on.the northern edge of the Parish. After it closed there was a brief unsuccessful attempt to turn the building into a Casino in the 1960s before it was torn down and houses built on the site.

Rothesay's Glenburn Hydropathic was the most palatial of all the Clyde hotels, built in 1892 to replace an earlier version which had been destroyed by fire, and it is still in business today though no longer as a Hydropathic: the last hotels to carry that name, to the best of my knowledge, are Dunblane and Crieff Hydros in Perthshire and Peebles Hydro in the Borders.

I'm not sure if Rothesay had donkey-rides in Para Handy's day but it had everything else! It was the premier Clyde resort and as well as a huge range of boarding-houses and hotels for all tastes and pockets, it offered a yacht club, boat hire, water sports, bathing both indoor and out, tennis, golf, cricket, an aquarium, camera obscura, concert halls and much more.

15

The Incident at Tarbert

There is a very genuine camaraderie amongst the vessels which crowd the Clyde. In part it stems from the struggle with the common enemy, the sea, which unites all those who go about their living upon it, whether on a crack transatlantic liner or an inshore fishing dorey.

What particularly binds the puffer crews on the Firth, however, is an even deeper tie than that.

It is the need to show solidarity against the slings and arrows of outrageous disdain to which they are all too often subjected by those 'establishment' figures who see their own calling or their own position in the marine hierarchy as being inherently superior to the humbler workhorses of the river.

Such solidarity has rarely been better demonstrated than by an episode which occurred recently in East Loch Tarbert and news of which has now filtered through to Glasgow. The *Vital Spark*, of course, was well and truly involved in events, although Para Handy insists that her role was that of supporter rather than instigator.

Given her reputation, coupled with Hurricane Jack's presence on board in Dougie's absence on leave (his wife was on the point of presenting him with their twelfth child), I have my doubts about that.

~

The Tarbert piermaster is notorious for his brusque treatment of the puffers which are such regular visitors to the busy harbour. The huge local fishing-fleet he will tolerate (but only just) because on its activities is much of the wealth of the community founded. For him, though, the proudest moment of every day comes with the arrival of the *Columba*, unmatched jewel of the MacBrayne fleet, on her Glasgow to Ardrishaig run.

Her posted berthing time on her outward passage — and rarely does she deviate from it by more than a minute or so — is five minutes before midday. By that time the pier is thronged with bystanders and sightseers, and traps and carriages stand at the pierhead ready to whisk those passengers bound for Islay or Jura across the narrow isthmus to the waiting steamer at West Loch Tarbert.

On a recent Friday morning the *Vital Spark* lay at the small stone jetty in the innermost recesses of the East Loch, in company with three other Glasgow-registered puffers, unloading building materials for a local contractor.

"Would you look at that," Para Handy suddenly exclaimed, "where does the *Tuscan* think she's goin'? McSporran will no' be at aal pleased when he sees this!" McSporran was the notoriously high-handed piermaster who presided over maritime proceedings at Tarbert.

Another puffer had appeared in the harbour and was edging her way alongside the main steamer pier with the obvious intention of berthing in an area normally reserved exclusively for the passenger vessels and, on occasion, larger cargo carriers such as the *Minard Castle*.

"No, Peter," said Hurricane Jack, joining Para Handy at the rail and shading his eyes against the morning sun to stare across the water at the new arrival. "She's aal right, she's cairryin' a flittin'."

There was an unwritten concession, usually honoured by all the piermasters in the large Firth ports, that a puffer carrying a domestic as opposed to a commercial cargo would be allowed to use the main piers. Sure enough, the *Tuscan's* deck was covered with a jumble of wardrobes, bedsteads, chairs and the like, and a horse and cart were waiting to receive them at the inner corner of the pier, where their unloading would not interfere with the berthing arrangements of the *Columba*, expected within the next half hour.

Since the new arrival's skipper was a cousin of Para Handy's whom he had not seen for some months, he and Hurricane Jack strolled round towards the steamer pier to exchange the gossip of the river.

They got there just in time to witness the events which

transpired as the *Columba* appeared round the protecting Tarbert headland, her decks thronged with passengers.

The unloading of the puffer was in full swing when McSporran came rushing out onto the pier from his office at the turnstiles, waving the silver-topped ebony stick which was his unofficial staff-of-office.

"MacFarlane," he shouted to the skipper of the *Tuscan*, "will you get this rust-bucket aff my pier at once, and away to where she belongs, ower there wi' the rest of the screpyard fleet!"

Para Handy bristled.

"There's no call for language like that, Mr McSporran," he protested before his cousin Tommy could get a word in. "Besides she's cerryin' a flittin' and it is chenerally agreed that the coal piers iss no place for hoosehold goods

"You keep oot o' this, Para Handy," roared McSporran. "Besides this is the Royal Route, and what may be good enough for the likes o' Wemyss Bay or Brodick is certainly not good enough for Tarbert.

"Get that thing shufted — and this dam' cart as weel!"

Before anyone could stop him, or take evasive action, he lifted his stick and struck the patient Clydesdale, waiting in the shafts of the cart, smartly across the rump. The horse kicked out once and careered off up the pier, the cart bucketing in its wake and spilling its contents onto the quayside.

Ignoring the rumpus which that created, McSporran loosed from their bollards first the forward and then the stern ropes securing the *Tuscan* to the pier, and threw them contemptuously onto her deck.

"Get oot of this, MacFarlane. And from noo on stick to where ye belong. This pier is for the gentry. The Coal Pier is for the likes o' you. And that's the way I intend to run this harbour!"

∾

"Somethin's goin' to have to be done aboot that man," said Para Handy half-an-hour later as the crews of the two puffers stood lined up along the bar of a shoreside hostelry.

"You can say that, Peter," said Tommy MacFarlane. "He's cost me a lot of money today, wi' the damage to the flittin' and me no' insured for it. Not to say the damage to my reputation at the same time."

"I know he's an awkward duvvle, boys," said the barman,

wiping the wooden counter with a damp cloth, "but he's under a lot of pressure because of what's happenin' the morn."

"Eh?" said Para Handy. "What's that, then?"

"Hiv ye no heard? The Chook o' Hamilton's taken a shootings on Islay for the month, and he's chartered the *Duchess of Fife* from Ardrossan to Tarbert first thing tomorrow, en route for Port Askaig, wi' a whole gang o' toffs.

"Ass weel ass a wheen o' Bruttish gentry there's a couple o' Princes frae Chermany or somewhere. Every carriage and trap in the coonty seems to have been hired to meet the steamer and take them ower to the West Loch chust after breakfast, and auld McSporran's up to high doh aboot the whole thing."

"Iss that so indeed," said Hurricane Jack. "well, well" — and he drained his glass. "Boys, I think we should awa' and have a considered word with our colleagues at the Coal Pier..."

~

Anyone up and about in Tarbert at three o'clock the following morning would have been aware of mysterious goings-on in the darkness of the harbour. The silhouettes of the steam-lighters moored at the Coal Pier seemed to be moving, though the engines were silent. Closer examination would have revealed that the dinghy of each puffer had been lowered into the water and, with two men heaving at the oars, was painfully towing its parent puffer across the water — apparently toward the steamer pier a couple of hundred yards away.

~

When McSporran strode onto the pier just after eight o'clock to inspect the arrangements for the arrival of the *Duchess of Fife* and her very special passengers, he could not believe his eyes.

Its entire length was occupied by a row of five puffers moored stem to stern. A skiff could not have been manoeuvred in to the jetty.

As for the expected steamer...

McSporran spent 30 frantic minutes trying to get the puffers shifted. But the crews had all mysteriously disappeared and, though he could cast off the mooring lines, he could do nothing to move the boats for not only were their anchors down (but no steam up to allow them to be raised again), they were also chained tightly together.

"It's naethin' to do wi' me, Mr McSporran," said the Tarbert policeman to whom the piermaster had appealed for help. "The boats iss chust berthed: they're no' breaking ony law that I'm aware of."

~

At nine o'clock, with the *Duchess of Fife* due in just 15 minutes, he admitted defeat.

The waiting conveyances were moved round to the only available berth in the harbour.

The Coal Pier.

From their vantage point on a hill above the town, the crews of the five puffers watched with some considerable relish as the chartered paddler approached the steamer pier, her captain plainly in ill-humour as he leaned from the wing of the bridge to hear a shouted apology from McSporran, and his instructions about berthing against the tiny, grimy puffer quay.

They watched the dozens of gentry on their way to Islay pick their way down the gangways and across the littered, coal-rimed jetty towards the waiting carriages.

They watched the retinues of servants who followed with all the massed paraphernalia of an Edwardian shooting-party at its grandest.

And, above all, they watched the mortification, embarrassment and humiliation of the snobbiest piermaster on the whole of the Firth.

"Weel, that's set his gas at a peep" said Hurricane Jack with some satisfaction. "I think it'll be some time afore McSporran kicks the *Tuscan* — or any ither puffer come tae that — from its berth again!"

FACTNOTE

The Glasgow to Ardrishaig Service was jealously guarded and promoted by David MacBrayne as the paramount Clyde route, as indeed it was. An end in itself for round-trip passengers on a day excursion, it was much more than that. It was the major water-borne through-route to the Western

THE OVERLAND CONNECTION — Although the town was very much the crossroads for passengers going west and north, there never were any scheduled steamer services from Tarbert to Campbeltown and intending passengers faced an uncomfortable, clattering coach journey over much of the length of the Kintyre peninsula. The 40-mile trip would have taken almost a whole day by horse-drawn omnibus. The first motor buses appeared in the area in 1907 — needless to say in MacBrayne livery!

and Northern Highlands and Islands and many of its patrons were the wealthy landowners and gentry (and their guests) who lived most of the year in city homes — in London as often as Glasgow — but spent much of the summer months on the Highland estates.

It truly was an express service. Despite requiring to make nine intermediate stops, *Columba* reached Tarbert after a 90-mile passage from Glasgow in less than five hours and arrived at her terminus and turning point, Ardrishaig, 40 minutes later.

Those bound for Islay or Jura disembarked at Tarbert while those headed further North or West — to Oban or Mull, Inverness or Skye — stayed on board till Ardrishaig and then transferred to the Crinan Canal packet.

The dovetailing with MacBrayne's West Highland fleets meant that a passenger leaving London on the overnight train could be in Islay in time for tea the next afternoon, a time-scale only possible today by air. Those travelling north from Ardrishaig could reach Oban for High Tea, Fort William for Dinner.

Excursionists were an increasingly important market and it can be said that David MacBrayne almost invented the concept of the inclusive tour — and assiduously promoted it. The full day trip from Glasgow to Ardrishaig and return cost in 1899 only 12/-(60p!) in first class and 7/- (35p) in second: both inclusive of a meals package consisting of breakfast, lunch and tea!

Demand on the route was such that as well as *Columba's* daily service there was an additional sailing in the peak months by her consort *Iona*, which left Glasgow at 1.30 p.m. and reached Ardrishaig at 7.15: here she lay overnight before returning to Glasgow first thing the following morning.

Sadly, there were harbours where the puffers and their ilk were treated very much as poor relations, with their own designated berths in some hidden corner, and with officials anxious to keep the main pier as the preserve of the steamers, the yachts and the occasional scheduled cargo service.

One has the distinct impression that Para Handy and his crew were always happier in the smaller communities where they were assured of a warm welcome at any time of the year!

16

The March of the Women

Para Handy consulted the tin alarm clock which hung
on a string from a nail driven into the fo'c'sle bulk-
head. "Nearly six o'clock: Jeck iss late," he
announced. It was a Saturday afternoon in August
and the *Vital Spark* was lying at Anderston Quay, loaded to
the plimsoll line with steel plates for the shipyard at
Campbeltown.

She was ready to sail and, indeed, Para Handy had
planned to be half way to Greenock by this time. But
Hurricane Jack, learning on their arrival in Glasgow the
previous evening that his old command — the clipper *Port
Jackson* — was docked at Leith, had taken the train to
Edinburgh then and there to see his former colleagues, with
the promise to return by early afternoon the following day.

"Ye cannae trust that man at all," said Macphail with
some asperity, "he's a mountebank! We've missed the tide
noo and we micht as weel wait till the morn'."

Before the Captain could leap to the defence of his oldest
friend there came the clatter of boots on the deck overhead
and the man himself came bursting down into the fo'c'sle.

"Sorry, shipmates," he said, "but it's chust been wan o'
those days and my head's aal spinnin' wi' the stramash of it
aal."

"Wass it a heavy night wi' your friends, then, Jeck?"
asked the Captain solicitously. "Jum will run up to the dairy
and get a bottle o' milk to settle you."

"It iss not last night that is the problem," replied Jack
with great vehemence, "and my head iss fine, thank you.

"No, I got back to Glasgow as planned, just before dinner
time. The trouble started when I came oot o' Queen Street

Station."

"Trouble?" Dougie put in anxiously. "What trouble?"

"He'll hae met a friend that owed him and they've been on the ran-dan for the last five hoors," chipped in the Engineer with rancour.

"Pay no attention, Jeck," soothed Para Handy. "Chust tak' your time and tell us exactly what went wrong and where, and whether you want anything done about it."

"George Square, my boys," said Jack, "that's where it's aal happening: but nothing went wrong! Everything went right! When I came doon the steps from the Station, the Square was chust packed wi' wummin: nothin' but wummin and gyurls ass far ass the eye could see!

"There wass some sort of a wudden platform put up at the far end o' the square, chust in front o' the Toon Hall, and there wass a wheen o' older wummin stood on it, wi' wan o' them aye rantin' on aboot somethin'. I wisna' much carin', so I paid no attention to yon.

"But aal the pavements at the station end o' the square wass chust choc-a-bloc wi' gyurls: red-heads and brunettes and fair haired gyurls that would stop a tram in its trecks they wass that bonnie." He sighed with pleasure at the memory. "Dozens o' them! Hundreds o' them! I have never in aal my life seen sich a tempting array o' feminine beauty aal in the wan place at the wan time!"

Macphail the misogynist snorted: "And Ah'm sure you made their day too, and they wis jist speechless wi' excitement at seein' you," he said dismissively, "bein' the fine figure o' a man you maybe used tae be — aboot 20 years ago. Your courtin' days is done, Maclachlan, and it's high time you admutted it and acted your age!"

"Pay no attention, Jeck," said the Captain. "He is chust jealous. Go on! Who were they aal?"

"Suffry-jets," said Jack. "Ye'll have read aboot them. Gyurls and wummin wantin' the vote."

"Wantin' the vote?" said Sunny Jim incredulously. "Whitever will they think o' next. Votes for wummin? Fat chance!"

That dyed-in-the-wool anti-feminist, the Engineer, nodded in vigorous agreement.

"Well, I don't know," began the Mate, who was notoriously (and unceasingly) henpecked. "Maybe they have a point..."

"When are you goin' tae hae the courage tae start wearin'

the breeks in your ain hoose?" demanded Macphail truculently and it was only the Captain's timely intervention that prevented a trading of insults between the two.

"Go on Jeck," he repeated firmly: "and tell us aal aboot these suffry-jets."

~

The suffragette movement, till now largely directed towards the thinking women of the London area, had embarked on promoting a more national support, and Hurricane Jack had by chance debouched onto George Square in the midst of their first ever rally in Glasgow. There had been a considerable degree of local interest generated by the placing of a series of advertisements in local papers, bills posted everywhere proclaiming the place and time of the event, and a discreet but fervent word-of-mouth campaign.

Holding the rally on a Saturday had been something of a stroke of genius since it made it possible for the factory girls of Glasgow to attend in droves, alongside the middle-class women who had been the main target of much suffragette proselytising till then.

While most of the Glaswegian males who came upon the scene passed by, as it were, very firmly indeed on the other side, it was not in Jack's character as a devoted ladies' man of many decades devotion to pass up the opportunity to mingle with such a vast number of members of the opposite sex.

So, setting his cap at a jaunty angle, and regretting bitterly that he lacked a brass-mounted telescope tucked authoritatively under one arm, he had infiltrated the crowds of young girls on the square opposite the station.

After so many rebuffs, and frequent rudenesses, from the male sex, the young ladies surged eagerly and winningly around their new-found supporter and soon Jack was in his element.

He accepted the leaflets they thrust into his hands: "I have aalways had a very high opeenion o' gyurls chenerally," said he gallantly: "and I wush you every success in your endeavours. I chust wush I wass able to be of some help..." and he bowed and touched his cap to every side.

"We are planning to demonstrate forcibly, Mr MacLachlan," cried one particularly stunning red-haired

girl with a wide-brimmed white hat and an enormous parasol, "we will show our sisters in London that we are prepared to follow their example."

There was a chorus of approval.

"We would be chaining ourselves to the very buffers of
the trains," she continued, "but they will not even let us
into the station. Or to the railings of the City Chambers:
but the Council has placed guards in front of them."

Once they had established that Jack was a sea-faring
man, they showed particular interest in his ship and the
unfortunate Hurricane, carried away somewhat by the
heady glamour of his surroundings, gave into the temptation of gilding the lily somewhat both in his description of
the puffer: and in regard to his position on board her.

"The finest vessel on the Firth," he said firmly, with a
pride and enthusiasm of which Para Handy would have
most thoroughly approved, "sailing tonight for distant seas
and far horizons under the command of yours truly."

And when, reluctantly, he dragged himself from their
midst on the plea that he must return to his ship, the red-
haired girl insisted on walking with him to Anderston Quay.

"Not as big as I would have wished," she said mysteriously when they reached the *Vital Spark* at her berth. "But
she will do." And resisting Jack's clumsy attempt to place a
farewell kiss on her cheek she jumped nimbly aboard a
city-bound tram and waved him goodbye from its upper,
open deck.

∾

"So there you have it, shipmates," said Jack, beaming on
the company. "Bonnie gyurls and a friendly atmosphere!
D'ye think they wud have *me* for a suffry-jet for I would
enlist tomorrow chust for the sake of the cheneral frivolity?"

"You're some man for the high jinks," said Para Handy
enviously and the crew climbed on deck and started to prepare for their delayed departure.

Macphail scurried into his den to stoke up the boiler fires
and Sunny Jim and Dougie lashed the puffer's dinghy firmly across the hatch of the hold.

As Para Handy, Hurricane Jack just behind him, opened
the door of the wheelhouse, they were all suddenly aware
of the music of a brass band a few streets away — but com-

ing rapidly nearer. It sounded too as if a crowd was singing along with the playing of the band, and there were periodic excited whoops and cries.

Then the clash and crash of the band and its followers became overwhelming, as the head of a substantial procession appeared round the corner of one of the warehouses and headed straight towards the *Vital Spark*.

There were several hundred women trailing the band, singing enthusiastically at the tops of their voices, and a handful, all bearing suffragette placards, heading it. In the very van was a tall, red-haired girl wearing a broad-brimmed white hat and twirling a parasol on her shoulder.

The song died away as the band came to a halt on the dockside immediately alongside the puffer. The marchers massed behind it in a semi-circle and a repeated staccato chant went up: "Votes For Women! Votes For Women! Votes For Women!"

With a smile and a wave to the perplexed Hurricane Jack, the red-haired girl and two others stepped forwards and suddenly producing sets of hand-cuffs from, it seemed, thin air, they attached themselves to the hawsers holding the puffer fore and aft onto the quayside and threw the keys into the water.

"Jum," said Para Handy glumly, "wull ye go an' tell Macphail he needna bother gettin' up steam: and Jeck, seein' you got us into aal this, wull you go and fetch a polisman? You know where I'll be if you need me."

And, turning his back on the triumphant, chanting crowd, he made his way slowly along the deck and vanished down into the fo'c'sle.

FACTNOTE

Glasgow's George Square has for generations been 'centre stage' for rallies, protests and public meetings ranging from the sublime to the ridiculous. It thankfully escaped the worst ravages of the city's post-war architectural vandalism and is still overlooked by the magnificent Victorian facades of the City Chambers, the General Post Office, and other properties in keeping with its scale and character: but one doesn't need to look further than the adjacent skyline to see the philistine treatment which parts of the city received in the fifties and sixties.

The Queen Street and Central Stations have survived

A FORMIDABLE MATRIARCHY — The sole man in this family group looks appropriately worried about the encroaching feminism! Victorians were still getting used to the whole idea of photography and the only member of this particular group who looks at all happy about having a picture taken is the dog!

more or less intact but long gone, and much lamented, are the more modest but characterful Buchanan Street: and the most imposing of them all, St Enoch's, with its sweeping carriageway and the towering gothic frontage of its integral hotel.

The Suffragette Movement was at its zenith in the first decade of the century, spurred on by the leadership of Emmeline Pankhurst. As well as political protest and pressure, it relied on less peaceful means of promoting the cause and what we would now call publicity stunts ranged from the relative innocence of protestors chaining themselves to railings at the Houses of Parliament, Buckingham Palace or anywhere else where they felt attention would be focussed upon them: to the tragedy of the Derby of 1912, at which the Suffragette Emily Davidson threw herself under the hooves of King George V's horse, brought it down, and was herself trampled to death.

Many historians feel that the public revulsion stimulated by such activities was counter-productive to the cause, and that what in a sense 'saved' the Movement was the First World War, in which women played an incalculably valuable role. Indeed some commentators see the easing of suffrage restrictions which followed that holocaust as the country's way of recognising the service of the nation's womanhood.

One of the more colourful, though less high-profile, supporters of the Movement was the composer Ethel Smyth, who joined the suffragettes in 1911 and in the same year composed for them what became their Battle Hymn — the splendidly up-beat and instantly memorable 'March of the Women'.

It is one of the few of her compositions recorded and marketed today. But she merits a much wider audience for such stirring programme music as the Overture to her opera *The Wreckers* and above all for her magnificent and moving Mass, written in 1891 and first performed in 1893 — but not heard again for more than 30 years. Now available on CD it memorably deserves acclaim and recognition.

17

The Missing Link

Para Handy looked up from his perusal of the *Glasgow Herald* with considerable surprise. "My Chove," he said, "did you read this piece in the paper aboot the Piltdown Man, Dougie?"

Captain and Mate were alone in the fo'c'sle: Macphail was carrying out some running repairs with, to judge from the baffled curses which could occasionally be heard even from the forefoot of the vessel, scant success. Sunny Jim had been sent ashore with a long shopping list, for this brief stop-over at Partick would be their last chance to stock up the provisions cupboard for some days.

The puffer was on her way from Rutherglen, where she had loaded a farm flitting, and would shortly be sailing for the remote clachan of Bellochantuy on the western shores of the Kintyre peninsula. It would be some days before they were within hailing distance of a shop again.

"Piltdoon Man?" asked the mate: "and who might he be when he iss at hame?"

"He iss not at hame any longer," said the Captain, "for he hass been dead now this many thoosands o' years: but he used to live in the sooth of England and some professor or somethin' hass been and dug him up again, and says he iss the 'Missing Link', whateffer that might be.

"Chust look you at this picture, Dougie," he commanded, handing over the paper, opened at the page carrying the story of the Piltdown discovery under a banner headline, and bearing beneath that an artist's impression of what the 'Link' was thought to have looked like.

"It is quite uncanny!" continued the Captain with considerable conviction. "Did you effer in your naitural, if you were chust to shut the wan eye and look at it sidey-ways, see onythin' that pit ye mair in mind o' Macphail on wan o' his aff days?"

The Mate peered quizzically at the sketch.

"He certainly disna look too healthy," he said at last: "but iss he not raither mair like thon English chentleman that wass up for the shootings at St Catherine's last year, and shot himsel' in the foot, and we had to gi'e him a hurl across the loch in the punt, ower to the doctor's at Inveraray?

"I think it iss a wee bit unkind o' ye to be comparing him wi' poor Macphail, Peter. Even after 30 years shuvveling coal Dan's airms iss no' quite ass long ass that."

"Whateffer you think yoursel', Dougie," said the Captain: and carefully folded the paper before placing it on top of the mess table: "but I will be interested to have Jum's opeenion when he gets back wi' the proveesions."

~

At that very moment Sunny Jim was coming to the end of a longish grocery list in a branch of the Glasgow Co-operative on Dumbarton Road.

"And six pounds o' best pork sausage," he concluded.

"Links or Lorne?" asked the grocer.

Jim thought for a moment. "Mak' it links," he said at length "and a couple of black puddin's, and twa mealie wans too, jist for a wee divershun tae go alang wi' the sausages."

The grocer weighed out the goods, wrapped them in grease-proof paper and perched them on the top of the large cardboard box into which a full week's supplies for the crew of the *Vital Spark* had now been consigned.

"Onything mair?"

"Seein' I'm here, Wullie," said Jim, you could jist open me a screw-tap o' Worthington and I'll get ootside that while you're doin' the sums."

And he leant sociably on the brass-edged counter pulling at his beer while the Co-op man, licking the point of his pencil at intervals with a sigh of fierce concentration, totted up a long column of figures once, then twice to check it, and finally a third time — apparently for luck.

"That'll be five pund fifteen and saxpence," he said at length, straightening up and handing the document to Jim: "and anither saxpence for the ale."

"Mercy! Near on six pound! I'm sure I didna think I wis

buyin' the premises when I cam' in." said Jim. "And a tanner for the beer! Are you no' throwin' that in for the good wull o' the hoose?"

"Ah canna dae that," said the grocer. "For it's nae ma hoose and the chentlemen in Morrison Street wud soon be throwin' me oot of it if they foond Ah'd sterted tae gi'e the goods awa' on a whum.

"Whit Ah can dae for ye is send wan o' the delivery lads doon wi' the box on a bike tae the boat. That'll save ye a pech. And I'll gi'e ye a nip o' my ain whusky."

And on that offer the bargain was struck. Sunny Jim paid with six crumpled pound notes, pocketed his change, swallowed a generous dram poured from the bottle gifted to the grocer by one of his suppliers, and saw the box safely loaded onto the metal cradle at the front of the delivery bike.

"See and no' cowp it," he admonished the youngster who was to pedal it, "for there's eggs in there, and as we dinna like them scrambled you'd best get them tae the shup in wan piece. Put the meats in the wire safe on the foredeck, and the rest o' the stuff in the fo'c'sle. And tell the Captain I'm on my way."

~

The puffer slipped down-river in the gloaming with Dougie at the wheel: Para Handy passed the article about the Piltdown Man to Sunny Jim as the two of them sat on the stern gunwale.

"Dan to the life," he said in a deliberately loud voice: "but when I showed it to the man himsel' an hoor ago, he wass not at aal amused. You wud think he wud be prood tae be taken for onythin' ass important ass a 'Missing Link', but no. He chust ran awa' from the suggestion: he iss like the Gabardine Swine in the Scruptures, that had the pearls o' wusdom thrown tae them, but chust went dashin' awa' into the wilderness!"

A furious clang of metal from the engine-room at their feet indicated that the unfortunate engineer was reduced to taking out his feelings on a pile of coals.

"We wull put in to Bowling for the night," Para Handy added pointedly, "and mebbe Dan wull obleege the company by givin' us aal a Piltdoon performance at the Inns!" But, despite their cajoling, Macphail huffily refused

127

to join the rest of the crew when they went ashore after a herring supper to quench the thirst it had given them.

When they returned on board, though, he was in his bunk and fast asleep — with a somehow satisfied-looking grin on his face which made Para Handy bristle with suspicion. "He's been up to something: wait you and we wull see!"

~

The *Vital Spark* continued down the Firth after an early start the following morning and mid-day found her just off the south end of Bute.

Sunny Jim went below to make a start on preparing dinner for the crew. With the potatos peeled and set on the stove to boil in a pan of sea water, he went up on deck, opened the door of the meat safe and reached for the link sausages.

They were not there.

Cursing the delivery boy for his perfidy, Jim made the best of a meal he could from the black and mealie puddings.

"Ah'm sorry, boys," he said: "but yon wee duvvle has pinched the sausages on us, and there's nae mair I can do by way o' a meat dinner."

Para Handy and the Mate accepted the situation, grudgingly, but Macphail refused to eat any of the fare on offer and retired in high dudgeon to his stokehold.

"To bleezes!" said the Captain: "The man's still in an upset over the ribbin' we gave him yestreen: well, aal I can say iss that he'll be hungry afore we are," and he tucked into a forkful of mealie pudding with apparent relish.

~

In fact, Macphail refused to join them for any meal over the next two days, surfacing only to butter a few slices of bread and make himself a cup of tea at regular intervals, as they rounded the Mull, beached just off the farm to which the flitting was consigned, and unloaded the strangely mixed cargo into the new tenant's waiting horse and dray.

Then, on the morning they were due to sail for home, Sunny Jim squeezed his way into Macphail's domain, anxious to make peace with the engineer for the air of gloom and doom which hung over the little ship went quite contrary to Jim's nature.

And he found Macphail frying a pound or thereby of finest pork sausages on the back of a shovel held over the glowing ashes in his fire-pan!

His yell of outrage brought Para Handy and the Mate dashing to the engine-room.

"You're a duvvle, Dan!" Para handy,protested. "Can you no' tak' a bit o' a joke wi'oot complainin', or at least wi'oot losing the heid and stealin' from your shupmates!"

"Ah'm no' complainin' noo," said the engineer: "that's been the best grub Ah've ever had on this decrepit auld hooker. Two solid days o' meat meals and I'll say wan thing fur ye, Jum, ye ken a good sausage when you see it.

"Ah'm fair vexed that's the last o' them — or Ah'd offer you all a taste.

"Mebbe that'll teach you a lesson. Never mind aboot the Missin' Link: it's the missin' *links* that you should all be a lot mair concerned aboot!"

And with a satisfied laugh to himself, he swallowed the last morsel of sausage with evident, if exaggerated, relish.

∽

A few minutes later, the farmer appeared with his cheque-book to pay for the flitting and as he perched on the seat of his cart to sign it, he had his first sight of Macphail (who had been seated unseen in the engine-room throughout the unloading process of the previous hours) as that worthy came on deck to get a breath of air.

The farmer stared at him, transfixed, and was so put off his stride that he smudged the signature badly and had to start all over again and write a fresh cheque.

"My heavens, Captain," he confided to Para Handy in an awed whisper, "it's none o' my business, but that's some man you have as your engineer! You ken, he's the very double o' that 'Missing Link' that had his likeness in the Gleska Herald a day or two back.

"I hope I'm no' offending you saying that..."

FACTNOTE

The discovery of Piltdown Man was one of the great news stories of 1912, and one of the supreme academic hoaxes in history. For sheer audacity and confident theatricality it ranks with such classics of the genre as America's Cardiff Giant or the Berners Street prank in London, Scotland's 18th-century 'Ossian' literary imposture: or the hoax that went so infamously wrong when what had been intended as a slightly scary leg-pull turned to near-tragedy when Orson Welles' radio play, based on the H. G. Wells novel *War of the Worlds*, was believed by many of the listening American audience to be an accurate news broadcast, with whole families panicking and fleeing their homes.

Charles Dawson was an amateur antiquarian and archaeologist who announced to a startled academic world in 1912 the discovery of the 'Missing Link', the hominid which spanned the physical and intellectual gap between ape and man. For about two generations thereafter the skull and jawbone which he had 'excavated' to prove that theory held an honoured place in the pantheon of the British Museum and the site of his 'discovery' — a chalk pit in the Sussex Downs — became a place of pilgrimage for earnest and enthusiastic antiquarians both professional and amateur in the quest of further, momentous 'finds'.

All of which doesn't just help prove the truth of the old adage that 'There's a sucker born every minute'. It also demonstrates quite gratifyingly — at least to the layman — that as often as not the 'sucker' is a loudly self-proclaimed 'expert'.

Only in 1953 was the hoax finally exposed as what it was though even then (and, who knows, perhaps still today) there were voices raised in defence and protest against the destruction of a myth so dearly-held. The skull of the 'Missing Link' was proved, by dating techniques, to be that of a 20th-century man and the jawbone that of a 20th-century orang-outang, both cunningly stained to simulate great age.

I think the only individual involved in the whole scam who came out of it with honour intact was the orang-outang!

Scottish pork butchers, on the other hand, inherit a long and honourable tradition. Glasgow firms like McKeans, established in the 1870s, built up a worldwide reputation, winning awards and medals at food exhibitions (of which the Victorians were so fond) as far afield as Canada, and still trade today, changed beyond recognition by the demands of an evolving market.

Lorne sausage, for the uninitiated, is a coarse-chopped,

sliced sausage-meat in block form. The origin of the name
is unknown (the first maker perhaps?) but, when it is well
made and spiced to perfection, it is tastily addictive.

18

The Cadger

Macphail and Sunny Jim watched the Mate come disconsolately towards them along the quayside at Lamlash, his head down, and his hands deep in his pockets.

"Ah doot it's no' good news," said the Engineer. "We'll be here a week at the least afore the man's weel enough mended tae come back. A week in Lamlash! It shouldnae happen tae a dug!"

The accident had happened the previous afternoon, as they were unloading fencing-stobs for the Duke of Hamilton's estates. As a bundle of the posts was being swung upwards and outwards from the hold the knot on the rope binding them together had slipped and the stobs had come tumbling onto the deck. One caught Para Handy a hefty blow across the head, sending him flying across the hatch-coaming and into the depths of the hold.

The doctor, when he eventually arrived in a pony-and-trap from Brodick, was less concerned with the broken wrist which the Captain sustained in the fall than with the large area of contusion on the side of his head.

"I can strap the wrist no problem," he pronounced, "but I can give no guarantees about your the effects of that blow to your head, Captain MacFarlane. I'm not happy about it at all."

Macphail restrained himself with considerable difficulty from offering his own opinion on that matter, but the upshot was that Para Handy was removed within the hour by horse-drawn ambulance and taken the three miles over the hill to the Cottage Hospital at Brodick 'for observation'. Dougie went with him, partly to keep him company and see him safely installed, partly in order to telegraph the owner in Glasgow to advise him of developments.

"Whit's the news then?" asked Macphail as the Mate scrambled aboard. "Is he deleerious?"

"No, nor hileerious: but he's ass carnaptious ass a wagon-load o' pensioners for they're sayin' they want to keep him in for a week, and there's a nurse yonder built like a dreadnought wha's in cherge o' the ward and he's feart for her already, chust feart. No' that I blame him: if they'd had her at the Crimea it wud have been in the front line trenches and no' Florence's hospital they'd have pit her."

"So we're tae lie here for a week!" exploded Macphail. "A week in Lamlash in October! Nae wonder ye're lookin' as miserable as an innkeeper at a Rechabites meeting. We'll be oot o' wir minds wi' boredom, and here's me wi' naethin' Ah hivnae read, an' nae mair chance o' buyin' onything mair here than I hae o' gettin' a transfer tae the *Columba*."

"No," said Dougie, "it's worse nor that. I telegraphed Gleska and they said there iss a cargo o' scrap iron waitin' for us at Ardrishaig that's urchently needed up at Pointhoose so the shup hass to go and load it. Peter iss to choin us at Pointhoose ass soon ass they let him oot."

"Thank the Lord," said Macphail emphatically. "At least we get oot o' here. So whit are ye lookin' so miserable aboot then Dougie? I thocht ye always wanted a chance tae skipper the boat yersel'?"

"Indeed I did, Dan," replied the disconsolate Mate: "but the Gleska office will not let me do it! They say that for the insurance we have to have an experienced Captain and they're sending wan down to Brodick on board the *King Edward* tomorrow morning."

"Well, Ah'm vexed for ye," said the Engineer generously, "but at least we'll no hae to drum wir heels in Lamlash for a week. So why are ye lookin' like a wet December funeral?"

"For the same reason ass you will be in a meenit," responded the Mate dolefully. "Wance I tell you who the relief skipper iss goin' to be. They're sendin' doon Cadger Campbell."

Macphail blenched visibly. "Ye're jokin' Ah hope!"

"I wish I wass," said the Mate. "But I would not joke aboot ass serious a matter ass Cadger Campbell."

"Ah should hope not indeed," said the Engineer. "It wud be jist temptin' providunce if ye did!"

"For sure," agreed Dougie miserably.

Sunny Jim had been growing increasingly restive during this (to him) totally incomprehensible and infuriatingly repetitive exchange.

"And just exactly who," he managed to get in at last, "is this Cadger Campbell?"

"Dinna tell me that ye've never ever even heard o' the Cadger..." began Macphail.

"Look," said Jim in total exasperation, "if I had heard o' the man I wudna need tae be askin' who he wis, wud I? Noo are ye gaun' tae tell me, or no'?"

"He's wan o' the most notorious skippers that ever had command on the river," said Dougie. "He's lost wan chob after anither through drink an' fightin' an' he's been in the courts three times on a cherge o' wreckin' boats for the insurance only they could neffer prove it. What they did prove more nor wance though wass that he's a fist on him like a menagerie gorilla an' he's quite prepared to use it. The man's done fower spells at least in Barlinnie for assault. He's got a tongue on him as acid as a soor-plum and aal he can come by in the way o' work nooadays iss an occasional berth when the regular skipper's no' weel and there's an urchent chob to be done. Like noo, wi' us."

"By comparison wi' the Cadger," added Macphail, "Hurricane Jack is a teetotal pacifist wha kens every Moodey and Sankey hymn by hert an' sings them tae himsel' a' the day lang. Need I say ony mair?"

∽

The Cadger came aboard at half-past-eleven the following morning, bearing about him like a miasma an aroma reminiscent of a distillery and a brewery rolled into one, and carrying a grubby canvas hold-all which clanked noisily, as of bottles, when he placed it down on deck in the wheelhouse.

He was more than six feet in height, a hugely-built man in his early forties with more hair in his ears and nose than most men have on their beards, and a lived-in face the colour of a side of raw bacon and the texture of a pebble-dash wall.

He picked on Sunny Jim at once.

"And who the bleezes are you?" he asked, pulling the cork from a half-flask of whisky retrieved from the hold-all.

"Ah ken your shupmates fine — yon lanky streak o' a mate wi' the reputation o' bein' the most tumid man that ever set fit on a boat, an' the ither yin hidin' doon there pretendin' tae be a proper injineer when he cudna even wind up a waggity-wa' nock wi'oot breakin' the spring.

"But you, Ah've never clapped eyes on you."

Sunny Jim explained himself as best and as briefly as he could.

The Cadger's eyes lit up. "The Cluthas, eh! Weel, there's hope for ye yet: at least they wis boats wi' a turn of speed and a bit o' class aboot them. A bit o' a come-doon for ye tae finish up on this rust-bucket, though."

Gesturing to Jim to cast off the mooring ropes fore and aft, he pushed the unhappy Dougie unceremoniously out of the wheelhouse and, without granting him the dignity of employing the whistle and speaking-tube for the purpose, he bellowed his instructions to Macphail, grabbed the wheel, steered the puffer out from the pier and set a course which would clear the northern promontory of the sheltering Holy Isle, and move towards the open waters of the Firth.

∽

Four hours later the *Vital Spark* was well into Loch Fyne with the entrance to East Loch Tarbert just off the port bow, and their destination — Ardrishaig — only 12 miles ahead.

The atmosphere aboard was thick enough to cut with a knife. The Cadger, tipsy when he arrived off the *King Edward*, had been steadily demolishing firstly the half-flask of whisky, and then when it was finished the three quart bottles of stout which appeared to be the sole contents of the hold-all. Dan Macphail, hidden among his engines, had missed the worst of the relief skipper's verbal assaults and Jim, on the excuse of preparing the crew's dinner, had retired to the fo'c'sle — safely out of ear-shot, and out of sight as well: in fact though, so sudden and so unexpected had been the Cadger's departure from Lamlash that he had had no chance to replenish the ship's stores and the crew would go hungry till he could go ashore and stock up once they reached Ardrishaig.

The unfortunate Dougie, unable to make his escape, had suffered the brunt of the Cadger's unrelieved torrent of abuse, directed first at the boat, then at her ship's company one-by-one. Even the mild-mannered Mate was at breaking-point when the Cadger suddenly swung the wheel violently to port and headed into Tarbert harbour.

"It's no' Tarbert oor cargo iss at," Dougie protested, "but at Ardrishaig. We've near two hours to go."

"We're gaun nowhere wi' a dry shup," growled the Cadger with some menace, pitching his empty bottles overboard. "Unless you want tae go the same way as ma deid men, get intae the bows and get ready tae pit a line ashore when we come alangside."

Sunny Jim was summoned from the fo'c'sle, given a crumpled pound note taken from the Cadger's back pocket, and sent up to the village inn to buy two bottles of whisky.

"What the blazes kept ye," roared the Cadger when Jim returned 10 minutes later carrying not just the whisky, but two plain loaves, a bag of potatos and a couple of pounds of sausages as well, "and whit the hell d'ye mean by wastin' ma time and your money buyin' a' that breid and stuff?

"Never in a' ma life hiv I seen sich a bunch o' useless shilpit nyaffs as the three o' you. Macfarlane must be saft in the heid richt enough tae pit up wi' it: nae wonder the fenceposts did him sich a mischief at Lamlash!"

~

Para Handy came down the road to the jetty beside the Inglis brothers' Pointhouse Shipyard in the late afternoon of the following Wednesday, a bandage round his head and his left arm in a sling.

The crew welcomed him, like a long lost brother, with literally open arms.

"Now, now," he cried, retreating in some embarrassment, "I am chust fine, chust sublime, stop this fuss this instant and tell me how you got on with Mr Campbell, for I'm sure he's the only reason you are so pleased to see me back again! Iss he still here?"

"He never actually got here," said Sunny Jim. "Dougie brought her home frae Ardrishaig an' a right good job he made of it an' a'." Whereat the mate blushed like a young girl. "Naw, Campbell the Cadger is probably still somewhere on Fyneside, and lookin' for a cargo o' scrap — and his crew.

"By the time we got tae Ardrishaig he wis jist destroyed

wi' a' the whusky he'd been drinkin' an' he went oot like a light.

"We were to lift the cargo o' scrap that the auld Hay's puffer *Aztec* wis bringin' hame frae Furnace when her biler blew aff Lochgair. They've decided she's no' worth the repairs an' she's tae be scrapped hersel' wance they can fix a tow tae Faslane.

"So wance we'd shifted the cargo, we jist cairried the Cadger over tae the *Aztec* 'n' dumped him on a bunk in her fo'c'sle and changed the lifebelt wi' her name on for the wan wi' oors. Then Dougie brocht the shup tae Gleska.

"When Campbell finally woke he wud believe he wis still on the *Vital Spark*: he's probably huntin' through Ardrishaig for his crew richt noo!"

FACTNOTE

The Island of Arran, 165 square miles in area, about 20 miles in length and 10 in width, has often been referred to and (in tourist terms) promoted as 'Scotland in miniature'.

There is a logic to the claim. The island contains dramatic mountain scenery, fertile rolling farm country — both grazing uplands and arable lowlands — and a dramatic coastline from beetling cliffs to gentle beaches.

For generations Arran was a popular retreat for Glaswegians rich and poor and though the great days of doon-the-watter sailing have gone, and though more and more we desert our own land for sunnier shores when it comes to holidays, the island retains an immensely loyal following and maintains a mystique all its own.

The village of Lamlash was the first port-of-call for the steamers after the island capital, Brodick, and was a particularly popular haunt for break-takers during Glasgow's 'September Weekend' — always the last weekend of that month and the (unofficial) end of the holiday season.

Holy Isle, which shelters the bay of Lamlash, takes its name from the monastery founded there in the early middle ages. That tradition of sanctity is maintained today by the Tibetan Samye Ling Buddhist community who purchased the island in 1992, have renovated the farmhouse and lighthouse, and plan to build two new centres as refuges for interdenominational retreats at those sites.

The 'Pointhouse' to which the puffer's cargo of scrap-iron was consigned was the famous yard of A & J Inglis, builders of many generations of the most renowned of the Clyde steamers as well as whole families of ships great and small created for other owners, other waters and other purposes. The yard (sadly, like virtually every other Clyde ship-builder, long gone) stood on the north bank of the river Kelvin at the point where it joined the Clyde opposite Govan.

The character of Cadger Campbell is of course purely fictitious but it has to be said that there were always some notorious individuals on and around the river Clyde, as there were in any industrial environment anywhere! When researching background material for my factual study of Para Handy and his world (*In the Wake of the Vital Spark*, Johnston & Bacon, 1994) I was given much information which, even a generation or more after the event, I felt it unwise to specify. One snippet concerned a puffer captain reputed to have ingeniously 'lost' at sea not just three (as in Cadger's case) but *four* puffers in pursuit of fraudulent insurance scams!

19

The Blizzard and the Bear

The frost had scarcely lifted all the February day and now at three in the afternoon, with only a couple of hours of daylight left, the first flurries of snow began to tumble from a steely grey sky which seemed suspended only a few feet above the tip of the puffer's mast. From the engine-room came the clang of the furnace-door being thrust open and the rattle of Macphail's shovel in the bunker as he prepared to spread another layer of coal onto the glowing fire.

The three other members of the crew were squeezed into the wheelhouse in a vain effort to keep warm by dint of numbers but the only effect of their combined presence in that confined space was that their breath, condensing on the windows, had almost completed misted the glass.

The Captain wiped the pane in front of him with an oily rag and peered vainly into the gloom of the dying day. The curtain of falling snow now made it virtually impossible to see anything beyond the bows, which were rising and falling smoothly on an oily swell. Fully laden with a cargo of slate from the quarries at Ballachullish and en route to Port Ellen in Islay, the *Vital Spark* was in the unfamiliar territory of Loch Linnhe and Para Handy had intended to put into Oban for the night.

"Dougie," he now said: "I am thinking we would maybe be better chust to put her in somewhere close at hand and wait for this snow to blow over rather than risk the shup."

"Whatever you think yoursel', Peter." said the mate, who had been increasingly uneasy about the prospect of picking a blind course through the boneyard of the Lynn of Lorn when the only navigational aid on board for these strange waters was a school atlas Para Handy had bought second-hand from a Glasgow book barrow prior to their departure from the Broomielaw three days earlier.

And so, with the lights on the northern end of Lismore faintly visible as a guide on the starboard bow, and Sunny Jim perched reluctantly in the bows as a shivering look-out, they picked their way into the tiny harbour at Port Appin and tied up at the stone pier. There was not a breath of wind and a silence as of the grave lay on a landscape rendered all but invisible by the snow, which fell more thickly than ever. The crew prepared to make the best of a bad job by creating as much comfort as possible in the cramped fo'c'sle. Macphail carefully carried a shovelful of red-hot coals from the engine-room furnace to get the stove going: Dougie carefully trimmed and lit the two oil lamps hanging from the deck-beams: Sunny Jim filled a basin with water and began to peel potatos for their evening meal.

"I have neffer seen weather like it!" said the Captain, "The snow we get on the Clyde is chust a handful of confetti compared wi' this."

"You call this snaw!" derisively snorted Macphail, who had 'gone foreign' before returning to Glasgow and his berth on the puffer several years previously. "You should see the winter in the Baltic. The Rooshians get that much snaw the hooses get totally buried in it: it's only the lums sticking oot and smokin' that let folk ken whaur their hooses is at."

"That's a bit of a whopper, surely, Dan" said Sunny Jim. "Whit wye could they get in and oot o' them?"

"The hooses is all built wi' special doors in the roofs beside the lums, of course," said Macphail. "And I know for a fact for I've seen it that they can build railway lines ower some of the lakes in winter, the ice gets froze that deep. So if Para Handy wants tae conseeder some real winter weather then he shouldna be greetin' aboot a puckle snow in Appin, but raither remember whit things can be like for the Tsar and his weans and a' the ither folk at St Petersburg: it isnae all snowmen and sledges there, that's for sure."

"Is that so," said the skipper with heavy sarcasm. "Weel, that sounds like a spring mornin' compared wi' the conditions that Hurricane Jeck had to put up wi' wan year when he wass on the cluppers.

"He wass first mate on the *City of Lisbon*, wan o' they nitrate shups, and they wass on a voyage home to Liverpool from Chile wi' a cargo o' phosphates. Efferything wass smooth enough till they came to Cape Horn and here they wass hit by the most terrible storms for you should know, Jum, that this iss a place most weel-thocht-of for wund and waves the like of which you'll no' see anywhere else in aal the seven seas. Dougie himself will tell you."

"Right enough, Peter, right enough," affirmed the mate with alacrity, though he had never been further west than Barra nor further south than Belfast all his days at sea. "It iss a most terrible place, to be sure."

"For six days and nights they wass forced to run under bare poles, they daurna' show a scrap o' canvas, and the men on the wheel wass lashed to it for fear they would be washed awa' wi' the seas that wass sweepin' her from stem to stern. And aal the while they was bein' blown sooth, way off their course and aye nearer and nearer to the Sooth Pole.

"Then wan night the wund stopped chust as sudden ass when it started, and there wass a deathly silence, and a night chust as black ass the Earl o' Hell's weskit. In the mornin' when the daylight came they foond to their horror they wass becalmed in the mudst of a whole fleet of icebergs, effery wan of them as big ass a land o' hooses.

"It wass so cold you would not credit it. The riggin' wass ass hard and ass brittle ass icicles, and if you made the mistake of knocking against ony pairt of it, it wud just snap in twa like a stick o' seaside rock. The men off-watch below wass aal frozen solid into their hammocks and had to be chipped oot o' them by the men on watch. If you would try to tak' a billy of tea from the galley to the fo'c'sle it wass chust a lump of ice by the time you got it there and in the officers' salong the rum froze in their glasses afore they could drink it, and they had to sook it chust ass if it wass a cinnamon ball.

"Worst of all, the compass wass froze in the binnacle and they couldnae tell north from sooth so that even if the ice let up a bit, and a wind cam' up and they had the chance to pit some sail on her, they would have had no wye of knowin' which road to tak'."

"Ye're a haver, Para Handy," cried Macphail. "Whether the leear iss yourself, or whether it wass MacLachlan, I dinna ken: but wan o' ye is talkin' nonsense and it's wrang tae pit sich daft notions in young Jum's heid."

Para Handy paid no attention. "Jeck said," he continued, "that the only thing that saved them wass a perty of

Eskimos oot huntin' polar bears who happened by in their kayaks, and wass able to point oot where north wass tae them, so that when...

"Eskimos!!!" shouted Macphail. "Eskimos at the Sooth Pole! And polar bears forbye! Ye done it noo, even Jum must know that you only get Eskimos and Polar Bears in the Arctic."

"Whit d'ye mean 'Even Jum'?" cried Sunny Jim angrily. "Are you makin' oot I'm some sort of eejit or somethin'? Of course I ken the whole story's rubbish — but it's gey entertaining rubbish and it wis whilin' the time awa' very nicely.

"Why not get back tae wan o' your novelles, Dan, and leave the rest of us tae enjoy a harmless baur if we want tae..." And the enraged Jim picked up the potato knife and took his feelings out on a half stone of Kerr's Pinks.

~

Once their supper was finished, the engineer retired to his bunk, while the rest of the crew played a good-natured game of pontoon for matches.

After about half-an-hour, with the harsh sound of Macphail's stentorian snoring echoing through the dimly-lit fo'c'sle, Para Handy climbed up the ladder and opened the hatch to have a look at the weather.

The frost was harder than ever, but the snow had stopped and a crescent yellow moon hung in an inky black sky peppered with stars. For the first time it was possible to see something of the tiny harbour in which they had taken refuge. The village, and the village Inn, lay less than a hundred yards away but were totally hidden by an intervening hillock. Indeed there was not a single house to be seen anywhere from the deck of the puffer.

Even the shallow sea-water in the harbour was covered with a thick layer of ice, such was the severity of the frost: and the further harbour wall was so blanketed and smothered in snow that it was unrecognisable as a man-made object but looked more like a floating mass of ice.

At the edge of the jetty against which the puffer was moored there stood — coated with snow — a wooden tripod about six feet in height, surmounted by a round ball which, when aligned with the ball on a similar construction just visible half-way up the hill behind the harbour, would form a guide-mark for incoming vessels.

The tripod had two wooden arms projecting to either side about five feet off the ground. From each there hung a life-belt.

Para Handy tiptoed back down the ladder into the fo'c'sle and beckoned to Dougie and Sunny Jim.

"I'll treat you both to a dram," he said. "But come up quiet and dinna wake Macphail. Will you, Dougie, set the alarum clock to go off an hour from now: and Jum, bring yon shovel Dan used to bring the coals from the enchine-room. There iss a wee chob to do before we go up to the Inn..."

~

Ten minutes later he stood back to admire their handi-work. The lifebelts had been removed from the arms of the tripod and snow had been built up round it in a rough cone shape as far as the ball which topped it.

Snow had been carefully moulded onto the horizontal arms, and five short twigs of wood added claw-like at their tips. Around the ball at the top a muzzle-like shape had been created on the side facing the boat. Two large ear-like pieces projected from the top of it and three pieces of coal had been set into the head so created — one for a black snout at the front of the muzzle, two for eyes at its top.

"Not bad," said the Captain. "Not bad at aal. Enough to give Dan a bit of a fleg when that alarum goes off and he decides to come up on deck to find out why he's alone on the shup. Wi' an icebound landscape like this aal roond him I've no doot he'll wonder for a moment chust where he iss...

"He'll see then that there's polar bears in ither places than the North Pole — and maybe that'll teach him no' to be sich an auld misery next time, when aal we are havin' is a harmless baur!"

And with a spring in their step the three set off across the snow towards the companionship and warmth of the Appin Inn.

FACTNOTE

There are two villages carrying the name of Ballachullish, the North and the South, one at either side of the narrows where Loch Leven enters Loch Linnhe.

South Ballachullish was, until the middle of this century,

the unlikely venue for a major industry. It was largely to cater for that industry's needs that the isolated branch-line railway from the main Oban to Glasgow route (involving the construction of a cantilever bridge across the fierce rapids at Connell just north of Oban) was laid through the difficult Appin terrain and first opened for business in 1903. Passenger services on the line offered a faster route to link with connections from North Ballachullish onwards to Fort William and Inverness. Freight services took Ballachullish's industrial output to markets UK wide. But eventually more efficient road haulage facilities, and the growth of car ownership, precipitated an inevitable decline in demand and led to the closure of the line. Freight services ended in 1965 and the very last passenger train pulled out of the village the following year.

The industry which had spawned it all in the first instance was a slate-quarry, the highly-esteemed materials from which were exported not just throughout this country, but worldwide. First opened in 1761, it remained in full-scale production for two centuries. The scars which its operations inflicted on the West Highland landscape are only now beginning to mellow.

The Ballachullish narrows were one of the great natural divides between the North and the South. For generations there was a ferry between the two villages which saved travellers the inconvenience of a 15-mile detour round the roller-coaster road which circumvented Loch Leven. In the post-war years, the tiny vehicle-ferries with a capacity of just half-a-dozen cars were wholly unable to cope with the growth in traffic and delays of two hours or more became commonplace in the summer months. At long last a road bridge was built across the narrows, and opened for business in 1976.

Puffers did indeed carry slate from the quarries, and could be quite regular visitors to Loch Linnhe for other reasons. They operated on and through the Caledonian Canal, usually with cargos of timber. Sometimes it was newly-felled from forestry plantations in and around the Great Glen and ferried south: on other occasions it was processed and manufactured, and returned north as telegraph poles or fencing stobs.

But these Highland waterways would be unfamiliar territory to skippers who were more at home on the Clyde, where they could boast that they knew every one of its rocks, shallows and shoals (if not by name) at least by reputation!

20

The Launch of the Vital Spark

The hard work of the day was done, and a peaceful stillness lay across the *Vital Spark* like a balm. The only sound was the faint hiss of escaping steam from the derrick engine, abandoned and cooling itself down now after several strenuous hours spent loading timber from the nearby Forestry estate.

The crew were strewn across the deck-cargo of rough-cut planks in the late evening sunlight, in a companionable silence.

Dan Macphail was engrossed in a new paperback romance, dipping absent-mindedly now and again into a handily-placed bag of humbugs. Para Handy was sitting deep in thought, Sunny Jim was just sitting. Dougie was thumbing idly through the pages of a week-old Glasgow paper which he had acquired from the Forestry Manager.

"Mercy!" said the mate suddenly, "Would you credit this! Here's an Eyetalian liner sunk the very meenit she wass launched frae the slipway."

"Awa' ye go, Dougie, someone's chust makin' mischief wi' a bit o' a baur," said the incredulous Captain.

"Naw, naw, Peter: it's a fact," said the mate. "It chust proves that Clyde-built iss the only guarantee of quality in a shup. Listen to this!"

And, spreading the paper across his knees, he read aloud "Our Rome correspondent reports that the new Italian liner *Pri...Princip...Principesa Jolanda* sank within minutes of her launch in Genoa yesterday. The vessel had been fitted out with her masts and funnels rigged while still on the slip, as is the common practice in Italy, and was a proud sight as she slid down the ways. But within minutes of taking to the water she began to list to port and to the consternation of those aboard her, and of the thousands of spectators, she heeled right over and sank in the shallow water of the harbour, leaving only the plates of her starboard superstructure still showing above the surface..."

"My Chove," said the Captain. "Consternation's the word! Wass there ony casualties, Dougie?"

"Naw," replied the mate. "They wass aal rescued by the tugs that wass standing by her."

"Well," said Para Handy, it'll no' be the first time, nor the last, that someone's had to fish folk oot o' the watter at a launchin' perty."

Sunny Jim sensed a story. "Go on, Captain" he prompted.

Para Handy scratched the lobe of his right ear reflectively for a moment or two.

"Well," he said at length, "it was like this..."

∾

"Ass Dougie knows, I've been on the *Vital Spark* since the day she wass launched, first ass mate, when Hurricane Jeck wass the skipper of her, then ass Captain when he — er — retired, ass you might say. But that's another story," he said hastily, "of no consequence at all right now.

"Jeck and I had been hired by the owner chust a couple of days before the shup was due to be launched, and we were to stay on board her and oversee the riggin' of her and, (wi' an enchineer by the name of McCulloch from Clynder), the fittin' o' the biler and the machinery. Ass yet the owner had not decided which of us wass to be captain, and which wass to be mate. He had said he would put us through oor paces wance the vessel wass feenished.

"Now ass you can imagine, for aal that we wass the best of friends, both Jeck and I wass very anxious tae get the position for wirselves, and I think Jeck wass particularly keen for this wass no' long efter he'd lost his master's berth on the *Dora Young*, a Liverpool grain clupper. No' by way of ony shenanigans on his pairt, mind: chust the sort of bad luck the man could neffer seem to escape.

"So on the mornin' set for the launchin' of the shup, the three of us took a train from Gleska Buchanan Street Station oot tae Kirkintilloch."

"What on earth were you goin' there fur?" put in Sunny Jim.

"Where else would we go for her launchin'," asked a mystified Para Handy, "except the yerd she'd been built in?"

"She surely wisnae built in Kirkintilloch!" cried Jim. "That's miles frae the river, there's naethin' there except the canal and there's nae room tae launch a shup intae a canal!"

"Jum, I despair o' ye. Maist of the puffers have aye been built in either John Hay's or Peter McGregor's yerds at Kirkintilloch and they still are, on a slup parallel wi' the canal. They slide doon sidey-ways, wi' chains on them to stop them duntin' into the bank on the ither side.

"When we got to Kirkintilloch there wass a real cheery holiday atmosphere in the vullage, for the launch of a shup is always an excuse for a celebration. You'll understand though that the *Vital Spark* herself wass not then the handsome sight she is noo. She wass chust aal hull, wi' not even the wheelhouse on her, never mind a bonny bleck-topped scarlet lum, nor a gold bead, nor a smert boot-topping.

"For aal that, she was a splendid specimen o' the builder's skill, and Jeck and I were fair proud when we climbed the wooden ladder onto the deck ready for the ceremony.

"There wass a crowd like an execution to see her launched and the banks o' the canal, and the brudge ower it, were bleck wi' people, and there was ass many more hangin' oot the windows of effery building that gave a view of the yerd and the shup.

"There wass a wee wooden platform built up at the bow of the vessel to chust below deck level and on this wass the heid shupwright, and the owner of the *Vital Spark*: and his dochter, a bonnie gyurl of about 20 or thereby who wass goin' to name her and break the bottle on her bows.

"On the far bank wass aal the pupils from the local school who'd been brocht to see the launchin' and the teachers wass havin' some chob keeping them back from the edge, which aye got swamped wi' a sort of tidal wave whenever a shup wass slupped.

"The lassie said her wee speech and named the shup, and the men wi' the axes cut the last twa ropes holdin' her on the slup and doon she went. There wass twa chains attached to her at the bow and the stern, and from there to rings on the slup, so that they would bring her up short o' the far bank.

"Suddenly there wass a terrible cracking sound frae the

bows and afore Jeck or I or McCulloch could move, the wee platform sterted to fall ower, wi' the gyurl and her faither and the yerd's man on it. I found oot later that some fool had fankled the drag chain roond wan o' the legs o' the platform and when the shup went oot wi' the chain, it pulled the leg aff like snappin a twig.

"Well, the owner and the man frae the yerd chumped for the deck o' the shup, but the lassie never thocht to do that and she wass thrown into the watter.

"The rest of us wass so ta'en aback wi' aal this we chust stood and gawped, but Jeck moved like lightnin'. Quick ass a flash he threw his jecket off and dived into the canal, and caught hold of the gyurl and swum ashore wi' her.

"Aal the croods wass cheerin' by this time, and ass he cam' up the slup cerryin' the gyurl in his arms it wass chust like a scene oot of wan o' Macphail's novelles. The gyurl's mither ran to hug the lassie and her faither wass shakin' Jeck's hand ass if he wass pumpin' beer, and clappin' him on the back.

"The upshot wass that the actual launch o' the boat wass herdly noticed in the papers, but they wass aal full o' the exploits o' Jeck, and his photie wass on maist of the front pages under headlines like 'Hero of Canal Rescue' and 'Seaman Risks Life to Save Drowning Girl'. Oh aye, he wass the man of the moment in Gleska all right.

"So it cam' as no surprise at aal when the next day Jeck wass summoned to the owner's office in Gleska, and told that he had been chosen to be Captain o' the *Vital Spark*, wi' me ass his mate."

"That wass a lucky break for Jeck," said Dougie.

"There wass little enough luck aboot it," said Para Handy, "ass I found oot soon enough.

"I had my suspicions at the time, but it wass the next weekend that I walked into wan o' the Kirkintilloch pubs and found Jack in very close conversation wi' wan o' the riveters frae the yerd. Neither o' them saw me: but I saw Jeck slip the man a pound note, and thank him roundly. I knew then chust what had happened, Jeck had got the man to fankle the chain round the leg o' the platform. And stood by either to catch the gyurl, if she chumped: or dive in to save her if she didn't: reckonin' — and he wass right — that her faither would be that grateful he wouldna look past Jeck for the skipper's chob.'

"Whit a cheatin' rascal," cried Sunny Jim. "Could ye no'

hae telt the owner the truth?"

Para Handy pursed his lips, and then sighed. "Och no, Jum. It wass a ploy that wass chust typical o' Jeck's natural agility at the time — and you couldna grudge him that it had the outcome he wass hopin' for when he'd had the imachination and the foresight to pit the whole thing in place.

"Besides, if ye must know, I had plans o' my ain along similar lines.

"I'd arranged wi' McCulloch the engineer to fake a biler explosion when we wass givin' the owner his first trial run on the vessel efter the launch so that I could play the hero by divin' below tae rescue him.

"Jeck chust beat me to it, that was aal. Ass I should have known aal along he would, for you must mind he has aalways been a man of the greatest sagacity and deviosity — no tae mention sheer dam' umpidence as weel!"

FACTNOTE

The majority of the puffers were indeed built in the smaller, specialised yards established on the banks of the Forth and Clyde Canal. As well as those at Kirkintilloch there were others at Maryhill and Port Dundas.

The puffers were derived from canal-based craft and were originally built to operate on the canals, hence the restriction on their size dictated by the maximum dimensions of the locks through which they would have to pass. Even when they were intended for a working life on the Firth, there was still a limit on overall length — at about 75ft — for the boats which were actually built on the canal, as they had to navigate 13 locks between Maryhill and Bowling in order to reach the river.

Of the two Kirkintilloch builders, Hay's was the older, and also had a longer life-span. The first steam vessel from that yard was launched in 1869: the last, the puffer *Chindit*, in 1945. All but a handful of the dozens of vessels built by the yard over three quarters of a century were for the Hay family themselves, in their 'other' role as by far the largest owners and operators of puffers.

Some licence has been taken in the description of the launching of the *Vital Spark*. Though it is probable that the very first boats built on the canal were indeed built on its banks and then launched directly into it, very soon Hay's (and their rivals, McGregor's) had excavated basins and slips accessed from the canal: and future construction and launch took place there. However, the puffers (and other vessels) built in the yards were indeed sent down the slips sideways: and a launch was always something of an 'event' for the community, drawing large crowds to every vantage point.

No licence has been taken, however, in referring to the story of the unfortunate *Principesa Jolanda*. She was a two-funnelled liner of 9200 tons gross, 486ft in length, and (intended to operate a scheduled service on the Genoa to Buenos Aires run for Lloyd Italiano) she was launched on September 21st 1907. With masts and funnels in place, and dressed overall with flags and bunting, she slid majestically down the launch-ways, took the water with some aplomb, slewed 90 degrees off course, listed heavily and dramatically to starboard: and sank. In Williams and Kerbech's *Damned by Destiny* (Teredo Books, 1982) there is a splendid series of photographs capturing the whole sorry episode, from the confidence of the naming ceremony to her final, inglorious submersion.

No attempt was made to salvage her. At low tides, she was broken up for scrap where she lay.

21

Rock of Ages

Para Handy looked up at the great wall of rock towering above the little puffer with an expression of admiration mixed with wonder. "My Chove," he said, "she's a whupper, iss she not! It's only when you're in this close that you realise chust how big she really iss! From scenes like these…"

The *Vital Spark* was edging in under the looming shadow of Ailsa Craig, the great granite rock which stands sentinel at the entrance to the Firth of Clyde. 'Paddy's Milestone' has been for centuries the welcome confirmation of safe arrival at the estuary not merely for the seamen from Ireland who originally bestowed its nickname upon it, but for mariners from every country in the world.

However, though the puffer had often had Ailsa Craig in plain sight as she rounded the Mull of Kintyre on her journeys to and from Islay, or coughed her way into Girvan harbour for a load of Ayrshire coal, this was the first time she had had occasion to be so close to the remarkable monolith. Only three quarters of a mile in length, it soared to a 1100ft peak: sheer cliffs on the western side, but with a spit of rock and shingle on the east where the *Vital Spark* now found herself.

Her destination was the small jetty which served the rock's tiny permanent population, and periodic visitors. The residents were the lighthouse keepers and their families, and a tenant crofter who raised a handful of cattle and sheep, and grew a few vegetables. The occasional visitors, whose presence on the island right now were the reason for the puffer's visit, were the Ayrshire quarrymen who were from time to time contracted to extract a quantity of the fine granite for which the islet was world-famous.

~

Two of them were standing on the jetty as the *Vital Spark* came alongside, one wearing the traditional badge-of-office of the foreman, a rather battered bowler hat.

"You're late," said this worthy, without preamble. "We expected ye twa hoors ago."

"Chust so," replied Para Handy without rancour, "but what you contracted for wass the *Vital Spark*, no' the *Glen Sannox*. We are not exactly runnin' to a schedule."

"In fact," came a voice from the engine-room at his feet, "wi' the state o' this machinery it's a miracle we're runnin' at all!"

"Pay no attention to Macphail, chentlemen," said the Captain, unperturbed, "for bein' cooped up in that cubby-hole aal hoors of the day would turn anybody soft in the head."

Four hours later, her cargo of granite blocks in place, the puffer cast off from the jetty at Ailsa Craig and headed north towards Arran and her ultimate destination, the James Watt dock in Greenock.

"That's gey fantoosh stane tae be used for buildin' hoos-es in Greenock," observed Sunny Jim.

"Good heavens, it iss not going to be used to build anything at aal, Jum," exclaimed the Captain. "Surely you ken that Ailsa granite iss the nameliest there iss for makin' curlin' stanes, and they're sent aal over the world!"

"They must be weel thocht of stanes, then," said Jim, "if it's worth the labour o' folk tae go cairtin' them aboot the place like that. Who foond oot aboot them in the first case, oot on the Ailsa rock like that?"

"It will have been wan o' they gee-oligists, Jum. Like the man we saw last week at Furnace, the Englishman that wass stayin' at the Inn, and had thae sacks o' rock samples stored in the cellars, and him oot first thing every mornin' wi' his wee hammer and awa' along tae the quarries, afore they sterted blastin' for the day, to knock more lumps oot o' them."

"Whit's the point o' it all," asked Sunny Jim. "Whit dae they dae wi' the rocks when they've got them tae wherever they're takin' them?"

"Tae judge from the quality of coals we're gettin' on this

shup nooadays," observed Macphail, appearing at the wheelhouse door wiping his hands with an oily rag, "Ah doot they sell them aff cheap tae the coal yards, and whenever the merchants get an order frae the Gleska office tae fill the bunkers on the *Vital Spark* then they jist pit wan sack o' rocks in the cairt for every wan sack o' coals."

"There's times I think you could be right at that, Dan," said the Captain. "When I saw the rubbish we wass being given last week by MacFadyen's man at Craigendoran, I wass nearly sendin' for the local polisman to put MacFadyen on a cherge. There wass mair rock in it than I've seen in many of the shup's cargoes of roadstone!

"What they really do wi' it, Jum, iss to tak' it awa' and study it."

"Study it!" cried Sunny Jim. "Why dae folk want tae study a bit o' rock for guidness sake!"

"I don't know aal the ins and oots of it," admitted Para Handy with a shrug, "but it'll be for museums and the like. Then again maybe that's how they cam' to find oot in the first place that there iss good slate at Ballachullish and Seil Island, and tip-top granite at Ailsa Craig and at Furnace, and roadstone at Alexandria and aal the rest. Wee men in plus-fowers and sonsy bunnets crawlin' aal ower the country and chust chip-chippin' awa' wi' their hammers, and takin' great lumps of Scotland hame in their luggage when they're done. Nae wonder folk are aalways sayin' the country's no' half whit it was fufty years ago!

"Hurricane Jeck met up wi' wan o' them when we wass laid over in Portree for a day or two a few years ago, and sent him home wi' aal the wrang ideas aboot Skye, that's for sure..."

～

"It wass this way," he continued in a moment, once his pipe was going to his satisfaction, and the puffer had run the cheeky gauntlet of half-a-dozen youths in hired rowing-boats off Millport Bay. "Jeck and me wass crewin' a puffer that belonged to a man in Brodick, and we had gone to Skye wi' a cargo of early Arran potatos, and to pick up a load of peats for wan o' the Campbeltown distilleries.

"There wass a delay in gettin' the cargo in. I think mebbe it wass a deleeberate delay, for the skipper wass a Skye man and he chust went off hame for a few days, leavin' Jeck and me and the boy in the harbour at Portree.

"Jeck and I spent some time in the inns at Portree till oor money ran oot and it wass there that we met wi' this English gee-oligist. He was a hermless enough fellow, but there wass nothin' to him, he wass aboot five foot two in hiss stockin' soles and ass skinny ass a Tiree chicken. Effery mornin' he'd be off first thing wi' a hammer and an empty sack and effery evenin' he'd come staggerin' back into Portree bent double wi' the weight of whateffer he'd pit in it that day.

"It wass peetiful! There wass times you wud think he wud drop on the spot!

"Wan night he wass that trauchled that Jeck went up from the boat and gave him a hand to get the sack to his Hotel, and pit it in the cellar wi' aal the rest he'd collected. There wass mair than a dozen of them, aal whuppers, wi' big labels roond their necks sayin' where the rocks in them were from, and whit day he'd foond them.

"The upshot wass that he offered Jeck a chob for the next day to go out with him and help fill his samples and then, come the evenin', cairry them back to Portree. Five shullings he offered and Jeck chumped at it, for we wass oot of money except for a couple of coppers and some foreign coins the Portree Inns wudna take. 'I'll split the money wi' you, Peter', says Jeck: 'You stay here and keep an eye oot for our peats comin', and I'll go and help the mannie.'

"Next mornin' Jeck wass up at the crack o' dawn and up to the Hotel, and I saw the two of them headin' off, the mannie wi' a wee knapsack and his hammers, and Jeck wi' two huge empty sacks draped ower his shoulders.

"Six o'clock at night, Jeck appeared on the quayside and you wud not think he had walked a yard nor cairried a pound for he wass as fresh ass a daisy: but you must remember he wass at the height of his powers at the time, full of natural sagacity and energy, built like a brick oothoose and with the strength of three.

" 'You're lookin' quite jocko, Jeck,' says I, ass we made oor way along the harbour towards the Inns. 'It wass not too hard a day then?'

" 'It could have been,' says Jeck. 'Wud ye believe we went aal the way to Sligachan, a good eight miles along the main road, and then off we go into the hills and he leaps aboot the rocks wi' thon hammer hammerin' awa', and he fills the sacks till I could scarce lift them off the ground. He says it makes sich a difference havin' a fine strong chap to do the cairryin', and for sure he took advantage of it!

" 'When it comes to dinner-time and I'm thinkin' the least he can do iss tak' me and treat me at the Sligachan Inn, here he ups and opens the wee knapsack and brings oot some bread and cheese and two bottles of milk. *Milk*!

" 'Towards fower o'clock, when the sacks are full to the very top wi' lumps o' rock of effery shape and size and description, he thanks me very politely for my services, and gives me the five shullin's we'd agreed on for the feein'.

" 'Then he says that he'll go back to Portree the long way roond, takin' the track that runs along the coast beside the Sound of Raasay: but that I can chust tak' the main road hame for the sake of speed and comfort. So I did, and so here I am. There's no sign of him back at the Hotel yet but his sacks is aal safely snugged doon and labelled in his cellar.'

" 'You look very fit on it, onyway,' says I. 'The sacks couldna have been aal that heavy for you look chust ass fresh ass when you set off and there iss no' ass much ass an ounce of perspiration on you.'

" 'There would have been, if I'd let it,' said Jeck. 'But did ye think I wass goin' to be daft enough to hump half of Sligachan eight miles up the road to Portree? Wan stane is like any ither stane ass far ass I can tell, so I chust waited till he wass well oot o' sight and then I emptied the sacks oot at the roadside at Sligachan, hung them round my neck, and when I got back to the town I filled them up again wi' rocks from yon big pile of roadstone lyin' at the pierhead.

" 'He'll neffer ken the difference...' "

FACTNOTE

Lying at the mouth of the Firth nine miles west of Girvan Bay, Ailsa Craig has become familiar to anyone in the UK who has ever watched transmission of the Open Golf Tournament from the nearby Turnberry links. Cameras make a habit of zooming in on the dramatic silhouette of the rock when there is not much happening on the course!

For decades the very best curling stones were indeed regarded as those made from Ailsa granite. There was little else of any material value on the islet, though it was tenanted from the Earls of Cassilis, into whose estates it fell, for a tiny rental which, at least till the beginning of last cen-

THE ARRAN CONNECTION — *Here in all her late Victorian, splendour is the Glasgow and South Western Railway Company's Glen Sannox, which gave 33 years service on the Ardrossan to Brodick crossing, her speed helping to reduce the Glasgow to Arran journey to under 90 minutes. She ran her trials on 1st June 1892 and it is probable that this photograph was taken then. This is obviously a 'new' vessel, and there are no members of the public on board.*

tury, was paid in kind — young gannets for the table, and seabird feathers and down for bedding and cushions. It was still tenanted just a generation or so ago, but the fisherman's summer bothies, the remains of which can still be seen on the north-east coast, have been deserted for much longer.

Most of the eminent travellers in Scotland, from Monro in the 16th century onwards, have visited and been overawed by the rock. Many of them, coincidentally, were geologists — though their travels were not solely motivated by that specialised branch of science. John McCulloch, who criss-crossed the Western Highlands and Islands in the first two decades of the 19th century, has left the most comprehensive account. Much of it may be almost unreadably turgid but nobody, not even Pennant in the late 18th or Muir in the late 19th centuries, covered so much ground. McCulloch visited virtually every rock and atoll in the north west and left a unique account of their society as well as their geology in four volumes published in 1820.

It is interesting how early travellers in Scotland seemed to come in surprisingly well-defined categories in an evolutionary progression.

The enquiring — such as Monro or Martin. The curious — Johnson or Boswell. The polymaths — Pennant or Garnett. The geologists — Jamieson or McCulloch. The antiquarians — Cordiner or Grose. The economists — Newte or Anderson. The historians — Selkirk or Logan. The natural historians — Kearton or Harvie-Brown.

And (at regular intervals) the downright eccentric, such as the formidable Englishwoman, the Honourable Mrs Murray Aust of Kensington, who undertook a journey through the Highlands which included the crossing of the notorious 2,200 feet Corrieyairack pass from the Spey Valley to the Great Glen *in a post-chaise carriage and pair*, and wrote a two volume account (published in 1810) to prove it!

22

Taking the Needle

Para Handy stared, fascinated, at the approaching figure of the *Vital Spark's* engineer. "My Chove boys,
come and take a look at this! What on earth hass
Dan been up to?" The *Vital Spark* was berthed in
Campbeltown, and Macphail had just appeared in sight
staggering along the quayside with a large square wooden
contraption cradled in both arms, his face only just visible
peering over the top of it. Behind him came a man carrying
in one hand what looked like an oversize megaphone and in
the other a large brown suitcase.

"It looks like he went to that hoose sale right enough,"
Dougie observed, "and it looks ass if he bought the half of it
ass well."

Indeed, his eye caught by an advertisement in that
week's issue of the *Campbeltown Courier*, Macphail had at
breakfast announced his intention of attending a roup taking place that morning, at which the effects of a recently-
deceased citizen of the burgh were to be sold at auction.
Para Handy and Dougie had had enough of auctions for the
time being, following a couple of unfortunate experiences at
such occasions in the recent past and Sunny Jim was, as
usual, suffering from a chronic shortage of funds. So the
engineer had gone off on his own, announcing that he
would stay just a few minutes "for the entertainment
value".

"It seems you got more than chust entertainment then,
Dan," the Captain observed as the engineer puffed his way
on board and, with a sigh of relief, laid his burden on the
hatch-cover of the hold. His companion did the same, and
then, after a short consultation during which a few coins

changed hands, scrambled up onto the quayside and made off.

"What on earth is aal this?" Dougie asked as Macphail picked up the giant 'megaphone' and inserted its narrow end into a metal-rimmed hole in the top of the wooden box. This itself had, let into one side, a brass handle which was in shape something like a miniature version of the handle on the puffer's anchor winch and on the top, a circular plate with a convoluted brass contraption alongside it.

"What d'ye think," asked Macphail sharply. "It's a grammyphone, of course."

"And what might that be when it's at hame?" asked Para Handy.

"For peety's sake," said the exasperated Macphail. "D'ye live in the Erk or somethin'? Grammyphones is a' the rage in the big hooses nooadays. Listen and I'll show ye!"

And opening the leather case to reveal a stack of black shellac records, he pulled one out, set it on the turntable on top of the instrument, birled the handle to wind up the spring-driven motor, swung the playing arm over and carefully lowered the needle into its groove.

A tinny version of *Rule Britannia*, sung by an enthusiastic but breathless soprano who sounded as if somebody was standing on her foot, blared from the horn of the gramophone and across the harbour. Heads turned to stare at the *Vital Spark* from all directions.

Para Handy, Dougie and Sunny Jim retreated towards the puffer's bow.

"My Cot," said the Captain. "Whateffer wull they think of next? How on earth do they get the wumman to fit into the box — never mind the baun'!"

"Very funny," said Macphail sarcastically. "Ye ken fine hoo it works, ye've seen them aften enough in the shops.

"It's the thing o' the future! A concert hall in every hoose! A few years frae noo the harmonium and the piano wull be things o' the past. Nae mair frien's an' relations makin' eejits o' themselves tryin' tae play choons they cannae play and wraxin' tae sing sangs their voices wisnae built for. Instead a'body can hae entertainment tae suit every taste at their command jist so lang as they hiv plenty o' these!" And reaching into a small recess on the top of the machine beside the turntable, he held up a small, fancily-decorated tin full of tiny needles.

Sunny Jim, meanwhile, was picking through the selection of records in the leather case.

"There's no mich here for the likes o' us, Dan," he said. "This all looks gey highbrow stuff tae me. Who's Dame Nellie Melba and whit's an operetta when it's at hame? Whit aboot Dan Leno or Marie Lloyd, or even some Harry Lauder? And I dinna see onythin' that wid be suitable for a baal or a soiree. Nae Gay Gordons, nae Dashing White Sergeant: jist waltzes and polkas an' that"

"Exactly," said Macphail, whose ideas of the appropriate sort of musical taste for a gentleman to assume had been honed and moulded by many years acquaintance with the glamorous world of his penny novelettes. "That's the point! None o' this popular trash, jist class, class at yer fingertips!"

"Cless!" said Dougie pointedly. "I've no' had a cless since I left the school and I'm no' stertin' noo! Jum's right, this iss aal right for the chentry, but it's no' the same as a good birl on the melodeon, when Jum's in good trum."

"Nor better nor yoursel' on the trump," conceded Para Handy generously. "Mony's the spree we've had with them both."

"Jist wait you and see," said Macphail defensively. "Every hoose in the land will hae yin o' these afore lang. And besides ye can get every type o' music ye care tae think of for it, so if ye wantit onything at a', from the Hokey Cokey to the Reel o' Tulloch, ye wud jist awa' oot and buy it."

"Fair enough," said Jim, "if ye could afford it! But there'll aye be a place for the melodeon, and the trump come tae that."

~

Over the next few days, though, the Mate and Sunny Jim became more enamoured of the new-fangled plaything and for most of the time the puffer was on passage, the instrument sat on the hatch-way and blared out a selection chosen from a collection of records which proved, if nothing else, that their departed owner had been a man of eclectic, not to say strange, tastes.

Only Para Handy remained aloof, and lost no opportunity to play down the worth of the new acquisition, and stress the value of having available for entertainment purposes on board any vessel such extempore live musicians as Dougie and Jim.

The performances of Macphail's travelling open-air

concert hall received what the newspaper columnists would have referred to as 'mixed reviews'. Some of the river traffic detoured towards the puffer in search of the source of the mysterious sounds but others beat a very hasty retreat to distance themselves as much as possible from it.

Which reaction occurred, and how quickly, usually depended on what particular record was in concert at the time. Italian opera did not, as a general rule, go down very well with either mariners or yachtsmen on the Firth: American brass band music on the other hand was very much more popular — and nothing more so than *Liberty Bell*, which acted like a magnet for approaching vessels and which, as a result, Macphail aired so frequently and repeatedly that Para Handy remarked that in no time at all the groove would be worn right through to the other side of the gramophone record.

Matters came to a head at Arrochar, where the *Vital Spark* arrived one Saturday afternoon to discover that a dance was being held that evening in the village hall. Jim was sent ashore to acquire tickets for all, and the senior members of the ship's company spent a couple of hours on a toilet as elaborate as it was unusual.

"Look at the three o' ye," said Jim sardonically, "three merrit men that should ken better gettin' all spruced up tae dance wi' lassies young enough tae be yer ain dochters! You should tak' shame at it!"

"What you should take shame at, Jum, iss the way you aalways cairry yon melodeon wi' you to the country soirees, for you ken fine that you'll aye be asked to perform when the band iss at its refreshments, and it gives you a shameless chance to flirt wi' aal the gyurls and impress them wi' your general agility on the unstriment!" retorted the Captain. And sure enough, Jim had already looked his melodeon out and was wiping it with a cloth to bring out the shine on its brass fittings.

"Not," continued the skipper, "that I aaltogether begrudge you that, Jum, for you're a better player than maist of the bands and I fair enchoy a good selection on the melodeon myself!"

∾

The crew's consternation, therefore, when they reached the Hall to find that the band which had been booked had not arrived on the steamer from Helensburgh, and that the organisers were thus intending to cancel the event, may be imagined.

Macphail was the first to recover his composure.

"There is no need for that at all," he said. "For on the shup Ah've got a cracker o' a grammyphone, wi' a fine section o' music. Jist gi'e me the len' o' a couple o' your chaps tae get it up here and this'll be the best soiree Arrochar ever had!"

And so, indeed, it seemed.

The vaunted instrument — or 'implement' as Para Handy had now christened it — was indeed a great hit with the folk of the village, and Macphail found himself the unaccustomed centre of attention of a flattering coterie of ladies — young, and not so young.

Sunny Jim, who had taken his melodeon back down to the puffer in despair earlier in the evening, looked on in disgust.

"Stole my thunder, so he has," he complained. "And him a merrit man that age! Arrochar's aye taken kindly to my melodeon in the past but the nicht, they never even wantit it!"

And he went to sulk at the far end of the hall and sat with his back to the posturing engineer.

⁓

Five minutes later Para Handy tapped him on the shoulder and winked in conspiratorial fashion.

"Jum, I think it would be no' a bad idea if you wass to go on doon to the shup and retrieve your melodeon. You could bring Dougie's trump at the same time, for there's goin' to be a demand for some real music here in a few minutes, and it wudna be fair if you had to play aal night. You should be allowed to enchoy the dancin' too, and I know fine that Dougie wull be only too pleased to spell you every noo and then so that you can have a circuit or two o' the floor wi' some o' the gyurls."

"Chance wud be a fine thing," said Jim. "Naebody wants the trump or the melodeon so long as Dan's holdin' court wi' thon portable concert-hall."

"Ah," said Para Handy, "but that's the whole point, Jum. I have a feelin' that Dan's reign is chust aboot drawin' to a close and that we'll no' be hearin' much more from his band-box the night."

"Whit way?" asked the mystified Jim. "Is it broken?"

"No, nor broken," said Para Handy. "But I think he is chust on the point of runnin' oot o' these..." And he thrust his opened right hand under Jim's nose. On the palm rested the brightly coloured tin of gramophone needles.

"Look lively then, Jum. Fortune favours the bold!"

FACTNOTE

Edison registered his patent for a 'sound-recording' machine in August 1877, yet for the next 20 years the implement was regarded as little more than a curiosity and little effort was made to commercialise it.

During this period, the cylindrical record was superseded by the new disc record, carried on a turntable: the earliest of these were a mere seven inches in diameter. Not till 1904 was the first machine with an 'internal' loudspeaker manufactured. Till then, all instruments were of the type immortalised in HMV's famous logo of a horn gramophone and a listening dog.

Grove's *Dictionary of Music and Musicians* affirms that in those early years 'various well-known musicians played or sang into the instrument, but they did so more or less for the fun of the thing: there was no attempt to market or duplicate their efforts.' Then when commercial production started in the early years of this century 'it was found that powerful notes caused trouble with the primitive instruments of the day' and that 'the grooves in which such notes occurred were liable to rapid wear'. So Para Handy wasn't altogether mistaken in his comments with regard to the possible foibles of Macphail's machine!

Puffer crews often carried their own entertainment, in the form of musical instruments. Melodeons were a popular smaller version of accordions — both of which were relatively recent creations. The humbler 'trump' or 'Jew's Harp', to give it its proper name, was by contrast an instrument of very considerable antiquity and surprising universality as well. There were many and various forms of this small, horseshoe-shaped gadget with its vibrating metallic tongue, held between the teeth and played by striking with the fingers and using the lips to create notes of a different pitch. Almost unheard-of in this country today, forms of the 'trump' have been known throughout Europe, Asia, and the

Far East for centuries, and it can be seen depicted in Chinese illuminated manuscripts of 900 years ago. It briefly ranked as a serious orchestral instrument in Europe in the early 1800s with acclaimed soloists performing recitals — and even a concerto — on the orchestral platform.

Harry Lauder, born in 1870, was enjoying a worldwide reputation by the early years of this century which, given the lack of any seriously-marketed gramophone records, was quite remarkable — a reputation built up, literally, by word of mouth. Originally a miner, he quickly established himself — both as singer and as raconteur — as the archetypal 'pawky Scot' and toured the world from the USA to Australia, with considerable and constant success. He died in Strathaven, Lanarkshire in 1950.

23

High Life at Hunter's Quay

L ow tide at Sandbank often produces a spectacle which is most unlikely to conjure thoughts of a glamorous maritime career in the imaginations of any passing landlubber.

The world-renowned boatyards of the Holy Loch village may be the cradle of some of the finest racing yachts ever constructed but the men working on the sleek speedsters taking shape on the slipways are treated almost daily to a timely reminder of the more mundane side of life at sea.

When the tide ebbs it exposes, at the head of the loch, a far from romantic stretch of sandflats (from which the village of course takes its name) to which the puffers are regular visitors. Slipping in at high tide, they are left high and dry as the water recedes, lying throughout the ebb period like stranded whales, their steam winches busy as the crews employ specially-designed grabs to load a cargo of sand before the tide creeps back in.

The value of such a cargo is slight — but the cost of acquiring it (apart from the aching backs and blistered hands of the crews) is nil, and there are always builders and contractors in need of large quantities of coarse sand for construction projects up and down the Firth.

∾

The crew of the *Vital Spark* loathed coming into Holy Loch. The job of loading the cargo of sand was hard and dirty work and had to be carried out at speed if it was to be completed in time to the movement of the tide. Worse, the Sandbank Inn was tantalisingly close at hand but quite unreachable, for if you were to stroll across to it on the dried-out sand of the ebb, then by the time you were ready to return, you would need a dinghy to take you back to your boat across the flooding tide.

One June afternoon the puffer, after unloading 50 tons of coal at Ardnadam, came up to the head of the loch on the flood and, as the tide neared the foot of the ebb, got ready to take on board a cargo of sand for delivery to Bowling.

Macphail attended to the steam-winch, Dougie attached the steel sand-grab to the pulley of the crane, and Sunny Jim took the boards off the main hatch. Para Handy, as befitted the status of Captain, surveyed all these preparations from the relative comfort of the wheelhouse.

There were three other puffers beached close to hand and soon the clatter of steam-winches and clang of sand-grabs echoed off the hillsides. As the day drew on a change in the weather was plainly imminent: a breeze got up, the clouds closed in and there was a hint of rain in the air. By the time the job was done, it was gone seven o'clock: as the *Vital Spark* began to lift off the sea-bed on the incoming tide, Para Handy came to a decision he he had been contemplating for some time.

"Boys, " he said, "we will chust stay in the cheneral area for the night. I dinna much care for the idea of pickin' oor way up river wi' no freeboard on her in dreich-lookin' conditions like this. We'll go back doon to Hunter's Quay and tie up overnight after the last steamer hass been in, and mak' a snappy start in the mornin' to get hame by dinner time."

A shouted consultation with the skippers of the other three boats ended with them all agreeing to do the same, and at eight o'clock the four puffers weighed anchor and headed in convoy towards the mouth of the loch.

∼

The paddler *Madge Wildfire* had just made the final call of the day and was pulling away from Hunter's Quay pier as the little flotilla of puffers came hiccupping round the point from Hafton House.

On the beach to the west of the pier were jetties serving the Royal Clyde Yachting Club, whose imposing Clubhouse towered above the shore road and gave broad panoramas up river. Half a dozen racing yachts rode at their moorings in the bay and on any normal day would themselves have been a fine and imposing sight. But this evening they were dwarfed into insignificance by a vessel anchored just beyond them in the mouth of the loch.

"My Chove," said Para Handy in admiration. "Issn't that the beauty! She's a whupper and no mistake!"

The vessel in question was indeed magnificent. Almost as big as the *Madge Wildfire*, she actually managed to look bigger, thanks to the optical illusion provided by her soaring masts. She was a white-hulled, three-masted, topsail schooner, with a bright yellow funnel proclaiming her auxiliary steam power.

Macphail stuck his head out of the engine-room. "That's the *Sunbeam*," he said. "Earl Brassey's yat. I read in the paper she wis comin' intae the Clyde. She's on a roond-the-world cruise."

"Chust so," said the Captain. "Well then, we wull go and tak' a roond-the-yat cruise, for I want a closer peek at her." And he spun the wheel to port and headed for the anchored ship. The three other puffers, their crews apparently more interested in the attractions of the Hunter's Quay Inn than those of the sailing ship, kept on course for the pier.

As the *Vital Spark* approached the yacht, a small steam launch was being lowered from her davits and a party of what looked to be very important people indeed was descending the companionway slung over the starboard side. "That'll be Earl Brassey himself," Para Handy surmised, "and the chentry that's sailin' wi' him."

To his considerable surprise, as he circled the *Sunbeam* at a respectable distance, the yacht's steam tender chuffed over to the puffer and began to circle round it. Para Handy was first bashful, then flattered, to realise the *Vital Spark* was under scrutiny through binoculars by the gentry seated in the launch.

"Man Dougie," he said. "Haven't I aalways say that the shup iss too good for the tred the owner hass her in? They think we're the *King Edward* and they want to tak' a look at turbine power in action!"

After a couple of circuits round the puffer, the launch pulled away and headed off at high speed for the shore, throwing out a gleaming bow wave and kicking up a great wake as she did so.

Para Handy gazed after the little boat with a somewhat wistful expression. "Or then again," he said resignedly, "maybe they were chust amusin' themselves at oor expense!"

~

The *Vital Spark* approached the main quay to find something of a confrontation in progress. The other puffers were bobbing in a semi-circle about a hundred yards off the pier-head, whence a uniformed figure, with a megaphone to his mouth, was bellowing something (Para Handy was just too far away to catch the words) to the skipper of the *Cretan*.

"Wha's yon eejit?" Macphail queried, "and whit's he bangin' on aboot tae puir Ogilvie?"

"I canna chust mak' it oot, Dan," said the Captain. "The man's the Chief Steward at the Yat Club, wan McCutcheon, I ken him by his face, but I doot he's no' givin' us aal an eenvitation to the Clubhoose for oor dinners'."

A surmise which was confirmed seconds later, when the other puffers could be seen turning away from the pier and heading slowly towards the open Firth, their crews indicating their anger at the Club Steward in one or other of a variety of tried and trusted ways of so doing by means of explicit hand-signals traditional to the West of Scotland.

"You too, Para Handy" yelled the megaphone-bearer, swinging that implement towards the approaching *Vital Spark*. "This is a gentleman's club and a gentleman's pier and I'll no' have trash like you littering the quay and the foreshore. Clear aff!"

Catching sight, out of the corner of his eye, of the *Sunbeam's* launch gently manoeuvring alongside the steps at the innermost wall of the stone quay, he rushed over to catch the line thrown ashore by a white-clad crewman: shouting, as he did "Get tae blazes oot o' this, Para Handy" in the one direction, followed immediately by an obsequious "Allow me to be of service, Earl Brassey!" in the other.

"My Chove," said Para Handy from the door of the wheelhouse, "there's a man that dearly loves a Lord, and is sore in need of bein' taken doon a peg or two. But to be honest, it hass been a long day and I am no' in trum for an altercation wi' McCutcheon right noo, hiss turn wull come! Dan! Let's head for home!"

But, as he turned back and seized the wheel, he was astonished to hear a conciliatory, one could almost say a grovelling voice on the megaphone.

"Er, Captain Macfarlane," enunciated McCutcheon in the strangulated voice with which he tried to impress people, and which he reserved for his dealings with the gentry: "would you be so kind as to lay your ship alongside the pier? Earl Brassey would like to have a word..."

Sure enough, while the main party from the yacht waited at the top of the stairs, the moustachiod peer strolled across to the head of the quay accompanied by a tall, angular man with a mane of white hair, and a smaller, sturdy man with a huge plate camera slung across his shoulder and a large wooden box full of its paraphernalia clutched in one hand.

~

An hour later the crew were sat round a table in the bar of the Hunter's Quay Hotel. On it, as well as four dram glasses and four beer glasses (all appropriately filled), were two golden sovereigns, glinting in the light of the tilley-lamps.

"My Chove," said the Captain. "Now there wass a true chentleman and no mistake.

"But what for did he want all those photies? Yon man wass snap snap-snappin' awa' for the best part of an hoor aal over the shup. Wheelhoose, hold, enchine-room, the fo'c'sle — above aal, the fo'c'sle. You would think we wass savidges on a sooth sea island rather than chust some o' Brutain's hardy sons gaun' aboot their daily business...

"And ass for the questions thon white haired mannie asked? Whit a cheek! And in any case, whit's an anthro...anthripolijist when it's at hame? Whit did the Earl mean when he said tae him that there wass mair to wonder at on yer ain front doorstep than there wass in the farthest outposts o' cuvileesation? And why did Brassey keep sayin' — the impertinunce o' it — that the shup was chust junk in British watters and shud be preserved for posterity or folk wudna believe it?"

"Not 'chust junk', Peter, 'chust *like* a junk', whateffer he meant by that," said Dougie.

"Onyway," said Macphail. "They wis real toffs richt enough. Twa whole sov'rins for wir trouble!"

"Aye," agreed Para Handy. "But best of aal wass the expression on McCutcheon's face when Brassey shook

hands with us aal — but ignored him!
"Some things are chust beyond price!"

FACTNOTE

Today there are few vessels in private ownership capable of worldwide deep-water cruising. Most large yachts are based in the Mediterranean, Caribbean or, rather more exotically, such fashionable Pacific islands as New Caledonia or Hawaii. But there they seem to stay, doing little more time at sea than some occasional island-hopping, as often as not used more as holiday homes and entertainment venues than as ships.

By contrast, the years at the turn of this century were the zenith of the great privately-owned ocean-going yachts, whose owners used them for ambitious voyages of many months duration to remote and inaccessible destinations as well as to the more expected or established ports-of-call worldwide. Very often places on them were available to zoologists and those of other scientific disciplines who must otherwise have had scant chance of visiting the distant islands which were their common goal.

Largest of them all was the Earl of Crawford's towering 245ft *Valhalla*, the only ship-rigged yacht in the world. Brassey's *Sunbeam*, though, was certainly the best known. For almost 40 years she spent much of her time at sea traversing the oceans of the world on an extraordinary series of voyages chronicled in her owner's book *Sunbeam RYS*, first published in 1917. His wife, who accompanied him on most of his travels, wrote her own account of them in *The Voyage of the Sunbeam*. in most years the yacht did indeed spend some time in Scottish waters either at the beginning or end of a longer voyage, or as a destination in itself.

Sunbeam was launched at Seacombe in Cheshire in 1875. She was 170ft overall and with all sail set carried 16,000 square yards of canvas! Lairds of Liverpool installed a 70hp auxiliary steam engine for which her bunkers carried 80 tons of coal.

The human history of the remote destinations he visited and the way of life of the (then) virtually unknown peoples and tribes he met, were a constant fascination to Brassey and his book gives many valuable accounts of strange societies, unfamiliar communities and unexpected life-styles.

The imposing Clubhouse for the Royal Clyde Yacht Club

was built above the bay at Hunter's Quay in 1888, a splendid psuedo-Tudor construction totally out of character for its location. With half-timbered gables and balconies, stone tower and parapet, it is about as 'un-Scottish' as it could be yet sits magnificently in its prominent location.

Today it enjoys new life as the popular Royal Marine Hotel and is thus a social as well as an architectural landmark in the Cowal community.

SUNBEAM, RYS — *By an astonishing coincidence, the MacGrory collection contains this photo of Brassey's Sunbeam in Campbeltown Bay. Initially filed as a Naval archive (for obvious reasons) this is beyond doubt that remarkable ocean-traveller, as a comparison with a plate in the Earl's own book confirms. The crew of the launch are not in naval uniform but the yacht's own issue, and were this a naval scene the launch would be flying an ensign. The Sunbeam was in Scottish waters 10 times between 1897 and 1909.*

24

Flags of Convenience

It was one of the puffer's periodic visits to Bridge Wharf in the centre of the city of Glasgow, and an urchin appeared at the quayside with a letter in his hand, the envelope carefully addressed to 'The Captain, Steam Lighter *Vital Spark*, Glasgow' on one of the new typing machines which were sweeping all before them in the city offices.

"My Chove," said Para Handy, perusing the contents with an increasingly puzzled expression, "whit a fine kettle of fush!"

"What is it, Peter," asked the Mate anxiously. "Is it from the owner? He surely hassna been and sold the boat over oor heads?"

"Sold the boat!" came a splutter from the engine-room, where Dan Macphail was busy with oil-can and wrench trying to make good a leaking joint in the shaft-casing. "Of course he's no' sold the boat: he couldnae gi'e it awa' as a prize for a Good Templar's raffle!"

"Pay no attention to him, Dougie: he's been in a paddy ever since John Hay's *Spartan* overtook us at Bowling this mornin' chust after he'd been blawin' aboot the difference he'd made to our speed since he'd cleaned oot the tubes o' the biler.

"No, the letter iss not from the owner, though he iss the cause of it, it's from the Board of Tred. They are holdin' some sort of classes aboot — how do they cry it?" He opened the letter up again, " 'signalling procedures'. The owner hass volunteered me to go to them. The Board iss sayin' that the coastal tred iss no keepin' up wi' new methods and there have been too many accidents caused by poor signals at sea, or by shups that dinna understand them at aal.

"The upshot of it aal iss that he iss buying a complete set of signal flags for the *Vital Spark*, and I have to learn how to use them, and then they say I must teach you laads the whole whigmaleerie ass weel!".

"It iss a liberty!" exclaimed the Mate. "The *Vital Spark* hass never been in any trouble! You've aalways had a grand voice for bellowin' wi', Peter, and that's all the signals we've needed aal oor years at sea."

&

Liberty or not the owner's instructions had to be complied with and Para Handy duly presented himself the following morning at the Glasgow offices of the Maritime branch of the Board of Trade, unaccustomedly scrubbed and shaved, and kitted out in his one good pea-jacket.

"I don't like it, boys," he said as he left the puffer. "But I will not let the vessel down. A MacFarlane will neffer disgrace himself or tak' the easy way oot when it comes to representing the reputation and the good name of his shup!"

The class itself was held in an empty bay of a warehouse at the Stobcross Quay on the north bank of the river — a dusty, drab, dreich and draughty venue where were assembled some two dozen unhappy seamen, almost all skippers of steam lighters and quite without exception as resentful as Para Handy about the liberty taken in inflicting the classes upon them. Their tempers were not improved when they discovered that they would be introduced to the new mysteries, not by some veteran old salt, but by a fresh-faced youth in a grey suit and a white shirt with an Eton collar and a flower in his button-hole.

There were few of his fellow-sufferers with whom Para Handy was not well-acquainted. One however — the skipper of Hay's puffer *Spartan* whom the *Vital Spark* had by coincidence encountered on her way up river the previous day — was a particular bete-noire of the usually placid Captain.

&

"The side of the man!" complained Para Handy to his crew when he returned to the puffer for his dinner at the end of the morning session. "Aye noddin' and makin' oot he knows it aal already, and then runnin' errands for the young whipper-snapper that's takin' the cless when he needs new flags or whateffer.

"I always thought John Hay made a big mistake when he put Alec Bain in cherge o' the *Spartan* and my Chove now I know I wass right!"

"But whit aboot the class, Captain?" asked Sunny Jim. "Whit d'ye huv tae do?"

"You may well ask, Jum. Jumpin' through girrs! They have wan flag for each letter o' the elphabet but of course if you wass to use them to spell oot ony messages it wud take foreffer, so they have devised a sort of a code. You put chust two of the flags up the halyard at wance and effery pair means a different message to aal the ither pairs, and you find oot whit it is by lookin' it up in this list." At that point the Captain pulled a closely-printed sheet of paper from his jacket pocket and waved it in the air. "It's aal so unnecessary! We have managed chust fine for years withoot ony o' this rubbish!"

Sunny Jim still looked mystified.

"Let me try to explain the way of it, Jum," continued Para Handy. "If we were runnin' oot of coal, for example, what would we do aboot it at present?"

"It all depends on the cargo we're cairryin' at the time," said Jim, puzzled but trying to be helpful. "Ah mean, if it's coals we're cairryin' then ye jist send me tae the hold wi' a few sacks tae fill, for neither the merchant nor the owner'll ever fin' oot aboot it an'..."

"No, no Jum," said the Captain hastily, "that's not what I mean at aal. What do we do if we're gettin' short and we're at sea and we're not cairryin' coals...?"

"Weel, then ye'd jist bellow on the next puffer we meet and get the len' o' a bag or twa that wud see us safe to the nearest harbour," said Jim.

Para Handy beamed. "Precisely, Jim," he said. "But these dam' Board o' Trade regulations want us to put up flags for aal the world to see." He consulted the printed sheet: "The two flags you wud need fur that situation are the G and the Y — and they mean *Can you spare me Coal?*"

"Whit genius thocht yon up!" snorted Macphail. "I can jist see Williamson stoppin' the *King Edward* in her tracks tae gi'e me a few shuvvles of the best Ayrshire nutty slack somewhere between Lochranza and Campbeltown, in the middle of the Gleska Trades weekend!"

"Chust so, Dan," said Para Handy. "But —" burrowing once again into the mysteries of the leaflet, "— we could maybe try flyin' the R and the H — *Can you supply me with anyone to take charge as engineer?* It wud make a pleasant change to have wan! Or maybe we wud put up the B with the J which accordin' to the list wud mean: *Engine broken down, I am disabled.* Not too unlikely for the *Vital Spark* on the days you're in bad trum, eh Dan?"

⁓

For the sake of peace and harmony it was probably just as well that that was the point at which Para Handy had to leave the boat to attend the afternoon session at Stobcross.

It was nearly seven o'clock before he returned, trudging along the wharf with his head down in dejection and his hands in his pockets. "Don't ask me a dam' thing till I've had my tea," he said as he stepped aboard. "I'm chust at the end my tether!"

"If I thought this mornin' was bad, boys, you should have seen this afternoon!" he commented quarter of an hour later after having disposed of a plate of fried herrings and two mugs of tea sweetened with condensed milk.

"I chust hope that the owner hass more sense than he hass money and iss not thinkin' of puttin' wan of these godless wireless contraptions on the shup, for that iss what yon young fella wass tellin' us aal about this afternoon. I do not like the sound of it aal, boys, it mean the end of the independence we aal enchoy in the coasting tred!"

"What is it, then?" asked Sunny Jim, who had heard the word bandied around in the past two or three years without having any real idea of what was involved.

"It iss almost impossible to believe," said the Captain, "but it iss chust like the telegraph, except there iss no wires to it, and your shup could be in the muddle of the Minch and the office could send you orders ass nate as anything."

"But how..." began the Mate.

"Dougie, I do not know, that's the plain truth of it. But it iss two boxes filled wi' electrucity, wan for pittin' messages oot and wan for bringin' them in. It iss chust ass if you have a collie dug that big its tail iss in the office and its heid iss on the shup. So if you stand on the tail in Gleska, the heid will howl on the vessel: and if you pat its heid on board the

Vital Spark, its tail wags in Gleska.

"I'm tellin' you, I will have nothin' to do wi' it. If he tries to put wan of them things on the *Vital Spark* then I am takin' a chob ashore."

∼

Fortunately, things did not come to this pass. The following morning, half an hour before the puffer left Glasgow bound for Skipness in Kintyre, a horse-drawn van clattered onto the quay and delivered a large black tin box addressed simply to 'Steam Lighter *Vital Spark*'.

On examination this was found to contain a complete set of 26 individual flags, one standing for each letter of the alphabet, complete with halyards and cleats for the mast together with a hard-bound copy of the printed set of codes from which Para Handy had quoted the previous day.

"No wireless, thank Cott!" exclaimed the skipper with some relief, "though these dam' things iss bad enough. Jum!! Put up the new halyards seein' they're here, and take all the rest of this rubbish to the fo'c'sle. We'll maybe peruse it at our leisure some ither time," he concluded dismissively, and the crew thought that they had probably seen and heard the last of the hated signal flags.

Not quite.

Two days later, as they were returning to Bowling having delivered their cargo of roadstone to Skipness, the *Vital Spark* came through the narrows at Colintraive and Para Handy spotted the *Spartan* in the middle distance, headed towards them, and very low in the water with a full cargo of unknown identity.

"Jum!" shouted the Captain. "Away you down to the fo'c'sle and bring oot the flags for S and P, and K and Z: and run them up the signal halyard ass fast as you can!"

"What's that aal aboot, Peter?" asked the Mate, puzzled, as the mysterious signal fluttered in the breeze.

"Och, chust a chance to get back at that man Bain and his fancy ways at the cless the ither day.

"It'll gi'e him somethin' to pause and consider aboot if no more than that — but maybe he'll be late goin' to wherever he's goin' — and serve him right! You see, I ken fine that he hassna the wireless, for he said Hay's wass not puttin' them in aal the shups because of the cost. But he doesna ken whether we have the wireless or not.

"S and P means *Have received orders for you not to proceed without further instructions*: and K and Z means *Anchor instantly*.

"If we're lucky, he may well do chust that — and I'd like to be in John Hay's office if Bain goes ashore at Colintraive and telegraphs to get those instructions."

Noticing with impish delight, as the two boats converged, that the unfortunate *Spartan* was indeed preparing to let go her anchor, Para Handy doffed his cap and waved cheerily to Bain, ignoring the other man's efforts to shout questions with a polite tap on his ear and an apologetic shrug.

The *Vital Spark* passed her at Macphail's best seven knots, and swung westwards round the tip of Bute and out of sight.

FACTNOTE

I picked up a copy of the 1904 edition of *Signalling for Board of Trade Examinations* for a few pence in a second-hand bookshop a few years ago. The little handbook, produced by the nautical publishers James Brown & Son of Glasgow, dates from the time of the watershed between the old and new ways of communication at sea.

There is a whole range of coded flag messages and those given in the story are all genuine. However, in 1899 Marconi had presented his paper on *Wireless Telegraphy* to the Institution of Electrical Engineers. It too is reprinted in the handbook and as it was published, the very first wirelesses were being installed in ships — though needless to say not in the humble puffers!

There were six shore telegraph stations set up by the Marconi Company to handle wireless communication to and from ships in the Atlantic, and 10 shipping companies including the 'big names' such as Cunard, Norddeutscher Lloyd, American Line and the French CTG, had specified wireless facilities on at least some of their passenger liners. Nevertheless, the total number of ships in the world's merchant and naval fleets so equipped (according to Marconi's own list in 1904) was still less than 50 though, of course, it would soon be being added to daily as first the convenience and then the necessity of the new technology became understood.

The James Brown handbook also details methods of ship-to-ship and ship-to-shore signalling using lamps, semaphores and quite complex (but widely understood) combinations of other masthead paraphernalia — cones, balls, cubes, coloured lights etc. The messages conveyed in signal code ranged from the banal to the dramatic and all points in between.

Thus inconsequential communications such as *Pay attention!* or *Has the mail arrived?* or *My chronometer has run down* appear in Brown's handbook alongside rather more pressing messages which include *War has been declared, I must abandon the vessel, Beware of torpedos* and *We are dying for want of water* — all conveyed by a pre-arranged combination of flags.

Puffers, even at the end of their long career on the Clyde, were rarely fitted with wireless transmitters. Skippers in West Highland ports had to telephone their Glasgow head offices for further instructions about their next ports of call. Inevitably this could lead to some hilarious interchanges when a city clerk, looking out of his office window at a calm, clear and cloudless sky, refused to believe the circumstances reported by some beleaguered skipper trapped perhaps in Stornoway by severe gales, or else marooned in Campbeltown in a thick fog.

25

Hogmanay on the Vital Spark

It was mid-day on Hogmanay, and in the front bar of the inn at Lochgoilhead the crew of the finest vessel in the coastal trade were being 'treated' by the local merchant whose consignment of best Ayrshire coal they had just finished unloading.

Para Handy put his empty glass down on the bar counter with unnecessary ostentation, peering into it as if incredulous that it could have held such a small and quickly-taken dram.

"My Chove, I wass needin' that," he said with some conviction. "Coupin' a cargo of coalss iss no' the best of chobs in weather like this." Indeed a snell north-easterly wind was sending a thin flurry of snow drifting across the windows that looked out onto the loch, and the aspect was of unrelieved shades of grey.

"Best respects to you Mr Carmichael, and the compliments of the season," the skipper continued, "but if there's nae mair business to be attended to" — fiddling with his empty glass as he spoke, more in hope than anything else — "I think the lads and me should be getting on our way, for it'll be a long cold trup, bitter cold, before we're in Glasgow tonight!"

"All right Peter," smiled Carmichael, signalling to the barman. "I can take a hint. Set them up again, Wullie!"

Surprisingly, given the day it was, the party had the bar to themselves, with one exception.

If the small man at the table in the far corner, nursing what looked suspiciously like a glass of ginger beer, was aware that he was the object of the crew's curiosity, he gave no sign of it but could not have been surprised. Strangers in

Lochgoilhead at this time of year were as unexpected as a snowflake in June.

"He's no' a traiveller, for sure," offered Dougie when Para Handy, in a very audible stage whisper, invited ideas about the identity of the mysterious stranger. "For he's got no cases and you never yet saw a traiveller withoot his samples."

"And he's no' a towerist," affirmed Sunny Jim, "for they all go away tae hibernate efter the September weekend."

The barman leaned across the counter. "I was going to speak to you about him, Peter, to see if you could do me a sort of a favour wi' yon man. He's no' exactly a towerist, chust a sort of an Englishman that's been biding here for the past week and he's desperate keen to get back to Glasgow noo — but wi' the ice and that, Mackinnon's trap couldnae get up the hill to connect him wi' the charibang at the top of the Rest this mornin', and there's no a steamer till efter the New Year. So he's kind of stuck."

"What d'ye mean 'no exactly a towerist'?" asked the captain.

"Nothin' really, Peter," said the barman: "chust that at this time o' year ye dinna expect ony o' them." And reaching to the shelves behind him for the bottle, he poured another generous dram into the skipper's glass. "It would be a great kindness if ye could tak' him wi' ye on the *Vital Spark*."

"My Chove, Wullie," said Para Handy, eyeing his refilled glass suspiciously. "You're surely awfu' anxious tae get rid o' him. Whit's wrang wi' him?"

"Not a thing, Peter, not a thing: chust tryin' to do him a kindness, it bein' the time o' year it is."

"That's right," chipped in Carmichael. "He'll pay his passage -and I'll donate a bottle to keep you warm on the way up river."

Para Handy studied the little man surreptitiously. He looked harmless enough, but this was Hogmanay, not Christmas, and the generosity of both barman and merchant were uncharacteristic to say the least.

"What d'ye think, Dougie?"

"Whatever you think yoursel', Peter," said the mate agreeably.

"Just dinna let Mr MacBrayne find out you're in opposition for he'd be sair vexed wi' you," snorted Macphail — but the bargain was struck, and the little man was beckoned to join the group.

"Mr Clement, this is Captain Macfarlane," said Carmichael, "and he's agreed to take you to Glasgow. On the conditions that you and I discussed earlier," he added with some emphasis. "So remember to keep to them."

～

Two hours later the *Vital Spark*, riding light and making her best speed with a following tide, had Kilcreggan to port with every chance of making her berth at the Broomielaw before darkness fell. To speed their getaway from Lochgoilhead they had not taken time to stow the puffer's dinghy, which was now bobbing in her wake at the end of a tow-line.

Carmichael's bottle stood — unopened — on the top of the wheelhouse cubby pending their arrival in Glasgow: and their passenger, who had not uttered a word since leaving the bar at Lochgoilhead, other than to agree his passage fare of a florin with the skipper, was perched shivering in the bows, seated on top of his sole piece of baggage — a large tin trunk — with his coat collar vainly turned up against the cold.

"Jum," said Para Handy, "Go and tell that man tae come in oot o' the cauld: he can come in here wi' us, or doon tae the engine-room wi' Macphail, but I'll no be responsible for him catching his daith by stayin' oot there."

"Ye'll no' send him doon here," protested a voice from beneath Para Handy's feet, but the problem did not arise, as the Englishman squeezed into the wheelhouse two minutes later having, with the help of Sunny Jim, moved his tin trunk from the bows to the stern.

"Yon trunk's some weight," protested Jim. "What have ye got in there — it's no' a keg of whusky, eh, this bein' Hogmanay?"

"Whisky!" cried the man, "I would sooner carry dynamite about with me for it's a sight less harmful than that devilish drink!" And throwing back the lid of the trunk he revealed a great stack of leaflets, seized a handful and thrust one into the skipper's hands. "Whisky! It's an abomination and a curse, fountain of all the evil in this wicked world!"

"My Cot," said Para Handy. "He's wan o' they teetotallisers so he iss!"

Sure enough, the leaflet proclaimed in large print 'Clement's Campaign: Down With The Demon Drink!!!' and went on to describe in gory detail the horrors apparently attendant on the consumption of the merest drop of alcohol in any form.

"Nae wonder they wanted rid o' him at Lochgoilhead," said the mate.

"A godless place," cried Clement dramatically. "But I have seen worse in my travels across Scotland these past months. I was making some progress there. When I stood at the doors of the Inn and harangued the poor, blind sheep who were being lured to its wicked temptations, some of them turned aside from the path of sin and went their way."

"I'll bet they did," said Para Handy. "The sight and sound of you and your damn' nonsense would turn milk soor, never mind put any man off his drink: it's a miracle you got out of there in wan piece. If my friend Hurricane Jeck had come across you he'd have thrown you and your tin trunk intae the loch."

As the Skipper turned back to the wheel, Clement caught sight of Carmichael's bottle and, before Sunny Jim or Dougie could stop him, he had seized it and, stepping out on deck, hurled it over the stern into the gathering dusk.

"That settles it..." cried Para Handy. "We're putting you off at Bowling, but ye'll pay for that whusky if you want to walk ashore dry-shod, otherwise you'll be swimmin' for it, and your trunk wi' ye."

Banished back to the deck, and five shillings the poorer after meeting the Captain's demands for recompense, Clement stood in aggrieved silence as the puffer edged her way into the little harbour where the Forth and Clyde Canal joined the river.

"Peter, ye can't do this to the good folk at Bowling," Dougie protested. "Many a fine spree we've had here. Now he'll be goin' round all the pubs and makin' a'body's Hogmanay a misery. Can ye no' tak' him up tae Gleska and let him loose there? He can't do mich herm in a city."

"Naw," said Para Handy. "He's goin' ashore here. But, Dougie, you've given me an idea. Tak' the wheel a meenit while I have a word wi' the man."

~

Bowling was unusually busy, even for Hogmanay, with

the little passenger boats loading for the journey up the Canal to Glasgow and beyond. Clement was unceremoniously dumped on the quayside with his precious trunk, and was last seen making his way not to the nearest Inns, but towards one of the canal vessels.

"Where's he awa' to noo?" asked Dougie as the *Vital Spark* resumed her journey up-river and Sunny Jim went to check on the dinghy's tow-line.

"Well, Dougie," said the skipper. "I think he might be on his way to Kirkintilloch: for I telt him that it was namely ass the most drouthy village in the whole country, and sair in need of some temperancising."

"Kirkintilloch!" cried the mate. "Peter, there's no' a pub in the place. It's wan o' the few 'dry' villages this side of the river ever since they had that stupid vote." His voice tailed off as realisation dawned.

"Chust so," said Para Handy. "Chust so. They do they're drinkin' at hame in Kirkintilloch. Mr Clement'll no manage to ruin onybody's Hogmanay up there!"

"And he's no' ruined ours either," a delighted Sunny Jim called from the stern, and a moment later bounced into the wheelhouse with Carmichael's bottle in his hands. "When he threw oor whusky overboard it went straight intae the dinghy. And didnae' break!"

"Well, well," said Para Handy. "It chust goes to show you, Jim, that as Mr Clement might put it — the duvvle looks after his own! Away you and get the mugs fae the fo'c'sle and we'll have chust the wan wee nip tae keep the cold out between here and the Broomielaw!"

FACTNOTE

Scotland has had some pretty arcane rules and regulations with regard to the sale and consumption of alcohol. This may have been the legacy of the somewhat ambivalent attitude towards drink which prevailed in Victorian times.

On the one hand, the 'upper' classes deplored the 'excesses' of the 'lower' classes while themselves showing a healthy appetite for brandy, port and claret. On the other, the working-class quarters of towns and cities were well-endowed with temperance societies — counterbalanced by the proliferation of all manner of shebeens and drinking dens.

Periodically therefore some odd pieces of legislation

(unique to Scotland within the United Kingdom) have been in force.

Glasgow had a ban on licensed premises in all munici-pally-owned properties, including housing developments, for three quarters of a century: a ban which was lifted only in 1966. There is little doubt that the absence of well-run public houses as community focal points in the new periph-eral re-housing projects, into which so many families were reluctantly decanted from the inner city in the post-war years, was one factor in the problem of building a sense of local pride and purpose to replace that which had been left behind with the move.

Till the early 1960s, on Sundays no Public House could open and Hotels could only sell drink to so-called *bona fide* travellers who had to enter name, address and destination in a book kept specially for that purpose, and open to police inspection, not to say public ridicule. The number of occa-sions on which the books revealed that Mickey Mouse had passed through en route to Hollywood was legendary!

More draconian still was the Temperance Act of 1913 which made provision for 'Veto Polls' in each and every community whereby a small number of electors could enforce a vote as to whether or not pubs should be licensed within it. Kirkintilloch was one of a number of villages voted 'dry' for more than 50 years as a result. Its near-neighbour Kilsyth was another. On the south side of the Clyde the rural Renfrewshire parish of Kilmacolm, in which I was born and brought up, was without a pub from 1913 till 1989 despite having had no fewer than seven before the veto was invoked!

There were also many real life equivalents of the Mr Clements of the story: peripatetic temperance campaigners were a common enough hazard in rural areas in which the population was too small, too scattered or simply too unin-terested to establish a permanent Rechabite Lodge or a Good Templar's Hall.

26

A Girl in Every Port

The long wet winter was over, and the cheery touches of a green and cheerful spring were at last appearing on the hills and in the fields and gardens on either shore of the Firth. The pleasant effects of the change of the seasons were not lost on the crew of the *Vital Spark* as she went about her business and the welcome May weeks rolled past.

Para Handy, as befitted a man of his position, deployed his energies and his natural enthusiasm with yet more bounce than usual. Even Dougie's lugubrious countenance positively beamed and Dan Macphail, interred in the stygian gloom of the echoing stokehold, whistled at his work.

It was Sunny Jim's behaviour, however, which at once manifested in very practical terms the joy of the returning spring, but at the same time gave the crew in general, and Para Handy in particular, cause for concern. In spring they say a young man's fancy turns to thoughts of love: but in Jim's case it was his deeds rather than his thoughts which were in evidence.

No matter where the puffer tied up overnight, or how late, her young hand seemed to have an assignation ashore — and an assignation that simply would not wait.

∽

"There he goes again," complained Dougie as they lay one sunny evening at Millport, watching Jim marching smartly up the quay towards the town, his hair uncharacteristically combed and dressed, his cap at a jaunty angle, and his face and hands shiny with scrubbing at the pump.

"And what did we get for oor tea tonight? Tinned sardines again. 'Quick and easy, shupmates for Ah huv tae go ashore, but jist rammed fu' o aal the goodness o' the sea!' " he mimicked disgustedly. "Huh! I'll ram him full o' somethin' and it won't be goodness, unless things improve — and soon."

"Dougie's richt," said Macphail emphatically. "It's aboot time ye dusciplined the boy before we all starve! Who's in charge on this boat, that's what Ah ask masel' — a whippersnapper of a laddie or a man auld enough to be his grandfaither?"

Para Handy, ignoring the disparaging suggestion as to his age, explained that his concern about Jim's misdemeanours was based more on an ethical than a nutritional consideration.

"The way things iss turnin' oot noo it's the laad's morals I am more worried aboot than I am aboot oor stomachs," said the Captain. "He iss tryin' to run when he can scarcely walk. I had expected him to be content wi' chust the wan gyurl in hiss life, maybe a sensible Bowlin' lassie that he could see every time we are in there. But that iss not good enough for oor Jum!

"It is wan thing for a man wi' the sagacity and devagation o' Hurricane Jeck — or indeed mysel' when I wass in my prime — to be on caalin' terms wi a gyurl here or a gyurl there ass we wass peregrinatin' aboot the river: it iss a very different matter for a young fellow such ass Jum, who hassna had the chance to learn aal the niceties of dealin' wi' the fair sex, for that sort of experience only comes wi' practice."

"Well, he's gettin' plenty of practice the noo, that's for sure," interjected the engineer. "The baker's dochter last week when we wis in Fairlie: yon dairymaid in Largs: the lassie frae the goon shop in Wemyss Bay. Ah'm tellin' ye Peter, if he parades anither yin past us the nicht to show aff hoo smert he is like he's done up till noo, Ah've a dam' guid mind tae remind her whit he really is — jist oor deckie, and no' the flash dandy he likes tae think! Ah wonder who it's gaun tae be in Millport?"

∾

Dan Macphail's question was answered half-an-hour later when the object of their criticism sashayed by on the quayside with his topcoat hanging on one arm and a tall red-haired girl in a blue silk gown hanging on the other, an opened floral-patterned parasol twirling across her left shoulder.

"What ho, shipmates!" called the errant deck-hand, making the introductions to his latest conquest with some bravura. "Why dinna ye come oot for a stroll instead o' hunkerin' doon there on the deck as if ye wis naethin' but the maritime equivilunt o' they Chelsea Pensioners! It's a richt bonny evenin' for a perambulation and me an' Liza is jist gettin' up an appetite for a McCallum at the Shore Cafe afore we look in on the Hielan' Night at the Quay Hotel, for it would be a shame if I kept the belle-of-the-ball away from the ball!"

"Chust so, Jum, a bonny gyurl and no mistake! Complements of the evenin' to you, Miss Liza" said Para Handy gallantly, "but I doot oor perambulatin' days iss done, ass you say. Unless it wass perhaps to look for a bite to eat," he added pointedly.

"Aye, weel," said Jim, reddening slightly. "There's a grand selection of restrongs in Millport for ye to choose from. The pick o' the Clyde!"

And with that he touched the tip of his cap with a cheery grin and swung away from the quayside and headed back towards the esplanade.

"That boy needs took doon a peg or two," grumbled the engineer as soon as the pair were out of earshot.

"What I canna understand," said Dougie, "iss how Jum thinks he can keep stringin' aal these lassies along. I mean, it would be bad enough if he wass chust takin' them oot and then forgettin' aal aboot them: but here he iss sendin' them aal cairds and letters frae every corner o' the Clyde, ass if he wass the faithful swain and they wass the only girl in the world for him! It's no' fair on them, it's chust no' right. He collects them chust the same ass if they wass cigarette cards."

"Aye, sure enough," agreed the Captain. "He hass no respect for the gyurls at aal, and that iss aal wrong. Jum iss not a chentleman when it comes to hiss dealin's with the lassies."

"Indeed no," affirmed Macphail, "and he needs to be taught a lesson, so he does."

"Aye, Dan: maybe so. And maybe I can see chust how it might be done."

∾

Three days later the puffer was moored at the Coal Pier in Dunoon. Arriving late the previous evening, she had discharged her cargo in the morning and the crew now had the prospect of a pleasantly lazy afternoon. She was due to take a flitting back over to Millport the following day — Saturday — but for the meantime there was nothing to be done. Para Handy's hints about freshening up the paintwork had fallen on deaf ears.

"Can ye no' leave a man in peace instead o' breakin' yer neck tryin' tae find him some work tae do?" Macphail protested, and the normally placid mate was equally adamant that he wanted nothing to do with any painting projects. Sunny Jim was already busy at the pump with soap and flannel, and did not even deign to reply.

Somewhat to their surprise, the skipper did not press the point and 10 minutes later, not long after Sunny Jim had left the puffer with a hunter's gleam in his eye, Para Handy himself went ashore.

"I chust have a little business to see to," he said, "and I'll be back in aboot an hoor." And he set off in the direction of the steamer pier, where the *Queen Alexandra* was just berthing.

He returned to the puffer in under the hour with a strangely smug look on his face.

∾

As the puffer approached the north end of Cumbrae the following afternoon, her hold chock-full of all the higgledy-piggledy merchandise of a household flitting, Para Handy scrutinised the Ayrshire coast and consulted his watch. Then, to that worthy's total astonishment (for normally he was the butt of constant complaints about inadequacies of his engines) he asked the engineer to slow down.

The *Vital Spark* continued slowly down the eastern shore of the island. Across the sound Para Handy watched as the paddler *Galatea*, on her way from Greenock and Wemyss Bay, called in at Largs and then headed on towards Fairlie.

At the same leisurely pace the puffer steamed on, eventually arriving at the entrance to Millport bay just as the *Galatea* was berthing at the steamer pier, where she would lie over for a couple of hours before retracing her route back to Greenock.

"Jum," called the Captain, "go doon and put the kettle on, like a good laad, and we'll aal have a cuppa before we stert gettin' this flittin' unloaded."

Sunny Jim, who had been busy writing a series of 'wish you were here' cards of Dunoon to his coterie of lady-friends, put his pencil and his correspondence in his pocket and disappeared down the fore-hatch to the fo'c'sle.

"Now, Dougie," said Para Handy, "away you and see that you keep the laad below deck till I give you a couple of toots on the whustle: then bring him up."

"What are you up to, Peter?" asked the mystified mate.

"You'll see soon enough," said the Captain enigmatically. "But if my plan hass worked oot then I think we'll see a change in the way Jum treats the gyurls from noo on."

As the *Vital Spark* edged in towards her berth at the cargo quay four conspicuous and attractive figures standing there watched the progress of the puffer with interest, and eyed each other suspiciously at the same time.

Dan Macphail scrambled up from the engine-room, in response to Para Handy's call, to throw a heaving-line to one of the pier staff and caught sight of the waiting group as he did so.

"Here!" he turned to Para Handy in astonishment. "Is that no' some o' Jum's conquests lined up up there?"

"Chust so," said the skipper. "That's Liza from Millport, and Ellen from Fairlie, and Bella from Largs, and Jean from Wemyss Bay.

"I thought mebbe Jum would forget to let them aal know he wass comin' back to Millport this efternoon. Ass I've a friend who's assistant purser on the *Queen Alexandra*, when I saw her lyin' at Dunoon yesterday efternoon afore she left for Wemyss Bay and aal points sooth, I went and asked a wee favour from him by way o' deliverin' some correspondence for me. I took the liberty of sendin' the gyurls a caird each on Jum's behalf, askin' them if they wud like to meet him here at fower o'clock today for a wee daunder, and their teas and mebbe a McCallum, before the *Galatea* took them back hame at six.

"It'll mebbe be a bit o' an upset for the lasses, but they'll soon get over it and it's better that they should see Jum for what he iss, raither than let him break their hearts. And it's no' his heart they'll want to break when they realise what's what.

"I doot he'll learn to treat a ġyurl wi' a bit mair respect from noo on."

And, with a cheery wave to the colourful bevy of beauties on the quayside, Para Handy reached for the lanyard and ġave a couple of short blasts on the puffer's steam whistle.

He watched with some satisfaction, and a considerable sense of anticipation, as the fore-hatch swung open and an unsuspecting Sunny Jim climbed up onto the fore-deck.

FACTNOTE

Though the island of Cumbrae, with its capital Millport, was never able to rival the premier Clyde resort destinations such as Dunoon or Rothesay, or the more distant and much larger Isle of Arran, it enjoyed a remarkably loyal and strong following among Clyde trippers and holidaymakers and indeed does so to this day. Excursions to the Millport 'illuminations', the only such attraction on the Firth, remain a popular September destination for *Waverley*, last surviving paddler on the river.

Millport was just not big enough to compete on equal terms with the largest resorts. The island's total population at the turn of the century was less than 2000. With an area of just five square miles and an unspectacular topography (its highest hill less than 500ft in height) it was dwarfed by Arran, with 30 times the area and mountains rising to over 2800 feet. Yet the tenacity and determination of the islanders, and their easy proximity to the Ayrshire coast a couple of miles to the east, have made it a prized destination for its *aficionados* who — quite rightly! — will not hear a word against it.

The town enjoyed the unique distinction of having two piers to serve it — the Old Pier and the Keppel Pier — and a complex and competitive steamer service to no fewer than three mainland railway towns, namely Wemyss Bay, Largs and Fairlie. For many years too there was a direct steamer service into the centre of Glasgow.

The *Galatea* was built as the new 'flagship' for the Caledonian Steam Packet Company fleet by Caird's of Greenock in 1890 and though she was a most handsome, two-funnelled paddler with a reasonable turn of speed at just over 17 knots, her owners were never satisfied about either her performance or her appeal. Her time on the

Clyde was as a result relatively brief and she was sold to Italian owners just 14 years later.

The *Queen Alexandra*, launched in 1902, had an even shorter career on the Firth. Badly damaged by fire at Greenock in 1912 she was repaired — but then sold to owners in Vancouver, which she reached by sailing round Cape Horn because, of course, the Panama Canal was still under construction! She was replaced by a new vessel of the same name which distinguished herself by ramming and sinking a submarine in the Channel in World War I and later by emerging from a refit in 1935 as MacBrayne's three funnelled *St Columba*.

A 'McCallum' was a popular West of Scotland courting delicacy for many decades and consisted of a sundae-glass of vanilla ice-cream smothered in raspberry syrup. Just who invented it, and who gave it the name, and why, can still be the subject of debate among enthusiasts!

THE HIGHLAND GATEWAY — *Only Rothesay pier was ever as busy as Dunoon: the Cowal pier is seen here at the height of its dominance as the 'Gateway to the Highlands' as well as an important destination in its own right. Here the paths of the North British steamers from their Craigendoran base criss-crossed (among others) those of the Caledonian Railway Company and MacBrayne, from Gourock: and of Captain Buchanan, from Glasgow. In this photograph, Eagle III to the left and, ahead of her, the first Lord of the Isles.*

27

Going off the Rails

Once her cargo of pit-props had been unloaded at Ardrossan harbour, the Captain of the *Vital Spark* went off as usual to the Post Office to wire back to the Glasgow office for news about their next assignment. The crew relaxed on deck in the early May sunshine, the mate perusing a copy of the previous week's People's Friend, Macphail poring over a new novelle.

Sunny Jim sat idly on the hatch coaming with a piece of tarry string with which he played cat's cradle while humming a tuneless, wordless song to the eventual, inevitable irritation of the other two.

Before too many harsh words could be said, fortunately, Para Handy was seen coming back down the quayside towards the puffer with the usual yellow telegram in his hands, and speculation replaced altercation on deck.

"Knowin' oor luck," said Macphail, "the office'll be sendin' us tae Glenarm for lime." That Northern Ireland port, serving a nearby limestone quarry, was the crew's most hated destination of all, for working that particular cargo was an especially foul job. "Whit Macfarlane has done tae offend them a' up at the Gleska office I dinna ken," continued the engineer: "but if there's ever ony dirty work tae be done it's aye the *Vital Spark* that gets tae dae it!

"I doot it's that, or even worse, by the look of the man," he concluded. And sure enough there was a puzzled frown on Para Handy's face as he jumped down onto the deck.

"Don't tell us it's Glenarm again," said Dougie disgustedly. Para Handy shook his head.

"Whateffer it iss, it's a misprint," he said. "There hass been some sort of a stoorie on the telegraph line and the message hass come oot wrong at this end. Listen to this, lads, and see if you can mak' ony sense of it. 'Rendezvous with puffer *Saxon* at Bowling and proceed together to Bridge Wharf to load cargo of trams for Rothesay.' Trams? *Trams??* Whit are they on aboot?"

"It should maybe be *Drams*, Captain," suggested Sunny Jim with some enthusiasm. "We're tae tak' a cargo o' whusky for the Rothesay Inns maybe?"

"Naw, Jum," said the Mate. "They aalways get their supplies wi' the *Texa* effery second Thursday. And even at the Fair Fortnight you wudna need a pair o' puffers tae tak' the necessary supplies for the visiting Glaswegians doon tae Bute.

"Could it no' be *Rams* they mean, Peter? Or *Lambs* maybe? For there's a wheen sheep on the island already."

"Aye Dougie," said the Captain, "but they're usually bein' sent oot, no' brocht in! It's beyond me. *Prams?* — there's no that mony weans in Bute. *Hams?* — they cure their ain.

"Cot knows whit it iss — but there's only wan way to find oot! Mr Macphail! If you can get your lang face oot o' that trash and get some steam up, we can maybe get awa' tae Bowling and see if Wullie Jardine on the *Saxon* kens ony mair aboot this than we do!"

~

The two puffers met up at Bowling harbour the following morning when the *Saxon* came in from completing a run up the Forth and Clyde Canal to Grangemouth, collecting timber which she had then delivered to McGregor's yard at Kirkintilloch.

"It's gobbledegook tae me tae, Peter," volunteered Jardine when the two Captains met. "We'd best get up there and fin' oot the worst. Ah wush Ah cud think whit way they're wantin' the twa boats thegither: that's the real mystery."

They found out soon enough.

Standing on the quayside at Bridge Wharf there were indeed two *trams*: two of the newly perfected electrical variety: and their destination was indeed to be Bute, as replacements on the 20-year-old Rothesay to Port Bannatyne tramway for the smaller horse-drawn vehicles which had served it till now.

The only means of getting them to their destination was

by the use of a pair of puffers, lashed together to form a broad square platform onto which the two trams could then be lowered gently by crane, laid transversely across the cargo hatchways of the boats, and secured with wire hawsers and ropes to cleats and eye-bolts on the decks and gunwales.

The delicate operation took the most of the day to complete and the two crews went ashore in the late afternoon for a badly needed refreshment at the Auld Toll Vaults.

Para Handy and Jardine looked back at the strange silhouette at the quayside.

"Skoosh-caurs!" exclaimed Para Handy. "Skoosh-caurs! I do not believe it, Wullie, I neffer, neffer in aal my born days thocht to see the smertest boat in the coasting tred (no offence meant Wullie, you understand) aal higgledy-piggledy wi' a cargo the like of yon. It looks chust like a tinker's flittin', it iss makin' a fool o' the shup!"

He changed his mind half-an-hour later when a raincoated figure with a snap-brim hat put a head round the doorway of the snug at the Auld Toll to enquire: "Is there a Captain MacFarlane here?"

"Aye, that's me," said Para Handy.

"Ah, Captain: my name is Farquharson. I'm a reporter from the *Glasgow News*. Your friend Mr Neil Munro sent me to see you, he thought I might find you here. You see we would like to write a piece about you — and about you too of course, Captain Jardine," he added hastily as Wullie swung round to give him a long hard look, "since you're both in the news, as it were, on account of the cargo you're taking down to Rothesay. The first of the new electric trams for the island! The first cargo of its kind ever on the Clyde, and carried by steam lighters! Our readers will be very interested to read all about it in tomorrow morning's paper."

Para Handy positively swelled with pride. "In the news, eh? Well, what else wud you expect when dealing wi' the smertest..." Tactfully realising, just in time, that that particular line of thought was best left unspoken, he said no more.

"Well, well," he smiled, "please sit doon and mak' yoursel' at hame, Mr Farquharson, and speir awa'. Jum! give the chentleman that seat, and get a stool for yoursel'.

"I am chust sorry I cannot offer you a refreshment, but we only came in for the wan wee gless of sherbet to clear oor throats and my money iss aal on the shup."

The reporter, well forewarned by Neil Munro, took the hint with no further prompting.

～

Sunny Jim was sent ashore first thing next day to buy a copy of the paper before the strange hybrid creation set off on its journey down the Firth.

There was a long article on page two of the *News* congratulating the Directors of the Rothesay Tramway Company on their 'brave investment in the remarkable new technology which would shortly revolutionise transport on both land and sea', as the writer put it: and complementing the shippers on their ingenuity in creating 'the first set of nautical Siamese Twins ever to have been seen on the Firth' to accomplish the task of transporting the cargo safe to its destination.

Only Macphail remained jaundiced about the whole enterprise and scathingly critical of the indignities heaped on the puffer.

"It's just a shambles!" he protested. "Wud ye tak' a look at whit we look like for peety's sake! Jist a broken-doon penny ride frae Hengler's Circus and Carnival, jist makin' a richt bauchle o' the boat."

Para Handy, on the other hand, once he had had the chance to study the piece in search of any hidden, unflattering innuendos (explaining to the mystified Sunny Jim, in the meantime, just what was meant by the allusion to Siamese Twins) and finding none that he could see, was quite delighted by the notice (or notoriety) which was, at last, attaching to his command — even if he had to share the glory with Wullie Jardine.

It was as well that the Captain of the *Saxon* was an old friend, for the actual passage down-river was fraught with considerable difficulty, and demanded considerable tact on the part of both Captains and both crews.

Which skipper was to be in overall command?

Which engineer and which set of engines was to dictate the speed at which the floating tangle of glass and steel should be progressed?

Which helmsman was to establish the headings to be steered, and how — when neither wheelhouse gave a view of anything other than the side of a tramcar three feet in front?

Para Handy was just about to broach this delicate question with Wullie Jardine when the latter, following an earnest discussion with his engineer in the wheelhouse, approached the Captain of the *Vital Spark* with the unexpectedly generous suggestion that Para Handy, as the more experienced man, should have overall charge: that Macphail, as a former deep-sea engineer, should set the pace for the voyage: and that Dougie, being taller than the mate of the *Saxon* and therefore better able to see where they were all heading, should be navigator-in-chief.

"My Chove, that's very gracious of you, Wullie," said Para Handy, and the two shook hands on the agreement, and gave orders for the lines to be cast off.

The twin-decked carrier moved slowly into the middle of the river.

∿

The twin-decked carrier continued to move slowly, very slowly indeed, all the way down the Firth.

"I neffer thought it wud tak' so long," said Para Handy with some exasperation as at last they came abreast of Toward Point and within sight of their destination. "The *Saxon* chust iss not in the same class ass we are for speed. I shall neffer, neffer be rude to Dan aboot the enchines again!"

The Directors of the Tramway Company, together with all the great and the good of Bute, were awaiting their arrival at Rothesay and for the first time in her long career the *Vital Spark* (and of course the *Saxon*) came alongside a flag-bedecked jetty to the cheers of a large crowd.

∿

"My Chove, Wullie," said Para Handy an hour later, as they sat in the bar of the Commercial Hotel, "I thocht we wass neffer goin' to get here. I chust hope we can make better progress back up river to Gleska!"

"I wudna bet on that, Peter," said Jardine guiltily. "Ye see, ye'll hae tae gi'e us a piggie-back again."

"A piggie-back? Again? Whit are you on aboot?"

"Well, it's like this. We cracked wir biler this mornin' jist as we were gettin' steam up at Bridge Wharf and had tae shut it doon. That's what the ingineer wis tellin' me aboot in the wheelhoose. But I wisnae goin' to miss the spree and the glory of it a' so I kept ma peace! The *Vital Spark* wis the only shup wi' ony power on the way doon river, and I'd be obleeged if ye'd just keep us lashed by ye for the trup back hame.

"We'd baith look awfu' schoopit if this got intae the papers Peter, wudn't we?"

FACTNOTE

The Bute Tramway was in existence for more than half-a-century, the first two miles of track being opened in 1882 between Rothesay and Port Bannatyne. For the first 20 years of its operations the service was provided by horse-drawn vehicles which took about an hour on the round trip. Though the initial impetus for its construction came from its role as a tourist attraction (Rothesay was then just about to enter its zenith years as the number one tourism mecca on the Firth) the service ran year round.

In due course, the winter operations were being provided by specially constructed enclosed vehicles, whereas the summer service (somewhat optimistically!) was always maintained by open-top carriages.

In 1902, the service was electrified. This involved closing it down completely for a few months to allow the necessary conversion to be carried out, before the new tramway opened for business in May of that year. Some three-quarters of a million passengers were carried annually at its peak, and there were 22 trams in service.

In 1905, following years of planning and discussion, the line was extended to provide a summer season service to the fine sands of Ettrick Bay on the south side of the island and though there was occasional talk of further extensions, none actually came to reality.

The tramway finally closed down in 1936, the victim of the expansion of more comfortable and reliable coach and charabanc service.

Most of the vehicles for the Rothesay tramway were indeed brought to Bute by pairs of puffers or lighters lashed together to provide the necessary beam, this being the most practical and above all the most economical way of transporting such a bulky and awkward cargo.

The limestone cargoes referred to earlier were confirmed

by most puffer crews as their real bete-noir. The loading and unloading process kicked up a positive stour of clinging dust which got into clothes, hair, lungs, and pervaded every nook and cranny aboard the boats.

By comparison, carrying a couple of tramcars down river really must have seemed like a relaxing holiday — especially since it would not have involved any back-breaking work with the steam winch or the shovel!

ROTHESAY TRAM TERMINUS — Here is the town terminus for the Bute Tramways at Guildford Square, Rothesay, with one of the new electric vehicles loading holidaymakers for Port Bannatyne and Ettrick Bay. To the left lies the inner harbour, destination and berthing place for the numerous puffers which served the island community, but it was unfortunately empty of shipping the day this photograph was taken.

28

The Cargo of Cement

S unny Jim had been sent up on deck to bring back a report about the weather as soon as the battered old alarm clock (the only item of any ornamental pretension in the fo'c'sle) had gone off as usual at seven o'clock.

"Sorry boys," he said as he returned. "It's rainin' as hard as ever, and no sign of a break in the sky at all."

The *Vital Spark* had lain at Berry's Pier on Loch Striven for four days now and, though the month was May, the rain had been unrelenting for nearly 96 solid hours. The tops of the hills in Cowal to the north and on the Kyles to the south were embedded head first, as it were, in the base of low grey clouds which pressed down to within a few hundred feet of the surface of the loch.

"Still rainin' on!" complained Para Handy, swinging his feet out of his bunk and reaching for his shirt. "I have neffer known weather like it and I am fair at the end of my tether wi' it aal.

"I shall go and talk to the builders again. We cannot lie here for effer and a day. What the owner must be thinkin' I hate to imachine. With there bein' no telephone in the big hoose for us to get a message to him, he'll be thinkin' that we iss aal lost at sea, and his shup wi' us!"

∾

Their enforced idleness had been caused by a combination of the constant rain, the nature of their cargo — and a very cautious clerk-of-works. The 'big house' at Glenstriven was in process of having some amenities added before the annual summer visit of its owners, a Glasgow merchant and his family.

Chief amongst these was the building of a large new boathouse beside the pier which served the estate: and the construction of a substantial flagstoned terrace at the front of the house, as a necessary adjunct to the quite unheard-of extravagance of the small outdoor swimming pool which had been installed there only the previous year.

The paving stones, bricks, tiles and miscellaneous items of hardware for these works had been delivered by the puffer the previous Thursday — together with the building squad, who had spent the weekend carting sand and pebbles from the nearby beaches to the site of operations. On Monday, the puffer had returned from the Broomielaw with the last and most important ingredient in the recipe — the bags of the cement itself.

And that, so far as the supervising agent of the contract was concerned, was the problem.

Cement.

Despite the skipper's assurances that they had trans-shipped such a cargo successfully many times in the past and that the specially-treated bags were rain-proof, the clerk-of-works, terrified of the effects of such an unending downpour on his precious cement, had refused point-blank to countenance its unloading till the rain had stopped. That was Monday. And today was Friday.

Thus the hatch on the puffer's hold was undisturbed. The heavy tarpaulin across it was still fastened down tightly, and the bag of rope netting which would transfer the cargo to a waiting horse and cart on the pier hung idle from the derrick.

On the puffer, the crew sat fuming in the fo'c'sle and getting ever more short-tempered with each other: ashore, the builders huddled under the leaking canvas roof of their ramshackle bothy and wished they were back in Glasgow.

And both sets of disgruntled and frustrated men individually and collectively cursed the clerk-of-works — who was himself safely ensconced in the considerable comfort of the staff wing at the big house, courtesy of the estate factor, though to the dismay of the domestic staff who were expected to look after his needs.

～

"He still insists that the bags would chust turn ass solid ass a rock," Para Handy protested as he climbed back down into the fo'c'sle and hung his dipping oilskins over a line stretched across the deck-beams next to the chimney of the iron stove in the fore-peak.

"To the duvvle," said Macphail with feeling. "Is your word no' good enough for the man, Peter?"

"He wuddna' believe it even if it wass written in the Good Book itself," said the skipper bitterly. "He iss that nervous for his chob. We must chust thole it oot for another day, boys, and see what comes.

"At least though we can get a wee break, for when I telt him we wass low on proveesions, instead of offerin' food from the big hoose, ass any Chrustian wud do, he chust said we could tak' a trup ower to Rothesay and stock up."

Within a short space of time, Macphail had steam up, and the puffer eased out from Berry's Pier for the crossing to the capital of Bute. Though the rain still swept mercilessly out of a grey sky, the prospect of a change of scenery, the chance of some company, and the promise of a quiet dram, went a long way to brightening the day for the crew.

For once, their optimism was not to be disappointed.

The owner, when Para Handy telegraphed his office to report on their problems and their whereabouts, was sufficiently moved by their plight to wire some money to them at once, care of the Rothesay Post Office.

Though this was probably through a sense of relief at learning that his investment was not lost with all hands somewhere off the Cumbraes, it at least made possible a re-stocking of the *Vital Spark*'s larder, and a welcome refreshment for the crew before they re-embarked for the return crossing to their berth in Loch Striven.

~

As the puffer edged in to Berry's Pier, two things immediately became apparent.

Firstly, the clerk-of-works was to be seen, waiting for them on the pier — and in a very agitated state.

Secondly, the rain had stopped for the first time in four days and though it seemed that the respite would be brief (for dark, laden clouds were rolling in from the south west) it was at least a break from the monotonous deluge which they had tholed for so long.

The reason for the clerk-of-work's agitation was soon made clear. Dunoon Telegraph Office had delivered a wire from the owner of the big house, advising the factor and the steward that his three sons, with a dozen or more of their friends, would be arriving at Berry's Pier on a chartered steam launch at six o'clock that evening, intending to spend the weekend at the house.

"You'll have to move the boat immediately," cried the frantic clerk-of-works. "They will need to berth the launch here and, besides, we cannot have the loch frontage of Glenstriven marred by the spectacle of a steam-gabbart at the pier."

Para Handy was with some difficulty restrained by the engineer and eventually was able to point out that he had a cargo for delivery here, it was still aboard, and he had no intention of leaving until it was safely ashore.

"The fact that it iss not," he concluded, "iss entirely your own fault, Mr Patullo, and I would be grateful if you would chust remember that before you miscall the shup!"

The wretched Patullo wrung his hands. "But we've got to get the boat away — and my gang, too, if you'll give them passage back to Glasgow. The gentry will want the place to themselves for the weekend."

"Well," said Para Handy. "Get my cargo off the shup, and we'll can do that for you. But so long ass my cargo iss aboard — here I stay!"

"But how can I do that," protested the clerk-of-works. "It may be dry enough to unload ye noo — but the weather for the weekend looks set to continue wet, and I've no place to store the cement under cover.

"Captain," said Sunny Jim suddenly. "I think we can maybe sort this all oot..."

～

Two hours later the *Vital Spark*, on passage to Glasgow in ballast with her cargo of cement safely ashore at Glenstriven and the builder's gang sheltering down in the fo'c'sle from the rain (which had returned with a vengeance), met a smart steam yacht rounding Toward Point and heading westwards past Ardyne.

"That'll be the chentry," said Para Handy. "Och, they'll neffer know we wass there."

Sunny Jim's idea had been ingenuity personified. The

sacks of cement had been hurried ashore by every manner of means while the rain held off: most slung onto the waiting cart but others taken by wheelbarrow and a few, the last few, even manhandled, up to the waterless swimming-pool.

Mr Patullo had supervised their careful stacking in the empty pool. To clean it out and prepare it for the summer was one of the jobs for which he had been contracted — a job which would have to wait until the work on the new terrace had been completed, hopefully next week when he and his men returned on Monday after the young gentlemen and their friends had gone back to Glasgow.

Meantime the sacks were safe under cover: Para Handy had been happy to lend one of the puffer's heavy hatchway tarpaulins and this was now stretched across the pool, weighted down on four sides by heavy flagstones.

"I'll can get that back from you next week sometime Mr Patullo, for we'll be passing through the Kyles on our way to Furnace sometime afore next Thursday."

~

It was, however, a stoney-faced estate factor who met the *Vital Spark* when she arrived at Berry's Pier early the following Wednesday afternoon to recover her property.

"Is Mr Patullo no' weel, then?" asked the Captain from the wheelhouse window, as the crew lashed the heavy tarpaulin to the eye-bolts at the fore end of the main hatchway.

"Not ill, Captain. Just — shall we say — in disgrace. I don't think you'll be seeing him in Glenstriven again.

"It probably was not entirely his fault, but the master can be very unforgiving at times. You see, the weather turned better on Saturday and the young gentlemen decided they would have a swim. So they opened the stop-cock to fill the pool — without looking under the tarpaulin first.

"I'm afraid we now need a new pool, as well as a new terrace."

~

And he inclined his head solemnly, pivoted on his heels and walked away.

Para Handy turned towards the deck below him with an agonised expression: "Jum!" he shouted: "Jum!!! I need to talk to ye!"

The deck was deserted, but the fo'c'sle hatchway had just crashed shut with an echoing thud.

FACTNOTE

Duncan Cameron Kennedy of Glenstriven ordered the building of the 'big house' on the estate in 1868. It enjoys a magnificent setting high above the loch, looking due south across the sheltered waters. I must confess that it has never had a swimming pool — though there were plenty of them in the resorts such as Rothesay, whose first 'salt water swimming baths' were opened in the 1870s.

In 1872 Walter Berry, a Leith merchant, acquired Glenstriven estate and it was he who commissioned the construction of the pier which bore his name. There were more than 80 piers on the Firth at the height of the steamer and puffer traffic. Most of those on the Renfrewshire and Ayrshire side of the Firth were built by the Railway or Shipping Companies: most of those on the Argyll coastline either by the local community or for it by a wealthy landowner — such as, for instance, the wooden pier erected at Lamlash by the Duke of Hamilton in 1888.

There were some wholly privately built and owned piers of which Berry's was one: it was one of the very few, however, which were large enough to accommodate steamers. Most of the private facilities constructed for the big houses, or for the isolated farms and estates, were merely jetties or slips designed to allow goods, livestock or passengers to be ferried to or from the shore on a flit-boat.

Of the original Berry's pier nothing now remains except a few stumps of the old uprights. It was never used for scheduled services, but as a destination for occasional special excursion or charter parties and there is a splendid photograph of one such group, coming alongside aboard the paddler *Diana Vernon*, in the book *Clyde Piers* published by Inverclyde District Libraries. Though it is difficult to be categorically certain (the photograph is a little indistinct as to detail) it seems as if all passengers aboard the steamer are men, and most look to be wearing some sort of uniform. There is a small welcoming party at the head of the pier, including a number of ladies.

The pier at Otter Ferry on the east side of Loch Fyne was also originally built as a private facility for the large house which stands at the shore end. There was an established local ferry service across to Lochgair from a stone jetty at the tiny hamlet of Otter Ferry a few hundred yards to the south — a service which had been running for many years before the pier was built in 1900. In contrast to the pier at Loch Striven however, that at Otter Ferry was for some years a port-of-call for steamers on scheduled services. Even today the structure seems to remains remarkably intact, though the last cargo was unloaded there just after the Second World War and the last passenger steamer called in 1914!

29

The Pride of the Clyde

Daybreak always has a hushed, cathedral-like quality about it but this particular dawn had broken in a spectacular silence accentuated by the visual crescendo of light streaming in from the east: first a delicate bluey rose, then a brightening but still pale off-white, and finally a dramatic, blinding golden sunburst which chased the last vestiges of the retreating night across the western horizon and into oblivion.

Seen from the uninterrupted vastness of the ocean that palette of colour would have been quite overwhelming, even from the upper reaches of the Clyde, where it was set against the gaunt silhouettes of the stone tenements of Govan and Plantation, it was unforgettable.

The Captain and crew of the steam-lighter coasting quietly down river with the current after an early start from Windmillcroft Quay were not unappreciative of this natural wonder unfolding before their eyes.

"Man, Dougie," said Para Handy reflectively: "if only it wass possible to tak' a picture of that and pit it in the paper, to let folk ken what they wass missin', the world and his wife wud be oot their beds betimes, and you wudna be able to move on the river for the crowds come to see it!"

It was June, and the *Vital Spark* was headed for the Kyles with a mixed cargo consisting of assorted building materials for Colintraive, hotel furnishings for Tighnabruaich, and fencing wire for Kaimes.

A mile or so past Renfrew Ferry an immaculately-groomed launch of the river pilot service, speeding upstream, closed in on the puffer.

"Steam-lighter ahoy! Where on earth do you think you're

off to?" shouted a uniformed figure, leaning from her wheelhouse window and gesticulating frantically. "The river's closed at Clydebank: you can't go any further downstream now till the afternoon! D'you puffer captains never even bother to read the navigation bulletins posted on the quays, or published in the Glasgow Herald?"

"No," replied Para Handy, with commendable but (in the present circumstances) ill-advised candour. "Never. Why?"

The master of the cutter turned an interesting purple colour.

"Because if you did, you'd have known that this is the morning the *Lusitania's* being launched from John Brown's yard. The river's closed to all traffic between the Cart and Dalmuir from eight o'clock till two o'clock! Now get in to the bank and stay there! Or do you want me to arrest the boat?"

"I wudna put you to the bother," replied Para Handy in a rather more placatory tone, and he put the wheel over and headed the puffer for the Renfrewshire shore.

The towering cranes of the world-famous Clydebank yard were now in sight, poised above the monstrous hull which had been growing beneath them for the past 15 months. Here had taken shape, and today was now ready for launching, the largest and most luxurious ship ever yet conceived by the designers, or created by the craftsmen, who between them had made the name of the Clyde and the reputation of its workers synonymous with shipbuilding perfection.

The river bank on the Renfrewshire side opposite the yard was black with crowds come to see the spectacle. From their modest vantage point actually on the water, however, the crew of the puffer had a grandstand view of the whole proceedings, and once the *Vital Spark* had been made fast to a convenient marker post they settled on the hatch-coaming with hastily-brewed mugs of tea and an early dinner of bread and cheese.

Stands "for the chentry", as Para Handy put it, had been placed facing the bow of the ship, immediately behind the platform for the launch-party. The men who had built her were crowded along the slipway the whole length of her hull, with a favoured few perched on the foredeck and as yet unfinished superstructure of the new liner.

The slip on which her foundation keel had been laid down and on which she had then been painstakingly raised over the preceding months — vertical rib-upon-rib, riveted plate-upon-plate — was placed at an acute angle to the river channel.

The Clyde itself was an artificial creation, a once sluggish stream dredged and broadened to its status as a birthplace for ships, a mecca for trade. At this point on its journey towards the sea it ran, despite the work of generations who had made it fit for an international commerce on which it depended, through a channel which was narrower, bank-to-bank, than the length of the hull which was about to slide into it.

Only the subterfuge of that angled slipway made the very launch possible and even with that heavy drag chains would have to be deployed to bring the enormous hull quickly to a stop, in order to prevent her running ashore on the opposite bank.

A small flotilla of tugs stood by to capture the vessel and then to manoeuvre her into the adjacent fitting-out basin where she would be transformed from an impressive but inanimate hulk into a living being, a ship (like all ships) with a personality and indeed a soul.

"Brutain's hardy sons," said Para Handy with some emotion when at 12.30 precisely Lady Inverclyde christened the ship in the traditional manner. To the roaring approval of tens of thousands of spectators, drawn from all walks of life but united by a pride in what had been achieved, the majestic hull took spectacularly to the water. In the process *Lusitania*, just as every ship before and since has always done, curtseyed sweetly and gracefully to the lady who had named her, and sent her forth to fulfil her destiny.

~

Fourteen months later the *Vital Spark* was lying against the easternmost extremity of Greenock's Princes Pier, ready to load a flitting for Furnace once the scheduled steamers had left.

In their more favoured berths ahead of her the *King Edward* and the *Lord of the Isles* impatiently awaited the arrival of the train from Glasgow St Enoch station and their cargo of on-going passengers for Campbeltown and Inveraray respectively.

Anchored in the middle reaches of the Firth at the Tail o' the Bank, however, was a vessel which commanded the attention and the respect of everyone within eyesight, to the total exclusion of everything else that lay or moved upon the firth.

Lusitania had, just the previous day, come down river from the fitting-out berth at John Brown's Clydebank yard: and was next morning to embark upon her speed trial over the measured mile at Skelmorlie, and her general proving, before being officially and formally handed over to Cunard.

The crowds massed on Greenock promenade and further along the western shores of the Firth towards Gourock almost matched those which had witnessed her launch the previous summer.

In due course the train, an inconsequential minute and a half late, came in from St Enoch: the Campbeltown and Inveraray steamers loaded, and departed.

Para Handy rose from the pierside bollard from which he had been watching the world go by and stretched luxuriously.

"Boys," he said. "let us chust warp her up to the railway yerd chetty, and get this fluttin' aboard: and then we can go..."

"Excuse me," came a quiet voice from behind the Captain, "but I wonder if I could ask a favour of you ?"

～

As the puffer eased alongside the liner, edging in towards the floating pontoon at the foot of the companionway stairs which soared, seemingly into space, towards the entry port umpteen decks above them, the *Lusitania's* hull was like a wall of sheer black cliff, dwarfing them into total insignificance.

Their passenger smiled his thanks.

"The least I can do," he said, "is invite you to have a quick look through the ship before she sails. If you'd like to."

An authoritative nod sent two seamen scurrying from their posts on the floating jetty at the ship's side to take up watch on the puffer's deck and secure her safely, bow and stern. With the First Officer of the *Lusitania* — for it was he — leading the way, the crew of the *Vital Spark*, moving as if in a dream, began to climb the companionway towards the upper decks of the liner.

"I can't thank you enough," said the First Officer to Para

Handy as they stepped through the portway and into the First Class Reception Foyer. "Most embarrassing if I'd been stranded on the pier at Greenock! They knew I was due off that train and there should have been a launch to meet me.

"There should be a lot of people in a great deal of trouble...

"But it has been such a pleasure for me to meet you gentlemen and be reminded of my own beginnings as a hand on the old Hay's puffer *Inca* all those years ago...

Even Para Handy was — almost — speechless, as wonder after wonder unfolded in front of their eyes.

The First Class Smoking Room, panelled in walnut with an open fireplace and an ivory ceiling: the First Class Lounge with its intricate carving and stained-glass domed roof: the Foyer, magnificent in wrought iron and with the gates of the first electric lift ever installed on a ship at sea: staterooms with marble baths en suite, carpets into which the feet sank at each step: works of art crowding every wall, carvings and statuary featuring on stairways and in corridors.

And, towards the stern of the great ship, spacious Third Class accommodation for the emigrant traffic which made the facility offered on board the poor *Vital Spark* seem like the very worst deprivation on the most notorious slaver in maritime history.

"Dinna you daur touch a thing," Para Handy commanded Sunny Jim in a piercing stage whisper, 'for I'm sure I dinna ken when you last washed your haun's. At least we got rid o' Macphail!"

Indeed the Engineer, in a paradise all his own, was on a tour of the ship's pioneering high-pressure turbines and her 25 boilers, courtesy of the Fourth Engineer, commandeered for such duty by their considerate host.

"I wish I could thank you properly," said that gentleman 20 minutes later as he ushered the crew back towards the waiting puffer: and reached instinctively for his notecase.

Para Handy was affronted.

"No, Cot bless you sir, no! Don't you even be thinking of such a thing. But there iss chust the wan wee favour, if you could see your way to obleege us with it, that wud mean more than we could effer say."

～

Which is why, if you should find yourself aboard the *Vital Spark* at the right time of the day: if the crew have taken kindly to you: if the prognostications are right: and if the Captain is in good trim: if all of these imponderables have fallen into place then you might, just might, be offered a mug of tea in the fo'c'sle of the finest vessel in the coasting trade.

Tea prepared in a very, very special tea-pot to be found on no other puffer, or indeed other vessel of any description, on the Firth.

A tea-pot, polished to blinding brilliance and handled with due ceremony and respect, bearing a proud legend: *RMS Lusitania.*

FACTNOTE

In the early years of the twentieth century supremacy on the lucrative and prestigious North Atlantic passenger services lay with the two German companies Norddeutscher Lloyd and HamburgAmerika (Hapag).

Ships like the *Kaiser Willhelm der Grosse,* the *Kronprinzessen Cecilie* and the *Deutschland* provided standards of luxury and levels of comfort and service hitherto undreamt-of, and helped the German shipping companies to capture more than half of the Transatlantic passenger business.

Cunard replied with two stunning sister ships (built with the help of government loans and subsidies), one — *Lusitania* — from John Brown of Clydebank: the second — *Mauretania* — from Swan Hunter on the Tyne.

With a length of 762ft and a beam of 88ft these vessels were the largest ships yet built. *Lusitania* was ready for launching three months before her sister. Her launch weight of more than 20,000 tons represented the greatest mass which man had ever tried to move. She came down the Clydebank yard's slip on June 7th 1906 and sailed from Southampton on her maiden voyage 15 months later — recapturing the Blue Riband from the Germans in the process.

Lusitania, as everyone knows too well, was treacherously and tragically torpedoed off the Irish coast by a German U-Boat in 1915 with appalling loss of civilian life. *Mauretania* survived the war and stayed in service (ending her days as a precursor of today's Caribbean cruise liners) before finally going to the breaker's yard in 1935.

Because of her short life-span and tragic end, *Lusitania* has tended to be overshadowed by her sister ship in the litany and legend of the North Atlantic. In fact she started as the more famous of the two ships — really by virtue of being the first into service. The Americans in particular adored the *Lusitania* and though *Mauretania* has been called, with some justification, the most famous and best-loved ship of all time, it has to be remembered that this was only because of the sad and early end of the Clyde-built vessel.

Had she survived, the two ships would undoubtedly have shared the honour, the esteem and the affection which they both — equally — deserved.

THE FASTEST WAY TO CROSS — Blue Riband holder Lusitania at speed was an impressive sight as the largest ship in the world thrust her 31,000 gross tonnes through the seas as fast as a family car. As well as a quicker crossing, she also brought to the passage standards of comfort and cosseting beyond the most sanguine expectations of her 2000 passengers as she wrested transatlantic supremacy back from the German fleets.

30

The Downfall of Hurricane Jack

I had always been intrigued by the chequered career of Para Handy's oldest and dearest friend, Hurricane Jack, who had for long been on a seemingly irreversible downward spiral from the heights of his time as the revered Captain of a record-breaking wool-clipper, then a temporary officer with MacBrayne's, and by way of the skipper's berth on the *Vital Spark* in her early days on the Firth, to his present state-of-affairs as occasional odd-job man on any vessel prepared to give him a part-time berth.

Para Handy would occasionally make some oblique reference to Hurricane Jack's departure from the puffer, usually in terms of 'Jeck's doonfall' but all my efforts to elicit more information about the circumstances of it were to no avail, and led merely to a swift change of subject.

Then one morning, as I was changing steamers at Rothesay on my way from Helensburgh to Inveraray, I came across the *Vital Spark* in a corner of the inner harbour with her skipper seated on an upturned fishing box on deck, and studying a copy of the Glasgow Herald. The intermittent sound of heavy hammering and the occasional muffled curses which came from the engine-room were evidence that Dan Macphail was struggling as usual with more running repairs to that temperamental piece of machinery, but of the Mate and Sunny Jim there was no sign.

I coughed politely from the edge of the quay and the Captain. looked up from his paper.

"Why, it's yourself then," he said. "What a surprise to see you in Rothesay: what brings you to Bute at this time o' year?"

I explained that I was merely killing an hour till the arrival of the *Lord of the Isles* from Glasgow on her way to Inveraray where I was to spend a few days with old family friends.

"The *Lord of the Isles*, eh? Well, now there iss something of a coincidence," said Para Handy. "for here I am chust readin' in the paper aboot that very boat, where I see tell that she is changin' owners, and thinkin' back to the time when it wass her that wass largely to blame for the circumstances that led to poor Hurricane Jeck losin' his berth on the *Vital Spark*."

"You know I've always wanted to know more about that sorry event, Captain," I prompted hopefully.

"Well," he said hesitantly: "I suppose there would be no much herm in tellin' you aboot it after aal these years for it wass a long time ago."

I scrambled down the iron ladder bolted into the quay wall and jumped onto the deck of the puffer and sat down on the coaming beside him before before he had time to change his mind. "Go on, Captain," I said encouragingly: "I'm listening."

~

"Ass you probably have realised," he began, "Jeck wassna the kind of a man that wud suffer fools gledly, so at times he could occasionally be chust a little bit impatient..."

"Impatient!" came a protesting voice from the engine-room. "He wisnae impatient at all! He wis the maist argimentative and pugnacious man on the Firth, and wis never happier than when he had his dander up and wis thrang pittin' the frighteners on some puir innocent body that jist had the sheer misfortune tae be passin'! His temper wis aye on a hair-trigger, he wis the sort of chap that if ye gi'ed him hauf a chance he could start a fight in an empty room!"

Para Handy paid no heed.

"...but at the same time," he continued, as if there had been no interruption, "he had the hert of a child and wass aalways happy to do a kindness to ony o' his fellow bein's wheneffer he had a chance: aalways anxious to introduce a ray of sunshine into a gloomy day and gi'e folk somethin' to enchoy at the time and talk aboot later. It wass that very spurit of goodwull that cost him his chob when he wass skipper on the *Vital Spark*.

"Wan time we wass lyin' at the Albert Harbour basin in Greenock waitin' for instructions from the owner. Jeck went ashore to go up to the telegraph office to see if there wass any message but ass he came oot onto the shore road he wass chust in time to see a smash between wan o' the Greenock to Gourock skoosh-caurs and a hackney cab. The caur had caught wan wheel o' the cab wi' its step-board ass it cam' roond the corner and though the horse, and the cab-man, wass chust fine, the passenger had been thrown onto the street and it wass clear the puir duvvle had broke his leg.

"He wass a ship's officer by his uniform so Jeck rushed over to see if he could help. It turned oot the man wass a Captain Fairlie, and he had been on his way to Princes Pier station to catch the Gleska train, for he wass to take ower next mornin' as a relief skipper on the *Lord of the Isles.* He wass pleased to see anither sailor and of course for aal he knew Jeck could have been master o' the *Oceanic,* no' chust a steam-lighter, he wass aalways so smertly turned oot.

" 'If ye could jist send a telegraph for me to the Inveraray Shuppin' Company's Gleska office and tell them whit's hap-pened to me,' he asked Jeck anxiously ass he wass bein' strapped to a stretcher by the ambulance men, 'I'd be mich obleeged. I'm no' wan o' the regular reliefs, in fact I wis engaged through their Greenock Agents so they only know me by reputation and I dinna want tae let them doon first time.'

"Jeck told him to relax, efferything would be chust fine, but ass soon ass the poor fellow wass off to the Infirmary he didna go near the telegraph office, he chust came back to the shup and told us he had to go to Gleska, the owner wanted to see him, but he'd be back the followin' night.

"If I had known whit wass goin' on I'd have told him no' to be sich a fool…"

"And ye'd have been at the Unfirmary yersel', gettin' a lesson in emergency repairs o' the human anatomy result-ing from an aggravated assault," shouted Macphail from the engine-room.

"…but nane o' us had ony idea whit wass whit, and so off he went. He spent the night wi' a kizzin o' his in Yoker and at half past six the next mornin' he presented himsel' on board the *Lord of the Isles* at the Brudge Wharf and let on his name wass Fairlie and that he wass the relief skipper.

"Naebody asked eechie or ochie aboot that at aal, he wass chust accepted ass bein' who he said he wass, for they wass aal expecting a new man and why should they jalouse that there wass shenannigans goin' on?

"Jeck wass in Paradise! He'd had plenty of high-jinks in the Hebrides two years earlier wi' Mr MacBrayne's *Flowerdale*, what wi' her twin screws and her cheneral mobility, but she wass ass an ageing cairthorse to a young thoroughbred compared wi' the *Lord of the Isles*, which wass less than a year old and chust at the height o' her powers! She wass one-third again ass big ass the *Flowerdale*, wi' enchines to match and, bein' a paddler, she wass chust ass lissom ass a greyhound and you could turn and spin her like a young gyurl dancin' the Gay Gordons!

"At 20 meenits past seven, Jeck gave the order to raise the gangplank, cast off the bow and stern ropes, and rang doon for half speed ahead, and off they went. The regulations on the river stopped him givin' her her heid till she wass past Clydebank, but then he whustled doon to the enchineers and promised them aal a dram from the first-class salong bar when they got to Inveraray if they made the trup in six hours, which wass 10 meenits less than her best time ever, and anither wan for effery extra five meenits they could knock off that!

"Jeck stayed on the brudge till efter they wass through the Kyles for they wass callin' in at maist o' the piers and he wanted to be sure they were in good trum on each occasion, but wance they had cast off from Tighnabruaich, wi' the next stop no' till Crarae, he left the First Officer in cherge on the brudge and went into the Captain's day cabin. There he found some oh-de-colong and macassar oil belonging to the regular captain, spruced himself up, set his kep on three hairs, then went perambulating through the first-cless salongs and the dining room.

"You know how gallant Jeck aalways iss wi' the ladies, and he wass at his best form that day, bowin' to aal the young gyurls and sweepin' his kep off nearly to the ground in a gracious manner it wass a privilege to behold, givin' the grups to their faithers, and kissin' the backs o' their mithers' hands ass if they had been royalty.

"He wass a great success wi' aal the chentry on board and by the time the shup reached Inveraray — which she did in a record time o' chust under five hours and fufty meenits — the maist of them was wishin' they didna have to go ashore to choin the Chook on a shootin party, or trevel on up to Loch Awe for the fushin', but could chust bide aboard for the return trup to Gleska in sich distinguished hands and stylish company!

"It wass that return trup — and Jeck's fondness for fun and his pleasure in bringin' high-jinks to his fellow man, whateffer the cost to himsel' — that wass his doonfall!

"They left Inveraray right on time and, since Jeck knew fine that he daurna reach Brudge Wharf earlier than the printed schedule or there would be questions asked, he took things easy on the trup back through the Kyles and then on by Rothesay and Dunoon.

"Their last caal before the run up-river to Bridge Wharf wass at Greenock Princes Pier, which wass chust a couple of hundred yerds from the basin at Albert Harbour where we wass waitin' for the man to return from Gleska where, you'll mind, we thought he wass in confabulation wi' the owner.

"Jeck chust couldna resist it. Ass he said to me after it wass aal over, 'Peter, I had to show ye whit wis whit, and let ye join in the fun! It would have been a poor hert that couldna rejoice and share the spree that wass on, given whit I had at my haun's that day!'

"What he did — instead of headin' oot into the up-river channel when he cast off from Princes Pier — wass to bring the *Lord of the Isles* through the narrow entrance into Albert Harbour at ass good a speed ass he could get up, and then throw her into full astern. By jinkin' from ahead to astern wi' the helm hard over he spun her roond in a tight pirouette not chust the wance but no less than three times in the muddle of the dock, whiles he wass oot on the brudge wing wi' the steam-whustle lanyard in his hands, givin us aal a cheery wave and blastin' oot on the shup's whustle like the early mornin' hooter at Singers's!

"You can imachine that the officers and crew, neffer mind the passengers, were taken aback wi' this: there wass somethin' of a commotion aboard the shup: and there wass proper uproar on the quayside ass well.

"The out-turn wass that somebody telegraphed the shup's owners in Gleska and when Jeck docked her at Brudge Wharf — which he did bang on time, and ass nice ass ninepence, like efferything else he did — the polis wass waitin' wi' the Directors o' the Company, and it wass the high chump for Jeck.

" 'My fault entirely, Peter,' he said when we met up the next day efter he'd been let oot on bail. 'If I had chust taken her up to Glesga and then disappeared, naebody would have been ony the wiser about who took Fairlie's place and there would have been no trouble at aal.

" 'That wass what I meant to do.

" 'But when it came to it, there wass no way I wassna goin' to share it wi' you! I'd been given the very best toy and the very biggest toy I ever had to play wi' in my whole life, so I chust had to let my oldest frien get at least a flavour o' the sheer joy and happiness of bein' a bairn again!'

"So that wass how Jeck took a tumble, and how I got the command of the shup, for the owner sacked him on the spot.

"But I wush it had never happened that way, for Jeck didna deserve such a fate when aal he wass tryin' to do, as aal he ever tries to do, wass to bring some sunshine into the lives of his fellow men."

FACTNOTE

Two Clyde steamers carried the name *Lord of the Isles*. The first was launched from D & W Henderson's Meadowside Yard in 1877 for the Glasgow & Inveraray Steamboat Company Ltd. She was from the first locked in rivalry with the *Columba* and that has been well-captured in John Nicholson's dramatic painting of the race between them.

It was something of a shock when the Company sold the paddler to English owners just 13 years later, in the autumn of 1890, and though she was replaced by the launch the following Spring of the second *Lord of the Isles* from the same builders it still remains a little mysterious that the changeover took place when it did.

The two ships were almost identical in dimensions, the second being just nine feet longer at 245ft: had similar machinery, though of slightly greater power in the 'new' *Lord*, giving her marginally more speed and (with a newly-developed steam steering gear in place) greater manoeuvrability: and they were of broadly the same appearance.

The main difference, and probable reason for the change, was that the saloons on the new ship ran the full width of her hull and thus gave significantly enhanced passenger space. As she had to compete with the *Columba*, whose onboard facilities were legendary, this may have been the logic behind the whole project, for the *Lord of the Isles* on the Inveraray run and her great rival on the Ardrishaig run were catering for the wealthy tourist, not the Scottish working class family on holiday.

Hurricane Jack's imaginary 'day out' is set in 1892: and the ship really did change hands — twice: firstly in 1909 when she was sold to the Lochgoil and Inveraray Steamship Co: and again in 1912 when they went out of business and the ship was bought by the pioneers of the new generation of civil marine power not just on the Clyde but worldwide, Turbine Steamers Ltd, who had come into being to operate the then brand-new *King Edward* just 11 years earlier.

Paddlers were, generally speaking, more manoeuvrable than their screw-steamer sisters, particularly in a confined space, partly thanks to a significantly shallower draft which allowed them to be 'spun' rather more easily through the resistance of the water: partly because the larger surfaces of the paddle-blades could more quickly bring the vessel to a standstill and get her moving again in the opposite direction.

And yes, I have grossly exaggerated their sprightliness but as any storyteller might claim, a tall tale should be a tall tale!

A FINAL VIEW — Stern views of paddlers are rare, which makes this fine plate from the MacGrory archive specially interesting. It illustrates perfectly the spaciousness afforded by the wide paddle-boxes in contrast to the fine lines of the hull itself, and the dramatic wake left by the twin blades. The steamer is the Duchess of Hamilton, and she has just turned away from Campbeltown pier and is heading out to sea towards the Ayrshire coast. When this picture was taken she was at the beginning of her career — in contrast to the unidentified square-rigged naval vessel anchored out in the bay, very much at the end of hers.